Murder From A to Z

V. M. BURNS

Kensington Publishing Corp.
kensingtonbooks.com

Murder From
A to Z

Chapter 1

"Her elevator doesn't go all the way to the top floor. If you know what I mean." Bethany Tarkington twirled her finger beside her head in the universal symbol for crazy and rolled her eyes at the petite woman sitting next to her. "She's my husband's aunt, but honestly, I'm not sure why she insisted on coming to this . . . thing."

I didn't like Bethany Tarkington, even before she insulted her aunt Alva in front of her face, but that last maneuver cemented my dislike. She'd spread her hands wide to encompass everything when she delivered her insult. The fact that we were sitting in the conference room at the back of my bookstore had got my back riled up. Market Street Mysteries may not have had the commercial appeal of big chain bookstores, but it wasn't a dump either. It was clean and homey. From the sturdy all-wood, custom bookshelves that were handmade by Amish craftsmen, to the comfy chairs covered with colorful hand-knit throws made by my Nana Jo's friend, Ruby Mae Stevenson. Market Street Mysteries was welcoming and inviting. Thanks to upgraded Wi-Fi, trendy marketing videos, promos, and displays that were the brainchild of my technology savvy and marketing genius nephews, combined with melt-in-your-mouth treats courtesy of my assistant Dawson Alexander, my bookstore had also become a hip hangout for old and young. How dare she. How dare this . . . this Bethany person insult my bookstore.

I heard a sharp intake of breath and felt steam rise from the dragon sitting to my right. If Bethany had been nicer, I might have tried to save her from the takedown I knew was coming. Instead, I sat back, folded my arms, and waited.

"Do you have a will, Mrs. Tarkington?" My sister, Jenna, flashed a cold, hard glance at Bethany Tarkington. Intelligent, professional, and hard as nails was the persona Jenna had perfected after years as a public defender in North Harbor, Michigan. Her face gave away nothing of the anger that was seething under her expensive suit, perfect makeup, and well-coiffed hair. As her sister, I saw the way her nostrils flared, and the slight narrowing of her eyelids. Sitting next to her, I could feel the electricity and heat radiating off her skin. To the uninitiated, she appeared cool, calm, and collected, but this was my sister. A storm was raging under that calm façade. Jenna leaned forward, a predator stalking her prey—a lioness. Bethany Tarkington was a gazelle grazing in a field, completely unaware she was about to be eaten alive.

"Well, no. But my husband, Carl, and I are young. We—"

"It's a common misconception by the uninformed that estate planning is only for the elderly."

Attack!

"We just haven't had time to—"

"If you were in an accident and unable to talk, does your husband know your wishes regarding medical care?" Jenna asked in a soft tone.

Attack!

"We've never discussed it, but I'm sure he—"

"If something were to happen to your husband, do you

know where your life insurance policy is? Or which company holds the policy?"

"I don't—" A red flush rose up Bethany's neck.

"What about something easier." Jenna squinted and leaned forward.

Ouch!

"If something happened to your husband, could you pay the bills to keep a roof over your head and the lights on for a year or two, which is the average time for probate?" Jenna raised one perfectly arched brow and tapped her pen.

"Two years?" Bethany's eyes widen to the size of a half dollar. "You're joking, right?"

"Nope." Jenna popped the *P* on the word and held up the documents that Bethany had brought in, which gave an estimate of Alva's assets. "Even with a will, an estate the size of Mrs. Tarkington's could take two years or more to clear probate."

Bethany gaped.

"Are you even listed as a beneficiary on these accounts?" Jenna pointed at the documents.

"Carl handled all of that." Bethany swallowed hard. "We're married, so if something happened, then I would get it, right? I mean . . . I'm his wife."

"It depends on how everything is set up, but probate could still take years, and there are no guarantees. There may be other claimants." Jenna leaned back. "However, if your aunt had an estate plan that included a trust, then it might be possible for her beneficiaries to bypass probate and save the thousands of dollars that you would spend on inheritance taxes, legal fees, and probate. So, if *Alva* insisted on coming today, then it sounds like *her* elevator is moving just fine."

Jenna's killer instincts had gotten her labeled as a pit bull. Although, most of the pits I've met were more marshmallows than my toy poodles, Snickers and Oreo. Still, she pushed down her inner pit bull and channeled her inner golden retriever instead.

"Pit bull: One. Mean Girl: Zero."

I nearly jumped out of my seat when my grandmother whispered in my ear. I hadn't realized she was so close until she spoke.

"She's good," I whispered.

Jenna forced a smile. She had Bethany Tarkington's full attention now. The woman had scooted to the edge of her seat, pulled out a pen, and furiously scribbled on the back of an envelope as though Jenna was revealing the secrets to eternal life.

"That's my girl." Nana Jo chuckled and walked away, and I glanced over at Alva.

Alva Tarkington was a frail woman with fluffy white hair that reminded me of cotton candy. Her skin was wrinkled, but free of age spots with only a mole near her right ear. She slumped in her seat. Head down. Her gaze had been focused on a handkerchief that she twisted in her hands.

I glanced at my phone. Only thirty minutes to go and we could call it a day. I wasn't a lawyer like my older sister and her husband, Tony, but Nana Jo was no respecter of persons. When she volun-told Jenna that she was teaching a class on "Getting Your Ducks in a Row," which was part of the bucket list courses offered at Shady Acres Retirement Village, I was volun-told that I was helping. My role was easy. I didn't have to deliver the content. I merely had to provide the venue, snacks, and assistance to my sister.

I stole a glance at Jenna. I had been glad to see the spark in her eyes as she took down Bethany. That gleam had also been there while she delivered her seminar. As a former high school English teacher, I spent years learning to take boring content and make it interesting. Jenna hadn't been a teacher, but as a lawyer, she was accustomed to talking to jurors and making her point. She'd done an excellent job with the seminar. For a few hours, she was her old self.

Both Nana Jo and I had been worried. Jenna didn't have that killer instinct that she once did. Instead of the lioness that walked proudly around the Serengeti, prepared to take down any interloper or antelope that crossed its path, she was the toothless, declawed aging lion at the local zoo napping on the concrete waiting for meat to be tossed through a sliding door.

When Nana Jo confronted her, Jenna mentioned being restless. Her blood pressure was high. Her energy was low. Plus, now that the twins had graduated from college and flown the nest, she wasn't sure what her next steps should be. Nana Jo hoped that teaching this seminar would help Jenna remember why she became a lawyer in the first place and would help her get her own ducks in order.

The seminar had gone well. Jenna's presentation was well received, and she was asked to repeat the course. Jenna did most of the discussion, but I helped by providing icebreakers and helping with discussions and the Q and A. Despite our differences, Jenna and I worked well together. Teaching is different from arguing in front of a jury, but I could tell that Jenna enjoyed herself. Without the state and local school boards dictating a curriculum, I enjoyed myself too. In fact, I was contemplating adding classes at the bookstore. Now that I was a published author, I'd met several other authors. I also learned that many of my patrons weren't just mystery readers, but like me, they were also aspiring authors. I was seriously thinking about adding a few classes on writing and publishing to the bookstore events calendar. The information Jenna provided was useful for everyone, not just mystery readers. Maybe I could attract new people into the bookstore.

"Earth to Sam." Nana Jo tapped my arm.

"Sorry, I was daydreaming."

"Make sure Jenna stays hydrated. She's been talking for hours." Nana Jo passed two bottled waters to me.

Jenna had spent hours talking about wills, trusts, and estate planning and was now providing private one-on-one consultations. Alva was the last.

I unscrewed the cap for my sister and slid a water to her. Then I prepared to zone out for the next thirty minutes while she talked. My skin tingled. Feeling that I was being watched, I looked up. Alva's eyes were focused and alert and directed at me. Earlier, Alva's eyes appeared cloudy. Now, the eyes gazing at me were sharp and aware.

I smiled.

That's when she blinked. And blinked. Over and over again, Alva blinked.

I wondered if an eyelash had gotten in her eye, but Alva never rubbed her eye, even though she had a handkerchief in her hand. Hypnotized, I sat and watched. That's when I noticed a pattern to the blinking. Three fast blinks. Pause. Three long blinks. Pause. Three fast blinks. There was a pattern that never changed. Three fast blinks. Pause. Three slow blinks. Pause. Three fast blinks. A chill went up my spine. *OMG!* That was Morse code. It had been more than thirty years since I learned basic Morse code as a Girl Scout, but that code was one that I would never forget. Alva Tarkington was blinking an SOS.

Chapter 2

Holy freakin' cow! I must be imagining this. She can't really be blinking an SOS in Morse code. Right? I blinked several times to clear my brain and shook my head like my chocolate poodle, Oreo. *Jeez Louise.*

Alva stopped blinking. Her gaze drifted over to Bethany before quickly locking back on me. Three quick blinks. Pause. Three slow blinks. Pause. Three quick blinks.

Alva was sending me a message and whatever that message was, she didn't want Bethany to hear.

I pulled out my cell and sent a quick SOS of my own. This time to my grandmother, Nana Jo, asking her to get rid of Bethany for fifteen minutes.

Within seconds, Nana Jo was by my side. "Bethany, dear. I've been meaning to talk to you about something. Do you have a few minutes?" Nana Jo gave Bethany a broad smile.

"No. I don't. Alva's paying for this private consultation, and we only have a few minutes left. I need—"

"Oh, pish posh. Sam and Jenna will be able to finish up without you. I really need to discuss something urgent with you."

Bethany scowled. She clearly had no intention of going off

with Nana Jo. She opened her mouth to protest. Obviously, she didn't know that resistance was futile with my family. She would have had an easier time convincing an angry rhino to roll around in the grass on its back like a puppy than she would in getting Nana Jo to let go of something once her mind was set. Yet Bethany's expression looked as if she was prepared to dig in her heels.

Jenna must have sensed that something was up because she stepped in. "Actually, that would be perfect. Why don't you go off with my grandmother? I have some routine documents I need to fill out anyway. And because of your inconvenience, I'll even throw in a free thirty-minute consultation tomorrow. That way, I can talk to both you and your husband."

Bethany hesitated.

I could see the gears moving in her head: Dig her heels in for the last ten minutes of Alva's consultation? Or get an extra thirty minutes free? You didn't have to be a financial genius to recognize the better deal.

"Well, I think that would be great, but I don't know if my husband can make the consultation. He works a lot. Maybe we could meet . . . just the two of us." Bethany shot a glance in my direction that indicated clearly I wasn't invited to the consultation.

Well, thank heavens, I would gladly forego any additional time with you too. I flashed a genuine smile.

Jenna's smile was more of a grimace, but she held it.

Bethany shoved the envelope she'd used for notes and her pen into her purse. Then she glanced at Alva, who had retreated into her dream world.

"You wait right here. I'll be back in a couple of minutes," Bethany shouted in Alva's ear.

Nana Jo steered Bethany toward the front of the bookstore.

Jenna stared at me. "What was that—"

Alva rubbed her ear. "I have no idea why people think just because someone is older, that they must also be deaf and barmy as a hatter."

Jenna had taken that moment to take a swig of water and nearly choked at Alva, who was anything other than barmy. "Sorry, I wasn't expecting . . . you're . . ."

Rarely have I seen my cool-as-a-cucumber sister at a loss for words, and I snickered.

Jenna turned her gaze to me. "You don't seem to be as surprised as I would expect."

I opened my mouth to explain but halted when Alva leaned forward.

"I'm sorry to interrupt, but we don't have much time before Bethany realizes she left me alone and returns. So, let's get this show on the road."

This time, both Jenna and I were equally stunned by Alva's quick grasp of the situation.

Jenna extended a hand for Alva to continue.

"Can you help me update my will before they succeed in killing me?"

Chapter 3

Jenna recovered quicker than I did. She leaned forward. "Kill you? Who's trying to kill you?"

I closed my mouth, which was gaping open, and looked around to confirm no one was nearby to overhear our conversation.

"My family, of course." Alva patted Jenna's hand as if she were calming an irate child. "But that's not important. What's import—"

"Not important? Are you jerking my chain?" Jenna glanced from Alva to me. "Is this a joke? Something you and Nana Jo cooked up?" She glanced around. "Where are the cameras?"

If I weren't so shocked, I might have denied the accusations my sister was leveling at me, but I was completely blown away. I raised my hands and then made an X over my heart, and shook my head in denial. "Cross my heart."

"I don't have time to go into the details right now. We need to hurry." Alva glanced around and then slipped her hand into the sleeve of her sweater to pull out a wad of toilet paper. "They never leave me alone. They're scared I'll tell someone what they're doing. The only time I have a moment alone is in the toilet."

Jenna rubbed her forehead and plastered a mask of benign acceptance on her face. "Mrs. Tarkington, I'm sure your family is only concerned about your well-being. They undoubtedly want to ensure you don't fall or—"

"Bull puckey. They want me dead so they can get their hands on the money, but that's not what bothers me."

"It's not?" I asked.

"If you aren't concerned that they'll kill you, then what . . . ?" I asked.

"I've lived a long life. I was an artist. My sister and I were both artists. We weren't masters, but we were creators." Alva looked off into the past and smiled. "I've seen the world. Lived. Loved. And, I've enjoyed myself. Most of my friends, family, and lovers are all dead. My sister . . . she wanted me to enjoy my life. We were very close. She—" Alva choked back a sob and wiped away a tear that had fallen from the corner of her eye before, but she quickly refocused. "No time for tears. The point is that at my age, death is more of a friend than an enemy. I have no regrets. That's the most important thing. No regrets. Plus, according to my doctor, I've got a short shelf life."

I covered her small, gnarled hand with my own and gave it a squeeze. Impending death without regrets. Here was something I understood. My late husband, Leon, had been the love of my life. We met young, married, and worked hard to build our life together. I had been a high school English teacher. Leon had been a cook. We'd worked hard day after day and year after year, hoping that if we worked hard enough, we could one day relax and live. One day, our ship would come in. The planets would align. One day, we dreamed, we'd stop working jobs that provided an existence but could actually *live*. We wanted to enjoy our lives. Follow our dream to quit the hustle and bustle of jobs that paid the bills, but also kept us bound. We both loved mysteries and dreamed of opening a bookshop specializing in mysteries. It wasn't until Leon was dying that the realization hit. We were simply hamsters on a wheel, running and running but not moving any closer to the dream on the other side of the finish line. When Leon died, I decided that life was too short not to follow your dreams—to live. That's when I quit my job. I bought the building Leon and I had dreamed about, and I opened the mystery bookshop. My only regret was the time I wasted before taking the leap of faith to pursue my dream, and that Leon hadn't lived long enough to experience it.

"No regrets." Alva returned the squeeze. "But I have some unfinished business and a limited time to make things right. I need to do what needs to be done before it's too late." She shoved the wad at Jenna.

Jenna unrolled the wad of toilet tissue. "What's this?"

"That's an addendum to my will."

Jenna gaped. "Addendum?"

"Sorry, dear, but the toilet is the only place where I could write in peace." Alva leaned forward. Her brow creased with worry. "Is it still legal, even if it's written on toilet paper?"

Jenna stared at the delicate document. "That depends. I mean, there are a lot of factors that could make an addendum invalid." She rubbed her forehead.

Alva chuckled. "You mean, if my family can convince the court that I'm really batty as a barn owl, then it'll all be for naught."

Before following my dream to Market Street Mysteries, I was a high school English teacher, and Alva's use of the English language brought joy to my heart. *When was the last time I'd heard someone use the phrase, "it's all for naught"?* Most of my former students probably didn't know what *naught* meant. They certainly weren't using it in a sentence. I reached out a hand

and squeezed Alva's hand. "Only a sane person would have the wits to write an addendum to their will on toilet paper and blink an SOS in Morse code."

"What?" Jenna asked.

"Look, I have no idea what you're talking about," Bethany's voice rose over the room chatter.

Alva's eyes moved from me to Jenna, asking the question she couldn't voice: *Will you help me?*

Jenna nodded, and pulled a piece of paper from her folder. She slid it to Alva. "Sign."

Alva scribbled a signature.

Jenna slid the paper to me. "Sign."

I didn't ask questions. I signed.

Jenna slid the paper back into her folder.

"They're coming back," I whispered.

"Your grandmother is as whacky as the rest of these looney toons." Bethany huffed as she flopped back into her seat. She glanced from Jenna to Alva and then to me. Her gaze narrowed. "What's going on?"

Jenna discreetly shoved the toilet paper under a folder on the table in front of her.

"We were just chatting with . . ." I glanced at Alva, but a shutter had closed over her eyes. Instead of the vibrant, alert, intelligent woman we just spoke to, there was an empty shell. Her gaze was unfocused and directed down at her lap where her hand plucked absently at a string.

Bethany frowned. She may not have been the brightest bulb in the pack, but she must have sensed that something was off.

The timer I'd set on my phone went off. "Our time's up."

Jenna stood and handed Bethany a business card. "Mrs. Tarkington, why don't you talk to your husband about a time to discuss your aunt's estate and give me a call?"

With no other choice, Bethany stood. She forced a smile

that didn't make it to her eyes. But there was nothing to be done, so she helped Alva to her feet and out the door.

It took another thirty minutes to clear everyone out of the bookstore. Everyone except for me, Jenna, Nana Jo, and Nana Jo's closest friends from Shady Acres, Irma Starczewski, Dorothy Clark, and Ruby Mae Stevenson.

I opened the door that led to the upper level of the building that was my home. Snickers and Oreo, my two chocolate toy poodles, ran downstairs, toenails clicking on the hardwood floors. I let them outside to take care of business.

Snickers was fourteen with plenty of attitude and an expressive face that indicated that despite receiving at least fifteen hours of sleep daily, she could use more. She stepped over the threshold, squatted, and was back inside in moments. Oreo, her brother, was two years younger than Snickers but was still very much a puppy. He ran around outside in the fenced-in courtyard that joined the back of the bookstore with the garage until he sniffed the perimeter and inspected every suspicious leaf lurking in his domain. Snickers and I watched from the door for a full five minutes. When Snickers looked up, I could almost read her expression. *Really?*

"He's a goofball, but you gotta love his enthusiasm," I said.

Snickers snorted. I guess she disagreed.

Eventually, Oreo remembered why he was there. He hiked his leg and then rushed to us, giving Snicker's ear a playful tug.

Back inside, we climbed the stairs that led to what had once been an industrial loft. After Leon's death, I sold the house we lived in together and renovated the bookstore's upper level. Moving had been Leon's suggestion. Our original plan was to rent out the upstairs to bring in additional income to support the bookstore. Leon knew me well enough to know that I would need a fresh start away from the home and all of the memories. He encouraged me to renovate the more than two-thousand-square-foot space into a two-bedroom, two-bath home, sell the house we'd shared and move into the upper level—a fresh start. Unlike the traditional style in my former home, this space was industrial, modern, and open. I never would have categorized my style as modern, but the beautiful oak floors, exposed brick walls and ductwork, floor-to-ceiling windows, and seventeen-foot ceilings converted me. Past Sam would have considered the modern loft cold and soulless. Present Sam enjoyed the earthy hues in the brick walls, the rich wood floors, and sun-filled space. It was natural, bright, and inviting. It was home.

Upstairs, Jenna, Nana Jo, and the girls sat at the dining room table snacking on leftover cheese, crackers, and cookies and drinking the sangria my fiancé, Frank Patterson, was testing for inclusion at his restaurant. Based on the fact that the pitcher was almost empty, I'd say the sangria was a success.

"Now, can you tell me what the heck you two were doing with Alva?" Nana Jo asked.

I glanced at Jenna, but she turned to me. Jenna may have been grappling with the issue of client confidentiality, but I wasn't a lawyer. So, the conversation wasn't protected. Regardless, I knew that any information we shared with Nana Jo and the girls was safe.

"Before I share, I need to ask you guys a question. Is there any chance that Alva Tarkington is . . . suffering from . . . diminished capacity?" I asked.

I wasn't sure what they expected me to ask, but that wasn't it. The women exchanged glances before they each answered.

"No."

"Not likely."

"Nope."

"How can you be sure?" Jenna asked.

Nana Jo frowned. "I've known Alva Tarkington since she moved to North Harbor a couple of years ago, and there's nothing wrong with her faculties."

"But you saw her today. How can you be certain?" Jenna asked.

"Well, she sure looked like she was out of it today." Ruby Mae Stevenson pulled out her knitting. She paused and sucked her teeth before adding, "I'm sticking with my original reply. Ain't nothing wrong with Alva's mind."

Born in Alabama, Ruby Mae still had a Southern drawl, despite nearly a half century of living in the North. She was the youngest of my grandmother's friends. I loved all of them, but Ruby Mae was my favorite. Skin like coffee with a touch of cream, she had salt-and-pepper hair which she pulled back and wore in a bun at the nape of her neck.

"She's probably faking to avoid having to talk to that idiot niece." Dorothy Clark was Nana Jo's closest friend and was nearest to her in appearance. At six feet and nearly three hundred pounds, Dorothy was a martial arts expert with a black belt in aikido. She was also an amazing singer with a rich, sultry voice as well as an incorrigible flirt.

"Probably repressed." Irma tossed her sangria back like a tequila shot, without the salt or the lemon wedge.

"Repressed?" Nana Jo stared.

"You know. She's been a widow for decades. She probably just needs to get lai—"

"Irma!" everyone yelled.

Irma swallowed whatever she was going to say, and then broke into a coughing fit. Irma Starczewski was in her mid-eighties and the oldest of Nana Jo's friends. Barely five feet tall and one hundred pounds, Irma dressed in short skirts, tight tops, and skinny-heeled shoes that she bought at Victoria's Secret. Nana Jo described her as a nymphomaniac, a label Irma loved and embraced wholeheartedly. Years of heavy smoking had left Irma's voice deep and raspy with a thick cough that sounded as if she were about to hack up a lung.

Nana Jo narrowed her gaze and stared from Jenna to me. "I'm not sure what you're digging for, but there's nothing wrong with Alva Tarkington's faculties. That woman's brain is as sharp as a meat cleaver. Now, what's going on?"

I told them about Alva blinking an SOS in Morse code and everything she told us.

"That proves she's not crazy, right?" Nana Jo turned to Jenna. "Someone who wasn't in their right mind would hardly have been able to do all of that."

"Not necessarily." Jenna took a long sip of her sangria. "It could just mean that she's paranoid or suffering from a persecution complex. I don't know."

"But Morse code?" I asked.

Jenna shrugged. "None of us are doctors. Without a medical diagnosis, there's no way to confirm Alva's mental state one way or the other." I revved up to argue, but Jenna held up a hand. "I'm not saying she's not competent. I'm just saying from a legal standpoint the question may need to be determined by the courts rather than what any of us *think*."

Silence settled on the room for several moments.

"Then we would be doing her a disservice by not giving her the benefit of the doubt." Nana Jo tapped her hand on the table. She lifted her chin and released a breath that was full of resignation. "We need to assume that Alva is sane and telling the truth. Her truth."

We sat in silence for a few moments. The hand that had been tapping the table smacked it, causing the glasses to rattle. "You know what that means." She glanced around. "It means someone is trying to kill Alva, and we need to figure out how to stop them."

Chapter 4

"We need a plan." Nana Jo pulled out her iPad and turned to Sam.

My brain went blank. After a few minutes, I glanced at the faces staring at me. "This is hard."

"Why? It's not like this is our first rodeo," Nana Jo said. "You've solved lots of murders."

"That's my point," I said.

Nana Jo stared at me.

"Usually, someone's been murdered. We have a place to start. I would talk to Stinky Pitt and get a look at the coroner's report, but I can't even do that. First off, Alva's not dead. And I'm fairly certain Stinky Pitt is out of town."

Detective Brad Pitt got the unfortunate nickname of "Stinky Pitt" as a kid. Nana Jo had been his second-grade math teacher and often used the name, especially when the detective was being cocky to bring him down a peg. I knew for a fact that Detective Bradley Pitt was indeed out of town. He'd developed a crush on my fiancé's mother, and had taken a long weekend to go visit. The fact that Stinky Pitt was attracted to Frank's mom wasn't surprising. She was an intelligent, beauti-

ful, successful surgeon. The surprising part was that Dr. Camilia Patterson seemed to be as infatuated with the detective as
he was with her. Both were close to the same age but couldn't
have been more different. Camilia was caviar and champagne
on a yacht in the Riviera, while Stinky Pitt was beer and brats
while floating on an inner tube down the St. Thomas River.

Jenna leaned forward. "Well, I'm going to see if Alva's
toilet-paper addendum is legal or not."

"You were smart to get her signature on that form," I said.

"It may not do any good, but at least we have her signature
for the addendum and our signatures as witnesses to her signature." Jenna shrugged.

"That was smart," Nana Jo said.

"No promises, but we did what we could," Jenna said.

"Good." I turned to Ruby Mae. "Maybe you could talk to
your nephew. Or is it great-nephew?"

"Daryl is my great-nephew." Ruby Mae smiled. "I'm supposed to have dinner with his mother tonight anyway."

Ruby Mae and the other ladies from Shady Acres Retirement Village all had a vast network of friends and family, but
none came close to Ruby Mae. Ruby Mae's extended family
was humongous. Everywhere we went, she had a niece, great-
nephew, or third cousin once removed that she could pump
for information. She had one of those faces people trusted. She
could sit in a corner with her knitting, and strangers sat down
next to her and poured out their life stories. Daryl Stevenson
was Ruby Mae's great-nephew and the chief of police for the
North Harbor Police Department.

I turned to Dorothy Clark. "Do you think Jacob would be
interested in a potential story?"

Jacob Friedman was Dorothy Clark's great-nephew, but he
was also a journalist who owned a magazine. Dorothy studied
journalism in college but stopped writing when she got married. The press was often able to gain access to information

and people that a bookstore owner couldn't. In exchange for press credentials, Dorothy had started writing freelance articles. Jacob was pleased and Dorothy was gaining a readership, so it had turned into a win-win situation. Some of her articles were even featured in regional magazines.

"Jacob's always interested in a story. What do you have in mind?" Dorothy asked.

"How about a write-up about the Estate Planning Workshop? I took some pictures for the bookstore's newsletter." I paused for a moment to collect my thoughts. "Alva Tarkington was an artist. Maybe if the killer thought she was going to be featured in a magazine, he or she might reconsider or at least delay drawing attention to themselves by killing her."

"I've already submitted something on Jenna's workshop. Jacob loved it. In fact, he thinks it might be worth a regular feature," Dorothy said.

"What?" Jenna gasped.

"He thinks you could do a regular feature with legal advice for the layman." Dorothy reached out and patted Jenna's hand.

"But I'm not a journalist," Jenna said.

"Journalists, real journalists, are nearly extinct. He just wants a short information piece." Dorothy smiled. "I'd be more than willing to help if you decide it's something you want to do."

Jenna blinked several times, but she still had a *deer in the headlights* look.

"I'm sure I can come up with some angle on local artists living in North Harbor." Dorothy tilted her head and stared at me. "But I don't know if it will be enough to stop a killer."

"Me either, but at least it's worth a shot. Plus, it'll be a reason to look into Alva's past."

"Got it." Dorothy nodded.

"Irma, are you still dating that accountant?" I turned to face Irma Starczewski.

"I date a lot of men, you're going to have to give me a little more to go on, Sam." Irma pursed her lips and applied a deep red lipstick.

Nana Jo rolled her eyes.

"I think his name was Clarence, but—"

"Oh, Clarence. Well, we haven't been out in quite a while, but I can give him a call. What do you want to know?" She patted her hair, which she dyed jet black and wore in a beehive style that had been popular in the 1960s.

"Bethany's husband, Carl, has something to do with investing, and I was hoping you might be able to see if he knew anything about him," I said.

"If he knows anything, you can count on me to get it out of him no matter what I have to do." She was also a shameless flirt who loved skirts and dresses that were too short and tops that were too tight. Irma flashed a big smile and pulled down her shirt, exposing more of her cleavage.

Nana Jo groaned.

"Jenna, maybe you could check on Alva's will." I gazed at my sister.

"I need to check into her toilet-paper addendum anyway, so I'll see what I can find out. Although, there's no guarantee that the actual will has been filed," Jenna said. "Her attorney may not have filed it."

I nodded.

"What do you want me to do?" Nana Jo asked.

"I was hoping you could ask some folks at Shady Acres if they've noticed anything . . . unusual about Alva. It's odd that all of you feel that Alva's mind is still sharp, but she certainly wasn't giving off that type of vibe when Jenna and I first met her. Maybe someone noticed something that might help us narrow down what's really going on."

"Certainly." Nana Jo updated her iPad, then she turned her gaze to me. "What are *you* going to do?"

I paused for a few moments. "I'm going to swing by and check on Alva."

Everyone started to object at once, so I raised a hand to stop the onslaught.

"Look, I will be careful. I'm just going to go and drop off a cake, pie, or whatever yummy baked goods Frank has at the restaurant. With any luck, I'll get to see Alva, and maybe I can nose around a bit. Maybe she's batty and spends her days alone in a room, staring at the wall or talking to people that aren't there. If there's any truth to her story, then maybe at least they'll know that someone is watching," I said.

"Well, I don't like it." Nana Jo frowned. "No way are you going alone."

"I'm not going alone. I'll bring Frank with me. If he can't make it, then I'll give you a call." I smiled at my grandmother.

Even though my grandmother was in her seventies, she was also close to five foot ten, nearly two-hundred-fifty pounds, and was a force to be reckoned with. She had a black belt in two different forms of martial arts and was also a crack shot with the gun she kept in her purse and referred to as her "peacemaker." But when it came down to my protection, Nana Jo had to concede that Frank possessed a particular set of skills that he'd honed from years in the military, which made him an excellent bodyguard.

We talked a bit longer, but eventually everyone went home, leaving me and my poodles alone. It had been a long day, and I was exhausted. Snickers and Oreo had spent their day napping, but you wouldn't have guessed it based on the way they acted. Curled up in a ball asleep, Snickers snored like she'd spent the last twelve hours performing heavy labor.

A text from Frank confirmed that he was both willing and able to accompany me to visit Alva Tarkington tomorrow. He offered to whip up a lemon meringue pie and pick me up at ten. I smiled when I got off the phone. Some women liked diamonds. Some liked pearls. My heart melted at the thought of a man who was willing to "whip up a pie" for me.

Frank retired from the military where he'd done things that he still wasn't at liberty to talk about to pursue his dream of opening a restaurant. North Harbor Café was his dream. He loved to cook, and he's good at it. He spent quite a bit of time at the restaurant, but with the approach of our wedding, he hired one of his friends, Garrett Cooper, to help. Garrett Cooper was also ex-military. I don't know the whole story, but apparently his "handlers" wanted him to lay low for a while, and North Harbor was as low as you could go when it came to hiding in plain sight. Frank trusted Garrett and I trusted Frank.

The physical exhaustion I felt hadn't extended to my brain, which hadn't gotten the memo that it was late and we needed to shut down for the night. Instead of drifting off into dreamland, my brain kept replaying the conversation Jenna and I had had with Alva. Was she faking? Did someone really want to kill her? Why would anyone want to kill her?

After tossing and turning for what felt like hours, I decided to stop forcing my brain to relax by giving it something else to focus on. Writing British historical cozy mysteries had been a dream. It had been a secret that I'd only shared with a few of my nearest and dearest. Thanks to a bit of pushing, prodding, and meddling from Nana Jo, the cat was out of the bag. My secret was not only out, but I had an agent and my first book, *Murder at Wickfield Lodge*, was out in the world and doing well. Initially, I started writing to fill the loneliness after Leon's death. Over time, I discovered that writing helped me sort through my thoughts. Nana Jo said writing allowed my subconscious to figure out the problems my conscious mind couldn't. Perhaps a trip in the British countryside would help sort through the muddle of what to do about Alva Tarkington. If nothing else, writing gave me something productive to do.

Cellar at Wickfield Lodge, England—September 1939

"Good Gawd! What is it?" Mrs. McDuffie, the Marsh Family housekeeper, frowned.

Mrs. McDuffie was a stout, middle-aged woman with a freckled complexion. Her fluffy red hair was thin and curly. Coarse and unpolished, Mrs. McDuffie didn't fit the image of a traditional manor house housekeeper. Hardworking and stern, she was also fiercely loyal to the Marsh Family and was a much loved and well-respected member of the household.

The wine cellar was cold and dark. While Mrs. McDuffie prided herself on the thoroughness with which she and her staff cleaned the large manor home, she wasn't as confident that the seldom-used wine cellar was as free of dust and cobwebs as the rest of the house. She frowned as she watched as workmen stacked crates against the brick walls.

"I . . . I don't rightly know, but I believe it's what is referred to as *modern* art," Thompkins stared at a painting that had hastily been propped against the crates.

Prim, proper, and rigid, the Marsh Family butler was the complete opposite of the housekeeper. Three generations of Thompkinses had served the Marsh Family and the butler was determined to uphold the tradition with dignity and pride.

A delicate cough interrupted the servants. "Excuse me, but this isn't just art. It's *Paul Klee*." The curator of the National Gallery, Nelson Wilmington's voice held a note of awe and pride. The man himself was short, and thin with average features except for a large beak-like nose.

"Never 'eard of 'im," Mrs. McDuffie said.

Eyes wide and mouth open, the curator clicked his heels and straightened his back. "Paul Klee is only one of the greatest modern artists of our time." He smiled indulgently and modulated his voice as if he were an announcer on a BBC documentary or a reel at the cinema. "Paul Klee was born in Münchenbuchsee in 1879. He—"

"Münchenbuchsee? That sounds German," Thompkins said.

"German? We're fighting a war with the Germans." Mrs. McDuffie frowned. "Why should we store their art in our English cellars?"

The war that had been looming on the horizon for years had finally arrived. In spite of the efforts of Prime Minister Neville Chamberlain, and the backroom dealings by the Cliveden Set to appease Hitler, Germany had crossed the line. Literally. England had turned a blind eye when the Nazis invaded Austria and Czechoslovakia, but when Hitler invaded Poland, England could no longer remain silent. England and France were bound to honor the treaty to defend Poland's borders and declared war on Germany. Unlike the Great War, this time around no one was under the illusion that this war would be quick and without heavy losses. Nevertheless, brave men and women both abovestairs and below knew their duty. Lady Penelope Marsh's husband, Victor Carlston, the Earl of Lochloren, and two of the Marsh Family's staff, Jim Leonard and Frank McTavish, were among the first to enlist and were away receiving military training. Lord James FitzAndrew Browning the 15th Duke of Kingsfordshire was abroad on a top-secret mission. Even Detective Inspector Peter Covington of Scotland Yard and Lady Clara Trewellen-Harper, Lady Elizabeth Marsh's cousin, had decided to forego their elaborate marriage for a civil ceremony at the Caxton Hall Register Office in London. Detective Inspector Covington enlisted in the Royal Air Force and would be shipped out as soon as he completed training. Lady Clara, meanwhile, was working on some top-secret things at Bletchley Park that the family knew had something to do with the war effort. Many brave men and women would fight, but even those remaining at home were preparing to do their duty to protect the home front, which was why strangers were unloading crates in Wickfield Lodge's wine cellar.

"Münchenbuchsee is actually in the Bern region of Switzerland." Wilmington paused for several moments before continuing. "But his parents were German and Paul Klee is indeed German."

Mrs. McDuffie's eyes flashed. Before she could rev up for an attack, Wilmington held up a hand. "Paul Klee is also Jewish."

"Lawd." The housekeeper released a breath and clutched the neck of her blouse. Before England declared war, there were rumors about the conditions that Jews were facing under the Nazis. However, ever since the Night of Broken Glass, or Kristallnacht, last November, the world got a chance to see the true face of the Nazis. Jewish homes, hospitals, schools, and even synagogues were destroyed throughout Germany, Austria, and the Sudetenland. Foreign journalists working in Germany reported the riots and destruction as it was happening. They estimated that more than thirty thousand men were arrested and sent to concentration camps.

Nelson Wilmington stepped closer to the two servants and lowered his voice. "Last year, Germany held an art exhibit depicting what they called, 'degenerative art.'" The curator pulled a handkerchief from his pocket and wiped his mouth as though that would remove the foul taste of the words.

"Well, I wouldn't put anything past those Nazis," Mrs. McDuffie said.

"What exactly is degenerative art?" Thompkins asked.

"Pretty much anything Hitler and the Nazi Party deem an *'insult to German feeling'* has been categorized as *'degenerative'* and banned. All modern art falls in that category along with anything created by personas non grata." Wilmington gave a knowing glance to the two servants and waved a hand at the portrait. "We've gotten word that the Nazis are even burning valuable paintings like this."

"Good Lord." Mrs. McDuffie stared at the

painting. "It's not my cup of tea, but that don't mean it should be burned. To each 'is own is what I always say."

Wilmington glanced around to make sure he wasn't being overheard, then leaned closer. "There's been an effort within the art community to save what we can to protect it for future generations. Some of the art—and artists—are being smuggled out of Germany."

"Good Lord. First Jewish children were smuggled out in the Kindertransport, then British women and children aren't even safe in London and had to be evacuated to the countryside. Now even art isn't safe." Mrs. McDuffie shook her head.

"Ah . . . you know about that, do you?" Nelson Wilmington gave the housekeeper and butler an approving nod.

The Marsh Family were cousins of the king, and Lady Elizabeth Marsh was also a cousin to the First Lord of the Admiralty, Winston Churchill. As trusted Marsh servants, they were privy to more than the average person. They were aware that one of the provisions that the government made in preparation for war was the evacuation of children as well as the permanent collection of the National Gallery away from London. The Kindertransport had been transferring children, mostly Jewish, from Nazi-occupied countries to England for nearly nine months. Now, the government's focus had turned inward. Vulnerable groups of children, pregnant women, and women with small children were being evacuated from urban areas and moved to the countryside.

"Sadly, the war will impact all of us, whether we're on the front lines or not. But we must protect our art for generations to come," Nelson Wilmington said. "Plans have been in place for more than a year to make sure that Mr. Hitler and the Nazis don't get their hands on British treasures like these." He waved his hand in front of the crates.

"We all know our duty and we'll keep the art safe." Mrs. McDuffie gave a fierce nod that didn't bode well for any Nazis who dared think they would take a single piece of art if she had anything to say on the matter.

"Most of the works are going to Wales, but we couldn't get everything moved without drawing undue attention." Wilmington glanced around again, then put his finger to his lips. "We must all be on guard. Fifth columnists are everywhere. In fact, some may be closer than anyone realizes." He sighed.

"I would like to see one of those fifth columnist come near Wickfield Lodge." Mrs. McDuffie scowled.

Nelson Wilmington winked and tapped the side of his nose before leaving to reprimand two workers who dropped a crate a bit too roughly.

Mrs. McDuffie leaned close to the butler and whispered, "What's a bloody fifth columnist?"

Chapter 5

Frank Patterson arrived at the bookstore just as Sam was finishing her opening routine. "Hey, did someone order a pie?" Frank handed me a lemon meringue pie and then pulled me close for a kiss.

Frank had soft brown eyes. His salt-and-pepper hair and closely groomed beard were more salt than pepper, but he looked distinguished rather than old. There was something about his straight posture and his bearing that screamed military; even if I didn't know he was retired military, I would know simply by looking at him.

I hugged him close and breathed in his scent of fresh Irish soap, bacon, and coffee. "Hmm. You smell good," I said.

Frank chuckled. "I should just bathe in bacon grease and coffee."

"Two of my favorite scents." I laughed. I put the pie on the counter and turned my full attention to letting Frank know how pleased I was to see him.

"Wow. I was just kidding about the bacon grease, but if that's the response I get I just might give it a try."

I gave his arm a playful swat. "I just wanted to thank you

for the pie. You didn't have to go to the effort, but I appreciate it."

"Sam, I own a restaurant, and I love to cook. It was no problem. Besides, lemon meringue is one of the easiest pies to make, so I whipped up several for the restaurant." He shrugs. "No big deal. Plus, I love baking for you."

"Still, you didn't have to do it." I kissed him again.

"Is everyone decent down here?" Nana Jo made an excessive amount of noise as she came downstairs.

"Of course." I pushed away from Frank.

"Well, darn it. Y'all aren't doing this courting thing right. Now, when me and your grandfather were courting that man knew how to send shivers down my spine. He could go from zero to sixty in five seconds flat."

"Nana Jo!"

"What?" she asked innocently.

Frank chuckled. "I guess I need to up my game."

"Your game is just fine, and don't get her started." I grabbed my coat and picked up my pie. "Are you sure you can handle things?"

Nana Jo waved us out of the store. She was the one who fueled my love of mysteries. Ever since I'd opened the bookstore, Nana Jo had helped me out several days per week. She had a knack for helping indecisive customers find just the right mystery by asking a few questions. Still, she was in her seventies, and I worried about her.

"I got this. Now, you and Frank go." Nana Jo shooed us out the door.

In spite of the fact that Shady Acres was located in South Harbor, Michigan, and I lived in North Harbor, the drive was short. Both towns shared the same Lake Michigan shoreline in the southwestern corner of the state. Despite the shared geography, the twin cities of North and South Harbor were worlds apart in demographics and economics. North Harbor, Michigan, had once been a manufacturing hub for the automobile industry. Large Victorian homes dotted the streets as a reminder of the wealth and opulence that once reigned in this lakeside community. Unlike Detroit, which was known for manufacturing cars, North Harbor was known for supplying car parts. When automobile manufacturers packed up and made the great exodus, taking the lucrative jobs elsewhere, North Harbor's economy went with them. The town never recovered. South Harbor had originally been a town for the working class with smaller, less pretentious homes. During the civil rights riots, a great racial and economic divide was created. While North Harbor was economically depressed, South Harbor was reborn as a tourist town with cobbled streets, a lighthouse, and multimillion-dollar beachfront homes.

North Harbor had a small number of diehards who refused to accept the towns decline without a fight. Leon and I had been among them. Efforts were made to revitalize the downtown, and renovate the now dilapidated Victorian homes that had been abandoned into lovely single-family homes. The renovation was slow, but Rome wasn't built in a day.

The drive highlighted the distinctions between the two towns. Frank drove the short distance to Shady Acres Retirement Village. Shady Acres was a senior community located on the shores of Lake Michigan. It was a private, gated community for active seniors with a variety of housing options. There were detached single-family homes the residents called villas, town houses, condos, and apartments. Each resident had a card that opened the gates and unlocked the main doors. Nana Jo owned a villa that she purchased when the development was just under construction, but she spent most of the week with me at the bookstore and stayed in her villa on weekends. I pulled out the card key that got us through the gates and Frank pulled inside.

Alva Tarkington's villa was larger than Nana Jo's but didn't have views of Lake Michigan. Homes with that sort of view went fast; lake-front with access went even faster. Nana Jo's home would be worth a lot if she ever decided to sell. Even without the views of a great lake, Alva's villa was nicely situated and had likely set her back a small fortune.

Frank pulled up to Alva's house, but the driveway had a surprising number of vehicles. "Looks like Alva has a lot of company."

I glanced out the window. "I wonder how many people live with her."

Frank parked on the street in front of the house, and we got out of the car and walked up to the driveway.

Before we could ring the doorbell, the front door opened. A woman stood in the doorway. Tears streamed down her face. One glance in those tortured eyes and I knew without one word spoken that Alva was dead.

Two men wearing dark suits pulled a gurney out through the door.

Frank placed a protective arm around my waist and pulled me against his chest, out of the path of the gurney.

I felt as though a rock landed in my stomach, and my knees shook.

Frank tightened his arm around my waist. "You okay?"

I wasn't.

We were too late. Alva Tarkington was dead.

Chapter 6

Dead. Alva Tarkington was dead. We failed her. The words bounced around in my head like the metal ball in a pinball machine. *Failure. Failure. Failure.*

"Stop it, Sam." Frank grabbed my shoulders and gave me a firm shake.

"What? How did you know?" Did I say those words out loud?

"I'm no mind reader, but I don't have to be to see the guilt written on your face." Frank took the pie from my hands and pulled me into a tight hug.

"Isabella, close the door and stop all that sniveling. You're—" A man walked up behind the crying woman at the door and halted when he saw Frank and me standing on the porch.

"Can I help you?" the man asked.

"We came to see Alva." I forced the words out of my mouth.

The man scowled and looked as though he would slam the door in our face, but I felt a growl rise in Frank's chest.

One look at my fiancé and I sensed danger. Gone was the

calm restauranteur that I fell in love with. In his place was the military veteran who knew how to kill with a paper clip.

The man tried to close the door, but Frank extended his arm. His hand slapped the door and it swung backward, barely missing the man. Frank stepped forward.

Then it was my turn to provide comfort. I wrapped my arm around Frank's waist. He was muscular with a six-pack that made my heart race, but he was wound tight as a spring and was ready to pounce.

"Who are you?" the man asked.

I tightened my arm around Frank and stepped forward. "My name's Samantha Washington and this is Frank Patterson. We were friends of Alva. We just saw her yesterday. Is she . . ."

"Sorry, but Alva died." The man frowned and waited as if he expected us to turn around and leave.

Frank's eyes were drilling a hole through the man's head like lasers, just daring him to say something so he could punch him in the throat.

"Are you Carl?" I asked on a whim.

The man's head jerked back. "How do you know my name?"

"We met your wife, Bethany, yesterday," I said.

A nasally voice from the back yelled, "Carl, what's taking so long? I checked every drawer, and I still can't find a will anyplace. Are you sure—" Bethany stepped behind her husband and stopped short at the sight of Frank and me.

We hadn't been invited inside and stood on the porch. Frank was still staring down the man I now knew was Carl Tarkington. The woman who first opened the door, Isabella, dabbed at her eyes with a handkerchief.

"What are you doing here?" Bethany asked, barely bothering to conceal the frost from her voice.

"We came to see Alva. We brought her a pie." I reached across and took the pie from Frank's clutch.

"A pie?" Bethany frowned and folded her arms across her chest.

"Yes, a pie." I forced a smile. "And when my sister, Jenna Rutherford, the lawyer you talked to yesterday, found out I was coming, she wanted me to find out if you and your husband had arranged for a time for her to continue the discussion on estate planning." With one hand wrapped around Frank's waist, trying to keep him from ripping Carl Tarkington's face off, and the other hand holding a pie, I wasn't able to cross my fingers. So I mumbled a silent prayer of forgiveness for the lie.

"Yes, I was going to call her," Bethany said quietly.

"Did you say something?" Carl asked.

"Jenna Rutherford is the attorney I was telling you about. She promised to give us a free consultation." Bethany flashed a smile that didn't make it to her eyes. "Don't just stand there, Carl. Let them in."

Bethany reached forward and took the pie, and then wrenched the door from her husband's hand to hold it open.

Carl grunted and marched into the other room.

Frank stepped inside, making sure to keep me firmly to his side. He leaned close and whispered, "That was strike one."

Once we were inside, Bethany closed the door and shoved the pie at the woman Carl called Isabella, who was still crying.

Bethany led us to a formal living room that was excessively formal with gilded Queen Anne furnishings.

Frank and I perched on an ornately carved white sofa in a room with white walls, white carpet, and white drapes. The only color in the room came from a large painting hanging over the fireplace of two young women who looked like mirror images of each other.

Bethany had flopped down in an uncomfortable chair across from us while Carl avoided making eye contact with

Frank. He leaned against the fireplace with his arms folded across his chest.

We sat in awkward silence for several beats before I mustered up my courage. "First, I want to convey my condolences to you both on Alva's passing."

"Thank you," Bethany said.

I waited a beat for an explanation. When none came, I tried again. "It seems so sudden. Yesterday she seemed completely fine and now—"

"Sudden? You must not have known her well if you thought her death was sudden." Carl rolled his eyes. "She's been lingering for a long time, too long."

"That's a surprise," I said.

"Shows how much you knew." Carl turned to Bethany. "I told you not to waste your time putting that hideous Victorian green wallpaper in her bedroom. Waste of money."

Frank growled and was about to rise when I reached over and squeezed his knee and he returned to his seat, but his gaze narrowed even more. He mumbled, "Strike two."

I wasn't a big baseball fan, but I didn't have to be to know that if Carl Tarkington threw out one more insult he was a dead man.

"She seemed fine yesterday," I said.

"Alva's been ill for a long time," Bethany said. "That's why she came back from Egypt a couple of years ago. She didn't have long, and she wanted to spend the time she had remaining with her family."

"Are you her only family?" I asked.

"Yes. Well, we're the only ones left." I must have looked puzzled because Bethany continued. "Alva married Carl's uncle, Oliver. They never had children. She had a twin sister, Zelda. They were both very close, but Zelda died in Egypt years ago."

I glanced at the painting. "Is that them?"

"Hmm. Yes. I believe Zelda painted it. She wasn't very good." Bethany frowned.

"They look identical. I can't tell them apart," I said.

"I'm told they were very close. Zelda never married. After Oliver died, Zelda moved abroad to be with her sister," Bethany said.

The crier who opened the door, Isabella, came into the room and hovered in the doorway. "Would you like me to prepare coffee or tea?"

Carl snorted, but was at least smart enough not to speak.

Based on the tension rolling through the air and vibrating from Frank, I needed to get him out before Carl was nothing more than a stain on Alva's white carpet. "We'd better be going. I'm sure you have a hundred things to do, and we don't want to bother you." I stood and pulled Frank to his feet.

"Refreshments won't be necessary, Isabella," Bethany said. "Why don't you go back to the kitchen and see to lunch."

"And then start packing. Now that Alva's gone, your services are no longer needed," Carl sneered.

Isabella clutched her hand to her mouth to contain a whimper.

"Strike three." Frank took a step toward Carl, but I pressed both hands against his chest, planted both feet into the carpet, and pushed.

Frank was strong, and all his protective instincts were engaged. There was no way I would be able to hold him back physically. I needed to defuse the situation, but my brain went blank. Then lightning flashed. "I'm not sure that's a good idea in light of the current situation."

"What's not a good idea?" Bethany asked.

"Letting Alva's staff go." I shuffled Frank toward the door. "I would think you might need to wait until the reading of the will or something, but then I'm not the expert. My sister,

Jenna, could probably tell you whether you're authorized to terminate staff, but I don't know anything about that stuff."

"What do you mean? We're Alva's family—her only family. Her heirs," Carl said.

Frank and I continued to make our way to the door.

"Wait. What do you mean?" Bethany asked.

"Like I said, I'm not the expert, but I think there are some rules around what you can and can't do when someone dies, but it's probably all in Alva's estate plan."

"Alva didn't have an estate plan. She had a will, but we haven't found it," Bethany said.

"Oh, well . . . maybe you should reach out to Alva's attorney." We were almost at the door.

Bethany rushed to the door. Her face was frantic. "Well, maybe you could ask Jenna. I mean, she did offer to give us a free consultation and we could really use it right now."

"Bethany! We don't need—"

Bethany shot a Darth Vader death glance at her husband. The words froze on his tongue. If looks could kill, Carl Tarkington would have choked to death instantly.

"I'll talk to my sister and see if she can come—"

"Today? Can she come today? With Alva dead, we need answers. We need to resolve this. Please, tell her that we will be available today." Bethany waited for a beat. "Please."

"I'll talk to her," I promised.

Frank shuffled me outside and into the car. He didn't speak until we passed through the gates of Shady Acres. "From the moment Carl Tarkington opened his mouth, I've wanted to smash my fist through his face. But . . ."

"But?" I asked.

"Then I met Bethany. Did you see the way her head whipped around when he started objecting to Jenna coming to talk to them?"

"She's pretty scary."

"I wouldn't have been surprised if she started spewing out green venom." He rubbed the back of his neck. "I almost felt sympathetic toward Carl."

I raised an eyebrow and turned to face him.

"I said *almost*."

"She's vicious, but is she vicious enough to have killed Alva?" I asked.

"My money is on Carl." Frank gripped the steering wheel as we made our way back to the bookshop.

Chapter 7

I sent a text to Nana Jo, Jenna, and the girls informing them about Alva.

After a slew of shocked, sad, and anger emojis from everyone, Nana Jo suggested we meet for lunch at Frank's restaurant.

My call to Jenna went to voicemail, but she sent a thumbs-up emoji about lunch, so I decided to wait to talk to her.

Frank's restaurant, North Harbor Café, isn't far from the bookstore, so we arrived roughly at the same time as Nana Jo and everyone else.

"Perfect timing. Dawson just arrived and is holding down the fort at the bookstore while we meet," Nana Jo said.

Dawson Alexander was one of my former students when I taught high school English. He was now a student at Michigan Southwest University (MISU) on a football scholarship. He had a turbulent relationship with his father. After a tough freshman academic year nearly cost him his scholarship, Dawson moved into the apartment over my garage and became my assistant at the bookstore. Nana Jo and I tutored him and while he wasn't on the Dean's List, he was doing well. Dawson wasn't a mystery lover, preferring fantasy instead, although he had become a fan of Jim Butcher's Dresden Files series featuring Harry Dresden, a Chicago P.I. who just happened to be a wizard. Dawson had also discovered a love of baking, which kept the bookstore amply supplied with baked goods.

Similar to my bookstore, Market Street Mysteries, Frank's restaurant was located in a downtown storefront. Unlike my building, where the upstairs had been converted into living space, his building wasn't. Frank planned to renovate the upstairs to provide additional seating and possibly space for private parties. It was off limits for most patrons, but whenever our group needed to meet, that's where we did it. Being engaged to the owner came with definite perks.

By the time everyone arrived and we were settled, Garrett Cooper came up to take our drink orders. Garrett was tall, dark, and extremely handsome.

I'd taken a seat in between Nana Jo and Jenna and was directly across from Irma. Even from the other side of the table, I heard Irma growl when she batted her eyelashes at Garrett.

Garrett jumped and a look of panic crossed his face. He forced a smile, but took two steps farther away from Irma.

"Five dollars says she just pinched our waiter's butt," Jenna whispered.

"I'm not crazy enough to take that bet."

Frank stopped downstairs when he arrived to check on things, but came upstairs with a pitcher of water with lemons, my favorite. He poured a glass and placed it in front of me. Then he reached down and kissed my earlobe and said, "Cooper was a sniper in the military, and has done things that would curl your hair. But he nearly swallowed his tongue when Irma squeezed his butt. I'm going to need to start paying hazard pay to my male servers."

Jenna nearly choked on her Moscato.

"I'll talk to her." I paused a beat. "Or I'll have Nana Jo talk to her."

Irma was still ogling Garrett, who was doing his best to keep his rear more than an arm's length distance from Irma. After the drinks were served, and he had our food orders, he wiped his brow and ran down the stairs.

"Irma! You have got to stop . . . manhandling the staff," I said.

"You're going to get slapped with a sexual assault lawsuit," Jenna said.

"But he looks so delicious. I just couldn't help myself. He looks just like Idris Elba. Every time I see him I just want to squeeze his—"

"Irma!" everyone shouted.

Irma broke into a coughing fit. She reached into her purse, pulled out a flask, and took a swig of whatever she'd brought with her, having already downed the amber-colored beverage Garrett had just dropped off moments earlier.

Jacob, Dorothy's nephew, was all in for the story.

"I suppose I can make it a memorial rather than a current feature." Dorothy released a heavy sigh. "I did find that Alva had dealings with the Linton Museum of Art."

"LIMA?" It took me several seconds to remember the museum's real name. Growing up in North Harbor, I rarely heard the museum referred to by its full name. In grade school, I spent many field trips wandering through the dark wood-paneled rooms, staring at paintings and artifacts while a family member droned on for what felt like years about the family's proud heritage.

"I didn't know there were any Lintons left," Ruby Mae said.

"Yeah. Ethan Linton is the last," Dorothy said.

"That place always gave me the creeps." Jenna shivered. "It was dark and gloomy."

"There used to be a suit of armor at the front door that gave me nightmares." I shook my head to erase the memory.

"Honestly, I thought that museum closed years ago. It's not like it's a major tourist attraction, especially since they opened that fancy new museum near the library in South Harbor," Nana Jo said.

"Does Ethan Linton still live there?" I asked.

"I'm meeting with him later today. I can find out." Dorothy shrugged. "I also learned a bit about Alva."

We waited while Dorothy pulled out a small notepad and flipped to the correct page. "Did you know Alva was a twin?"

"Identical or fraternal?" Jenna asked. As the mother of fraternal twins, Jenna was the person in our group who knew the most about twins.

"Identical," Dorothy said.

"Frank and I saw a painting of the sisters together when we were at Alva's house. Apparently, they were both artists."

Dorothy nodded. "Alva was a sculptor, while her sister, Zelda, was the painter."

"Were they any good?" Ruby Mae asked.

Dorothy shook her head. "From what I've seen, they were amateurish. Zelda lacked creativity and innovation."

"What about Alva?" Jenna asked.

"I'm certainly no expert on sculpture, but her work was better. She liked to include a bit of Egyptian style, but she hadn't produced anything in years. Not since her sister died," Dorothy said.

"Why?" Nana Jo asked.

"No idea. Maybe it's grief. I'll see if Ethan Linton knows anything when I meet with him." Dorothy shrugged. "Anyway, that's all I have right now."

"You did well." Nana Jo patted her friend's hand.

We hadn't expected to meet so quickly and most of the group hadn't had time to get any information yet.

We ate and made plans to meet tomorrow for lunch.

"I'll confirm that Alva's addendum is okay, then I'll meet with Bethany and Carl tomorrow morning," Jenna said.

"I never thought these words would ever leave my mouth, but I wish Stinky Pitt were here." Nana Jo glanced at the shocked expressions on everyone's faces. "At least Sam would be able to get the information about Alva's cause of death out of him."

"I don't know if he could help in this case," I said.

"Sam's right. The police would only be involved if Alva was murdered or if they had reason to believe that there was anything suspicious about her death. Alva's death will be declared natural causes. I don't think Carl is going to let anything like a medical examination stand in his way," Frank said.

"There has to be some way we could get the police to look into this," Nana Jo said.

"There might be one way we could get the police involved."

I hadn't noticed Garrett Cooper had returned until he spoke. I watched as he placed our drinks beside each of us.

"What's that?" I asked.

Garrett glanced at Frank, who gave him a brief nod. Garrett nodded. "You could use the old standby, an anonymous tip."

Six confused faces turned to stare.

"Anonymous tip?" I asked.

Garrett's lips twitched. "The police get them all the time. Someone calls the police station and leaves an *anonymous tip* that there's something suspicious about Alva's death and they might want to run some tests before the family has a chance to have her embalmed and evidence is destroyed."

Silence descended over the room like a blanket.

After a few moments, Garrett shrugged. "Sorry. I didn't mean to intrude."

Jenna was the first to recover. "That's not a bad idea. Seriously, the police get a lot of so-called tips."

"It happens all the time on television," Nana Jo said.

"It happens in real life too," Frank said.

"Why?" I asked. "Why not just man up and admit the truth?"

"Fear of retaliation. Not wanting to get involved. Or maybe they don't want to draw attention to something they've been doing." Frank shrugged. "Lots of reasons."

"Maybe they want to make money," Irma said.

We all turned to look at Irma, who was using her knife as a mirror as she reapplied her lipstick.

"What do you mean?" I asked.

"The police are always trying to get people to call that Crime Stoppers number to leave tips. They even offer rewards if your tip leads to an arrest." Irma puckered her lips and then used her napkin to blot the excess. When she finished, she glanced around the table. "What?"

"Who are you?" Dorothy gazed at Irma.

"Why are you looking at me like that?" Irma asked.

Nana Jo shook her head. "It's just that's the first thing you've said that makes sense and doesn't have some type of sexual innuendo."

Irma stuck out her tongue.

"There used to be a crime prevention program when I was teaching where the police went into schools and talked to kids. They had a cute dog mascot," I said.

"Detective McGruff," Jenna said.

"Their motto was 'Take a bite out of crime.'" I smiled at the fond memory.

Garrett Cooper filled glasses, but made sure to take a wide berth around Irma without turning his back to her, but Irma didn't let that stop her. She batted her eyelashes at him and growled—literally growled, "I'd like to take a bite out of—"

"Irma!"

"And now she's back to normal," Dorothy murmured.

Nana Jo turned to Garrett. "Will you make the anonymous call?"

Garrett nodded.

"I can drop a word into the district attorney's ear that he might want to look closer into Alva's death," Jenna said.

"I'm going to do the same thing to Daryl," Ruby Mae said. As North Harbor chief of police, Daryl Stevenson was aware of the assistance we'd provided in the past, but he had also been appointed to his role because of his reputation for integrity and strict adherence to the law. He wouldn't open an investigation simply because a friend or family member suggested it. He would need evidence.

"If the police get enough questions raised about Alva's death, they'll have to investigate, right?" I asked.

"Where there's smoke there must be fire." Dorothy nodded.

Jenna shrugged. "Maybe."

"With all of those tips, that should be enough to get the police at least curious," I said. "I know most of you haven't had time to get any information, but is there anything else we need to discuss?" Nana Jo pulled out her iPad.

"I'm going to go down to the courthouse to check on Alva's will. Plus, I'll give Bethany and Carl a call and schedule an estate planning session with her," Jenna said.

"I'll go with you," I said.

"Why on earth would you want to spend one more second near those two if you don't have to?" Jenna asked.

"Because you're my favorite sister." I grinned.

"I'm your only sister," Jenna said.

"Details." I waved away her objection with a quick flick of my wrist and smiled.

Jenna narrowed her gaze. "What do you want?"

"Nothing." I chuckled at our familiar routine for a few seconds and then got serious. "If you have the meeting at

Alva's I can try and talk to the housekeeper, I think her name was Isabella. She was the only person who genuinely seemed sad that Alva was dead. If I can get her alone, maybe I can find out what life in that house was really like."

We agreed to meet again tomorrow.

At the bookstore, I relieved Dawson and got lost in taking care of customers. Opening a bookstore that specialized in mysteries had been a dream that my late husband, Leon, and I shared because of our mutual love of mysteries. However, the reality of running a bookstore was different from my idealized dream where I spent my days reading mysteries and surrounded by books like Belle in *Beauty and the Beast*. I was surrounded by books, all right, but these had to be ordered, unpacked, shelved, and inventoried. I didn't think about the unending paperwork, long hours, and fussy customers, marketing, and hundreds of other tasks. I was fortunate to have the support of friends and family, but it was a lot of work that often left me little time to read for the sheer pleasure of reading. Still, I loved it. Between Frank, Dawson, Nana Jo, and my nephews, I had lots of help. Sales were good and I could afford to pay a couple of full-time clerks to help with the day-to-day work, but I liked talking to customers. I liked the smell of the books, and I loved seeing my dream come to life.

"Are you going to just stand there caressing those books?"

Nana Jo's question helped me take the detour away from memory lane and brought me back to reality.

Market Street Mysteries had a steady stream of customers for the remainder of the day, which kept me from spending too much time thinking about Alva. After the last customer left and we locked the door, I took a deep breath and allowed the exhaustion to sweep over me.

Nana Jo and I had developed a routine. We cleaned and prepared the store for the next day in a companionable silence. When we were done, I let Snickers and Oreo out to take care of business while Nana Jo prepared for a date with her boyfriend, Freddie. Freddie Williams was a retired cop and his son, Mark, was a state policeman. Between Freddie and Mark, Nana Jo would find out what information she could.

I spent an hour going through my emails, updating my social media pages, and doing the author-related things that I both loved and hated. I had not only dreamed of opening a mystery bookstore, but of writing British historical cozy mysteries. Now that I was a published author, I discovered that the reality of that career was a lot different from the lifestyle that I imagined based on watching Jessica Fletcher on *Murder, She Wrote*. Still, writing was an escape and at the moment, I needed to escape back in time.

⁂

Lady Elizabeth turned the corner at the bottom of the stairs and entered the servants' dining room. In the hall, Thompkins and the other servants were just finishing their meal but saw Lady Elizabeth and immediately stood at attention.

"Please, I didn't mean to interrupt." Lady Elizabeth motioned for everyone to relax and sit. She would have preferred to stand, but knew the servants wouldn't sit until she did, so she forced a smile and took a seat.

Mrs. McDuffie nodded to the maids as she took her seat.

At one time the Marshes, like many of the older aristocratic families in Great Britain, had retained a staff of more than fifty servants, but times had changed. Even before the war, it had gotten harder to find people willing to dedicate their life to domestic service. Both men and women had a lot more options. The Marsh Family had been fortunate. In addition to the housekeeper, Mrs. McDuffie, and Thompkins, the butler, the family had an excellent cook, Mrs. Anderson, and her daughter, Agnes, who lived in along with one of the maids, Gladys. Two other maids, Flossie and Millie, lived in the village and came daily. However, Lady Elizabeth knew that one or both were planning to join the WRNS. The Women's Royal Naval Service had been disbanded after the Great War, but there was talk of reforming the division. Lord William Marsh had it on good authority that Sir John Knox Laughton's daughter was being tapped to serve as director. Lady Elizabeth had met Elvira Sibyl Marie Laughton, whom everyone referred to as Vera, while working with St. Joan's Social and Political Alliance. The SJSPA had recently presented a paper on the "Condition of Women," to the League of Nations. Vera was a dedicated member of the military and a tireless advocate for women's equality. Lady Elizabeth had no doubt that with Vera at the helm, the WRNS would soon be in shipshape.

Lady Elizabeth glanced around the table, noting the empty seats that would normally have been taken up by the footmen, Frank and Jim. Both men had been the first in their village to enlist. She said a silent prayer that they would return safely to Wickfield Lodge when the war ended.

"First, I want to thank you for your help earlier." Lady Elizabeth nodded to Mrs. McDuffie and Thompkins.

Both the housekeeper and the butler nodded. Lady Elizabeth trusted these people with her life. They were fiercely loyal to the Marsh Family and to their nation. She knew they would die rather than reveal anything to the enemy, but then with all the talk of fifth columnists, it was getting harder and harder to know who the enemy really was. Plus, the artwork stored in the cellar wasn't her secret to reveal. Her cousin, Winston Churchill, a member of Parliament, had asked if they could store the art temporarily until arrangements could be made to transfer it to Wales where most of the other items were being kept. Lady Elizabeth couldn't object. Although, she had been tempted by her cousin's other request.

"Would Your Ladyship like a cup of tea?" Mrs. McDuffie asked.

Lady Elizabeth snapped back to the present. She nodded. "Thank you. I would love a cup."

She smiled as Millie hopped up from her seat and quickly brought a cup while Mrs. McDuffie poured the warm liquid. Mrs. Anderson placed a slice of her delicious lemon-seed cake onto a plate.

Lady Elizabeth took a few moments to enjoy the delicious tea and cake. She hoped that this casual encounter would ease the tension she felt from the young maids, afraid to make a mistake in front of her, but her presence only served to make matters worse. She put down her cup and glanced around at the anxious faces.

"I received a call from my cousin, Mr. Churchill. As you know, Winston was appointed as the First Lord of the Admiralty by the prime minister."

"It's about bloody time," Mrs. McDuffie said.

"Mrs. McDuffie!" Thompkins nearly choked.

Lady Elizabeth held back a chuckle, and raised a hand to prevent the butler from reprimanding the housekeeper too severely for her language. Mrs. McDuffie was a bit coarse and in bygone years, she would not have retained the lofty position of housekeeper. However, times were changing. She might not have the poise and polish of a housekeeper, but Mrs. McDuffie was honest, hardworking, and loyal. More importantly, Lady Elizabeth liked her. "It's all right, and I have to say that I wholeheartedly agree."

Millie and Flossie stifled a laugh.

"I'm sorry for my strong language," Mrs. McDuffie said, "but all that bending over backward to appease 'Itler and the Nazis was enough to make anyone swear."

Thompkins gave a discreet cough. "Was there something else that the Right Honorable, the First Lord of the Admiralty would like?"

"Yes." Lady Elizabeth took a deep breath. "Winston said the prime minister would like to hold a meeting here for the members of his war cabinet."

Milly gasped.

"Good Lawd, the prime minister?" Flossie whispered.

"But we're at war," Mrs. McDuffie said.

Thompkins's cough was much less discreet

as he shot the housekeeper a sharp glance. "Her ladyship and all of England is well aware of the fact that we're at war."

"Sorry," Mrs. McDuffie mumbled.

"If memory serves, there are eight members of the war cabinet. Nine counting the prime minister," Thompkins said.

Lady Elizabeth nodded. "Yes, but only four of them will be coming."

"When will they be arriving?" Mrs. McDuffie asked.

"This evening." Lady Elizabeth flashed an apologetic glance toward the housekeeper.

Mrs. McDuffie issued orders for Flossie and Millie to start getting the spare bedrooms ready. She hoisted herself up from her seat, but was halted when Lady Elizabeth placed a hand on the housekeeper's arm.

"You two get started on the rooms and I'll be up to lend a 'and shortly," Mrs. McDuffie said.

Flossie and Millie gave quick curtsies and then hurried to get the rooms ready for guests.

"Agnes, I have a couple of mince pies in the larder," Mrs. Anderson said.

"I'm sorry to spring a dinner party on you at the last minute. Please don't go to any extra trouble," Lady Elizabeth said. "I warned Winston that he can't expect meals fit for a state dinner with only a few hours' advance notice in the middle of a war."

"Pshaw." Mrs. Anderson frowned. "I know we all need to make sacrifices during wartime, but it's not every day the prime minister dines at our table, and I'm not going to serve fish and chips to the ruddy war cabinet." Mrs. Anderson, like many cooks, was known to be temperamental under the best of circumstances. However, Lady Elizabeth knew she would be humiliated to serve anything less than her best.

Lady Elizabeth nodded. "Whatever you feel is possible, but I don't want you to exhaust yourself."

"My friend gave me a recipe for a date and blue cheese dip. I can quickly whip that up really quickly, and toasted canapés. I have some salmon I was going to smoke, but I'll slice it thin, and it'll go over the canapés with sour cream and dill. Normally, I'd add caviar, but I'm sure capers will work just as well." The cook bit her lower lip and frowned. "We have plenty of mushrooms, and Agnes makes a lovely cream of mushroom soup that'll do for the first course. I can take the rest of the salmon and make fried fish cakes with grilled goat cheese for the second course. The main course will be sliced beef, potatoes, glazed carrots, and grilled courgettes."

"God knows we've got plenty of courgettes. That stuff grows when nothing else does," Mrs. McDuffie said.

"Which is why the Ministry of Agriculture is promoting it for Victory Gardens, but there's only so much courgettes anyone can tolerate." Lady Elizabeth glanced at the cook. "No offense."

"None taken. I'm thinking about trying something different. They hold a lot of water, which will make them ideal for a quick bread. I'm going to play around with different ways to prepare them so I can entice the boys to eat more vegetables," Mrs. McDuffie said.

The boys, Johan and Josiah, were the twins who were staying with the Marsh Family. The boys were part of the Kindertransport that had brought Jewish children from occupied areas of Europe to safety in the British countryside. Now that Britain was at war, a similar program, called Operation Pied Piper, was transporting women and children away from heavily populated areas of the country as well. Johan and Josiah and their baby sister, Rivka, had endured tremendous hardships and weren't normally picky eaters, but vegetables were not high on their list of favorite foods.

Lady Elizabeth trusted Mrs. Anderson's menu selections and quickly allowed the cook to get busy. She turned to the butler and housekeeper. "May I have a word with you both?"

Mrs. McDuffie and Thompkins nodded and waited for Lady Elizabeth to lead the way into the office that Thompkins used for paperwork.

The office was small, but large enough for Lady Elizabeth and Mrs. McDuffie to sit while Thompkins held his tall frame straight and rigid.

"I didn't want to say much in front of the rest of the staff, although I trust them implicitly. However, Winston was adamant that he wanted as few people as possible to know what was really going on," Lady Elizabeth said.

"What is going on?" Mrs. McDuffie asked. "Surely the prime minister isn't coming all the way out here for a dinner party when we've just gone to war."

Lady Elizabeth took a deep breath and then looked at her two trusted servants and friends. "You're right. This isn't just a dinner party. More accurately, this is going to be a hunting party. Instead of hunting pheasant or four-legged wild game, the prime minister's prey will be on two legs—a traitor in his inner circle."

Chapter 8

I woke up the next morning with a weight on my chest. I opened my eyes in time to see a long pink tongue stick out and lick my nose.

"Ugh!"

After nearly fifteen years. I should know better than to open my mouth when faced with my toy poodle, Snickers, mere inches from my mouth, but I must be a slow learner. Like a lizard, she managed to stick her tongue in my mouth.

"Yuck!" I rolled over on my side, dislodging all eight pounds of her.

Undeterred, Snickers licked my face. My arms. My hands. Before long, I was laughing and rolling around playing a weird game of Keep Away where I tried to avoid getting licked. It was a game we played before, and Snickers was adept at winning.

"Good. You're up."

I didn't hear Nana Jo enter the room until she spoke. The distraction took away my advantage and Snickers gave me a final victory lick.

"Snickers, come," Nana Jo said as she opened the door of Oreo's crate wider.

Unlike Snickers, who preferred to sleep in a dog bed on the floor or curled up on my bed, Oreo preferred the safety of his crate. I had long since stopped locking the crate, but given a choice, he always chose to sleep in his safe, enclosed space.

Snickers jumped off the bed and the two dogs did their morning stretches.

"Jenna called. She said you didn't answer your phone."

I glanced at the nightstand where I left my phone and realized I'd forgotten to put it on the charger. "Battery's dead."

"She'll be here to pick you up in thirty minutes. I'll let the dogs out while you get dressed."

My brain wasn't firing on all cylinders yet and it took me a few moments to realize what she'd said. I yelled down the hall, "Wait. Why is she coming? Picking me up for what?"

"To see Bethany and Carl Tarkington. She said it was the only time they all had free."

Good grief. It wasn't even seven. I grumbled, but hurried to get a shower. I wasn't a morning person, but Jenna was far worse. If she was making the effort to deal with people this early, then I could too.

By the time I finished my shower, got dressed, and beat my unruly curls into submission, the smell of coffee lured me to the kitchen where Nana Jo had a mug with my name on it. Yep, the mug literally had my name on it. It had been a gift and I loved it. A few minutes later, Snickers and Oreo alerted us that someone was at the door. Thanks to the marvels of modern technology, I checked my phone to confirm that it was my sister and unlocked the door with the app on my phone.

Jenna's hands were empty, so I turned on the electric kettle and pulled out the basket of tea and raw sugar I kept on hand solely for her use.

Unlike Nana Jo and me, Jenna never acquired a taste for coffee. Instead, her morning elixir was tea. Nana Jo described her as a tea snob and the moniker fit.

"Good morning," Nana Jo said.

Jenna grunted.

Nana Jo shook her head, but let the pre-caffeinated snub pass.

We drank in silence. Refilled our cups and then headed off. We were halfway to Shady Acres when Jenna's caffeine meter must have hit full, and she sighed. "I don't want to meet with these people, but I'm going to do it, for Alva."

"For Alva." I raised my coffee in salute and took a sip. "Why so early?"

"Alva's attorney is going over the will and Bethany wanted me present."

"Does she know about the addendum?" I asked.

"Not unless Alva told her." Jenna followed my directions to Alva's house.

There were several cars parked in the driveway, but we found a space on the street. We took a last swig of caffeine, girded our loins, and marched to the front door.

The same red-eyed woman from yesterday opened the door. This time I looked more closely. She was in her twenties with a Mediterranean complexion, brown eyes, and long thick, curly hair. "May I help you?"

"I'm Samantha Washington and this is my sister, Jenna Rutherford." I paused a few moments and added, "We were friends of Alva's. You're Isabella, right?"

Her eyes registered the shock for a few seconds. The shock was replaced by recognition. "You were here yesterday."

I nodded.

"Alva mentioned you." She glanced from me to Jenna. "You're the lawyer."

Jenna nodded.

"Miss Alva mentioned both of you. She liked you. She said you were going to help her."

"We're going to try." I wasn't sure how much help we would be, but we both nodded.

We followed Isabella into the living room, which I was surprised to see was crowded. I had braced myself for Carl and Bethany. I hadn't expected the other people who were at the house. The first person that I noted was a tall, slender man with silver hair and strikingly blue eyes. He was leaning against the wall examining a painting. Next to him was a rather dowdy woman with brownish-red hair that she had pulled back into a severe bun. She had dark eyes, thin lips, and a large nose. The woman studied the handsome man next to her with the same intensity that he applied to the painting.

The last attendee was a big man with a round belly, chubby cheeks, and a somewhat long beard. His eyes were bright and friendly. One look at Jenna and he was on his feet and headed our way. "Counselor."

"Andy?" Jenna stared at the man who had just given her an affectionate bear hug.

"Yes, it's me." He chuckled. "I usually head to Florida around this time every year so none of my Michigan colleagues see me like this." He flicked his beard.

"I wouldn't have recognized you if you hadn't spoken," Jenna said.

"Now you know my secret." He leaned close and whispered, "I'm Santa." He stood back and watched our reactions. His laugh indicated he got the response he was looking for. "Every year, I grow out my beard around this time. Then my wife and I head to Florida to spend the winter with our grandkids. By Christmas, I'll have a full beard. Amanda dyes it white and I get to be Santa . . . although she's having to use less dye each year. Besides"——he waved his hand around his belly—"I have the figure for it and it gives me the perfect excuse to eat lots and lots of cookies." He chuckled and gave a "Ho-Ho-Ho!"

"Wow! You're good," Jenna said.

"Thank you." He turned to me. "And you must be the woman who sells my wife all those blood-curdling murder mysteries that keep her awake until the wee hours of the morning."

"Guilty." I smiled.

"I'm sorry, I should have introduced you. Andrew Martin, this is my sister, Samantha Washington. Sam owns the Market Street Mysteries bookstore."

We shook and that's when the lightbulb came on for me. "Is your wife Amanda Martin?"

He nodded.

"Amanda took over the Mystery Mavens Book Club after their previous president died." I forced myself not to shiver at the memory of Delia Marshall lying dead on the floor of my bookstore. Or the thought that I was nearly arrested for her murder. "Amanda does a fantastic job with the book club. Everyone loves her and the group has more than doubled in size since she took over."

Pride shone from his eyes.

Carl Tarkington frowned from his position in front of the fireplace. "Can we get this over with?"

Jenna clasped Andy Martin's arm. "Can I have a word?" She quickly filled the attorney in on Alva's addendum. She didn't mention the blinked SOS, but pulled out a sheet of paper with a typewritten record of Alva's requests. "I can produce the original document, but it was in rather a fragile state."

Andy scanned the document and then gave Jenna a questioning glance. Whether he sensed something was wrong or not, he didn't say.

Carl approached us, but before he could speak, Andy turned on the Santa Claus charm.

"If everyone will take a seat, I'll get started."

The room was an open concept with a large dining room table that could easily seat ten people. Andy Martin took his seat at the head of the table and everyone else sat.

"My name is Andrew Martin, and my firm had the honor of serving Oliver Tarkington's estate for many years. Condolences on the loss of your aunt and friend." Andy turned a sympathetic glance to each person at the table.

"Look, can we skip the niceties and just get down to the nitty gritty?" Carl asked.

"Of course." If Andrew Martin was shocked by Carl's rudeness, he hid it well.

I could hear Frank in my head: *Strike 1* or *Strike 413*. I lost count. Frank wasn't here, but Jenna was and while I worried that my fiancé would throttle Carl, my sister could be far more dangerous without shedding a drop of blood. Her gaze narrowed and there was an electric energy that vibrated off her.

I reached out a hand under the table and gave her leg an *I'm here. Please don't go all pit bull on this idiot* squeeze. At least, that's what I hoped my squeeze conveyed.

Jenna shot me a look that looked a lot like Frank's umpire count, but I wasn't sure whether Carl or I was the one in danger of striking out. She took a deep breath, and I took it as a good sign.

"Yes, certainly." Andrew shuffled through the papers in front of him. He adjusted his glasses, and cleared his throat. "For the record and for my own benefit, I would like to get the names straight. So I know who is present." He paused for a moment and then continued. "We have Carl Tarkington. Carl is the nephew of Alva's late husband, Oliver."

"I'm his only family," Carl said.

"Carl's wife, Bethany." Andrew Martin nodded at Bethany and then proceeded to do likewise with each person. "Ethan Linton, owner and curator of the Linton Museum of Art."

Linton nodded.

"Margery Brooks, nurse and caregiver."

Margery bowed her head, pulled out a handkerchief, and wiped away an imaginary tear. Ethan Linton placed a supportive arm on Margery's back.

Andrew Martin glanced at the next person at the table. "Isabella Sadat, housekeeper and cook."

Isabella sniffed and real tears streamed down her face.

Bethany rolled her eyes.

"Samantha Washington, who I understand was an acquaintance of Alva's, and Jenna Rutherford." Andrew Martin cleared his throat. "Jenna is an attorney and recently met with Alva about an addendum to her will, but we—"

"She *what?*" Carl yelled. Carl's face was so red it looked purple. His eyes bulged and he stood up so quickly, he knocked over his chair. "That's a lie. There was no addendum. She couldn't have. You're a liar." Spit hung from his lips, making Carl look rabid.

If I thought Frank was a threat to kill Carl, it was nothing to the way my sister looked. If looks could kill, Carl Tarkington would have dropped to the floor like a lifeless rag doll.

"What did you call me?" There were only five words, but they were said slowly and with so much power that each one carried the force of a bullet. However, the words were nothing compared to the look. Something in Jenna's face changed. In one instant she went from Jenna Rutherford, counselor at law to *I'm-Going-To-Rip-Your-Face-off-Jenna-Rutherford-Pit-Bull* in two-point-three seconds. Her nostrils flared. The words were followed by a neck roll. I could swear that steam was coming from her ears.

I reached a hand to her arm and felt heat.

Carl may not have had any sense of self-preservation, but Andrew Martin recognized the signs of an apex predator about to take down a gazelle when he saw it. He set aside his Santa

Claus persona. Gone was the jolly ole elf and in his place was a round, chubby-cheeked, bearded Krampus. "Carl, sit down and shut up—now."

Shocked, Carl stared from angry Santa to Pit Bull. *Talk about being caught between a rock and a hard place.*

Jenna hadn't moved from her seat, but her gaze narrowed. She was wound tighter than a jack-in-the-box and was two seconds from popping. Or, leaping over the table and taking down her quarry.

Carl picked up his chair and flopped down.

Andrew Martin leaned back in his seat, took a deep breath, and adjusted his glasses. He turned to Jenna. "I apologize on behalf of my client's family."

Only then did Jenna transfer her gaze from Carl. She nodded to Andrew.

Bethany leaned across the table toward Jenna. "Mrs. Rutherford, I'm so sorry. Please accept my apology for the horrible behavior of my . . . for Carl."

"Thank you," Jenna said with a clipped tone.

After a few seconds, Carl mumbled an apology, which Jenna didn't bother to acknowledge.

"As I was saying, Jenna Rutherford shared an addendum which I will discuss after we finish with the major distributions." He cleared his throat. "The bulk of the estate of Alva Tarkington is to go to her nephew, Carl Tarkington, and his wife, Bethany."

Carl released a large sigh. "That's the way it should be. I'm the only family Uncle Oliver had. It was his money. Not Alva's. She just married into the family. It's only right that it should go to his blood relative."

Bethany rolled her eyes.

"Alva's designated twenty thousand dollars to the Linton Museum of Art along with several pieces of art which are listed here." Andrew Martin held up a paper with a list of items.

"I had hoped the amount would be larger, but . . . we are of course grateful for the generosity." Ethan Linton looked anything but grateful, but he at least had the grace to keep silent.

"Two thousand dollars to Margery Brooks for her care, and five thousand dollars to Isabella Sadat, cook and housekeeper," Martin said.

"Ha!" Carl snorted. "A measly five thousand dollars is nothing. I'll bet you thought you were going to get more. The way you fawned over her and it was all for nothing."

Isabella lifted her head like a dragon ready to spit fire. "I don't care about her money. I didn't do what I did for money. I loved Miss Alva, but you wouldn't understand that."

Carl snorted again.

Isabella's spark died and she sobbed into a tissue.

"Now, the addendum." Carl looked as though he was about to speak, but Andrew Martin held up a hand to stop him. "The crux of the addendum seems to be that Alva wanted to dispose of some of her paintings to the Linton Museum and to Miss Sadat. There are three paintings, *Daisies in a Vase, Woman in the Mirror,* and *Sisters,* which are to go to the Linton Museum of Art. Two other paintings, *Man with a Green Tie,* and *Horses on a Bluff,* are to go to Miss Sadat, along with a diary of poems that belonged to her sister, Zelda. She further stipulates that any of her or her sister Zelda's art that Carl and Bethany don't want is to be given to Miss Sadat."

"Is that all?" Carl asked.

"Yes. That's basically it." Andrew Martin removed his glasses and looked at Carl. "Now, if you want to contest the legitimacy of the addendum, that is within your rights. However, if you do contest the addendum, it will put everything on hold

until this matter is settled. I don't know the value of the paintings, but—"

"Nothing. Those paintings of Alva's aren't worth the money
she spent on the paint. If that's all that she put in the addendum,
then she can have them. I don't want any of that junk." Carl
waved his hand and grinned.

"I would be honored to have her paintings and Miss Zelda's
sculptures," Isabella said.

Andrew Martin nodded. "Then I think that's it."

"Let's go. I need to get out of here." Jenna rose and started
toward the door.

I hurried after her.

"Wait." Bethany rushed to meet us at the door. "Please,
Mrs. Rutherford. I'm sorry about Carl, but you promised to
help with estate planning. I understand if you don't want to
talk to Carl after he was so rude to you, but would you be
willing to meet with me?"

Jenna stopped, but the look on her face indicated she would
rather wrestle an alligator naked while rolling in a field of broken glass than stay.

"Carl is a jerk, and I'm sorry he insulted you, but please?"

Bethany was excellent at groveling, but I still didn't think
she stood a chance at convincing Jenna to stay and share her
expertise. Then Bethany surprised me.

"Please. I need your help. If you don't help me, then I'm
just going to end up like Alva."

Chapter 9

Talk about a mic-dropping bombshell.

"What do you mean?" Jenna asked.

"Not here. Let's go someplace quiet." Bethany glanced over her shoulder. Her unspoken gesture indicated that she wanted to go someplace away from Carl, which was fine with Jenna and me.

We followed Bethany down the hall and through a breezeway that led to a greenhouse. There was a sign on the greenhouse door that sparked a memory.

"Danger. Do Not Open. Door to Death," I read.

"Interesting sign," Jenna said.

That's when it clicked. "Nero Wolfe." I pointed at the sign. *Door to Death* was the title of a Nero Wolfe mystery. My brain was overloaded. I turned to Bethany and tried to hide my surprise. "You read mysteries?"

"Alva read mysteries, but when she discovered my hobby, she gave me the book and painted this sign." Bethany removed the sign and unlocked the door. She pushed the door open and stepped aside for us to enter.

Jenna stepped forward, but I grabbed her sleeve and pulled her to a stop. "If I remember the Nero Wolfe book, that sign was used to warn people not to enter a greenhouse where poisonous gas had been used to fumigate."

Bethany gave a devilish grin, and stepped past us and entered the greenhouse. "I just keep the sign to scare Carl away."

Jenna and I hesitated a few moments and then followed Bethany inside.

"So, you don't use poisonous gas?" I asked.

"I use Cyanogas G, which is calcium cyanide, but I'm always extremely careful. I have excellent venting."

The greenhouse wasn't huge, but it was a colorful and exotic oasis. The walls were lined with shelves that were full of strange and vibrant blooms. There was a long bench covered in colorful plants in various stages of development.

"Wow!" I stood in one place and turned in a circle taking it in.

"Are those orchids?" Jenna asked.

"Yeah. It's a hobby." Bethany looked around at the vibrantly colored plants that appeared to be from a completely different world.

"This is amazing." I tried to make sure that my tone was one of awe rather than shock, but I'm not sure I succeeded.

"This used to be Alva's art studio," Bethany said.

"You work fast. She just died yesterday," Jenna said.

"Alva stopped painting and sculpting months ago."

Jenna and I took a few moments to appreciate the beauty that surrounded us. It truly was an amazing space.

"This is my escape. I've always wanted to travel. See the world. Go to tropical islands where plants like these grow on the side of the road like weeds or wildflowers grow in Michigan." Bethany shrugged. "Carl isn't big on travel." She puffed out her chest and put her hands on her hips. " 'No wife of mine is going to go to some third-world backwater and bring home some disease that'll make your skin fall off and your hair fall out.'"

Her tone was as domineering and arrogant as her husband.

"Leprosy? Seriously?" I asked.

"You met him." Bethany chuckled.

"Couldn't you have found a compromise and maybe gone to Hawaii? My husband and I love Maui and all the islands," Jenna said without the frost that had coated her words since Carl stuck his foot in his mouth and insulted her.

"Carl doesn't believe Hawaii is part of the United States."

Stunned, Jenna and I both stared at her.

"Wait, what do you mean he doesn't *believe*? This isn't a question of faith or magic. What's to believe?" I asked.

Bethany shrugged. "Now you get an idea of what I'm dealing with. And I've had enough. That's one of the reasons I wanted to talk to you."

Jenna shook her head and gave Bethany a closer look. "I'm afraid I don't understand."

"I'm planning to leave Carl and I'm hoping you can help me."

Chapter 10

I was getting whiplash trying to keep up with the shocking twists and turns in Bethany's conversation. My sister and I don't look alike, but one glance at her and I saw the same confusion I knew was mirrored on my face.

"I'm a criminal lawyer, not a divorce attorney. Although I can recommend someone who you can talk to, I'm not the right person—"

"Wait. Just hear me out before you turn me down." Bethany pulled two stools from under the bench, walked over to a corner and pulled a third stool out.

We sat and waited while Bethany got her thoughts together. After a few moments, she started. "Carl hasn't always been a butthead. He used to be thoughtful and kind, but lately all he talks about, all he thinks about is money. We had to have money. He works as an investment banker and he earns a good salary, but he barely lets me spend a dime. Save. Save. Save. Invest in our future. In twenty years, we can retire and enjoy our lives." She shook her head. "In twenty years, we'll be too old to enjoy our lives."

"Was Carl obsessed with more than just your money? Was he also obsessed with Alva's money?" I asked.

Bethany nodded. "He said it wasn't her money. It was his uncle Oliver's money."

"Oliver was Alva's husband, right?" Jenna asked.

Bethany nodded. "Carl said that didn't matter. She was his wife, by marriage only. He was blood. He felt he had a stronger claim on the money than Alva."

"That's not the way the courts look at things unless Carl inherited the money and it was entailed," Jenna said.

"It wasn't. Carl's father, Henry, and his brother, Oliver, grew up poor. Oliver worked hard and got a degree in archaeology. He went to Egypt, which is where he met Alva. They fell in love and got married. Oliver was a professor and archaeologist. He headed a dig that unearthed some remarkable finds. He became an expert in his field and was highly regarded by Egyptologists. But all Carl cared about was the money that he made and that he thought Alva was squandering."

"Well, it looks like Carl is going to get what he wants, Alva's money," Jenna said.

"Alva couldn't die fast enough for him."

Bethany's words landed like two tons of concrete.

"Are you suggesting that your husband may have killed Alva?" I said quietly.

Bethany paused for several moments and then shook her head. "I don't know, but I'm scared. He was getting more and more desperate and . . . cruel. A few years ago, I never would have imagined Carl capable of murder, but now I don't know."

"If you have reason to suspect that Carl killed his aunt, then you need to go to the police. You need to—"

"No. No way. *If* Carl killed Alva, and I'm not saying that he did, but if he did then he's more than capable of killing me too. Either way, I'm done. I'm outta here. I have put up with his penny-pinching, Neanderthal ways far too long."

"Why'd you stay?" Jenna asked.

"What?" Bethany tilted her head and looked at Jenna as though she wasn't speaking English.

"Why did you stay with him? Why didn't you leave him sooner?" Jenna asked.

Bethany colored. A flush rose up her neck and expanded to her cheeks. She looked away. After a few moments, she choked out a laugh. Bethany came to a decision. "Why not." She turned toward us. "All of Carl's talk about investing must have finally sunk in. I've invested too much time and effort into this marriage to walk away with nothing. If Carl was going to get a big windfall, then I was going to hang around and get my share. Now, I just need you to tell me who I can talk to in order to make sure that I get every dime that I'm entitled to from his estate."

Chapter 11

"As a public defender, I've had to deal with some of the worst criminals in North Harbor, but none of them were as cold and calculating as Carl and Bethany Tarkington." Jenna gripped the steering wheel as she drove us back to my building.

"Do you think Carl killed Alva?" I asked.

Jenna shrugged. "No idea. If what Bethany said is true, he had the motive. He was living in the house and had the opportunity. We don't know what killed her . . . if she was killed. So we don't know if he had the means. As long as Alva didn't die of something exotic like the toxin excreted from a poison dart frog that's only found in the tropics, then I'd say there's a good chance that he had the means."

"Poison dart frogs?" I stared at my sister's face. Surely she wasn't serious.

"According to Bethany, Carl would never leave the United States and as far as I know, those frogs are only found in Central and South America," Jenna said. "If he thinks Hawaii is a different country, then no way would he travel to South America to get frog poison."

I laughed. After a few moments, Jenna joined me. It wasn't funny, but the laughter helped to relieve the stress and the tension of the past few days. We finally stopped when she pulled up in front of Market Street Mysteries.

There weren't a lot of people inside. I relieved Nana Jo, not because she was tired and needed the break. There was something therapeutic about working at the bookstore. Restocking the shelves didn't take a lot of thought. I could zone out and allow my mind to wander while I performed the repetitive tasks of bending, shelving, scootching books over, and then bending to grab the next books and repeating the process. It didn't require major brain power, yet I got the gratification of seeing the shelves organized and bursting with color and possibilities. The occasional customer came in, which provided a much-needed break. I loved talking to customers about mysteries and helping them find books they loved. Nana Jo was excellent at helping customers discover the right subgenre of crime fiction and even targeting the right book. She asked a series of questions: *What's your favorite hobby? What do you do for fun? Who is your favorite sleuth?* Her system wasn't scientific, but she could hone in on the types of books that a particular reader would enjoy, whether they liked British historical cozy mysteries or paranormal mysteries like Kay Charles's Marti Mikkelson, a sleuth who sees dead people.

Books made me happy. My bookstore wasn't large, but the shelves were lined with old friends and exciting new puzzles to be solved. This was my happy place. Running a bookstore was a lot of work. I didn't have the time to read as much as I once imagined that I would, but being here always felt like I was wrapped in a warm, cozy blanket. Immersed in my world, time passed quickly.

When it was time to close, I hadn't made much progress in figuring out if Bethany or Carl killed Alva, but I had a lot of questions. Surprisingly, I had to admit that it was a lot harder to solve a mystery without Stinky Pitt. That realization was shocking. It's not like Detective Pitt was a genius like Nero Wolfe or a great thinker like Hercule Poirot. I chuckled at any comparison between Poirot, the fastidiously dressed great Belgian detective, and Detective Bradley Pitt with his too-tight and too-short polyester clothing. At least he'd eliminated the combover he'd used to hide his bald dome. It was amazing what love could accomplish. One look at Dr. Camilia Patterson and Detective Pitt not only let my nephew cut his hair, but one of the last times I'd seen him was the first I'd seen him wearing anything other than polyester. I guess love could indeed conquer all.

Detective Pitt wasn't Columbo, but he was a detective. If he were here, I could have called and told him about Alva. He would have argued and fought with me, but I'd helped him avoid the embarrassment of arresting the wrong person by solving several murders in the past. He would complain, but ultimately he would have given in and looked into Alva's death. Then I would know what was happening. I would know what she died from. I'd also know what, if anything, the police were doing. But Detective Pitt wasn't here. On a whim, I picked up my phone and called my soon-to-be mother-in-law.

"Sam, this is a pleasant surprise." Camilia's voice was warm, and I could hear her smile even though I couldn't see it. We spent a few minutes on pleasantries. When the conversation began to lull, she abruptly got to the point. "Is everything okay?"

"Yes, of course." I hesitated. "I was just . . . wondering if Stinky—I mean, Brad was around. We have a situation, and I was hoping he might be able to help me."

"Sure, he's right here." Camilia had a muffled conversation with someone I recognized as Detective Pitt, who didn't seem to be interested in talking to me. Even if he hadn't been head over heels in love, I knew Camilia would get him to talk to me, which was why I called her even though I had Pitt's cell number. After a few moments, he gave in to the inevitable and took the phone.

"This better be good. I'm on vacation," he said sharply.

"It's good to talk to you too," I said.

"Look, if you don't get to the point, I'm going to hang up. Like I said, I'm on vacation and—"

"I'm pretty sure Alva Tarkington was murdered, but because she's old I think her nephew is going to cover it up so he can get access to her money."

The phone was quiet so long that I worried that he'd hung up. I looked at my screen to make sure the call was still connected.

There was a heavy sigh. "I'm going to hate myself for asking, but who is Alva Tarkington?"

I started telling him about meeting her at the "Getting Your Ducks in a Row" seminar, but he interrupted me.

"Yeah. Yeah. TMI. Get to the point. What makes you think she was murdered?"

I was reluctant to tell him about the blinked SOS and the addendum to her will written on toilet paper, but I did. "It was just a few paintings."

"What?"

"Why go to so much trouble for a few paintings? She snuck into the bathroom and wrote an addendum to her will on toilet paper. Who does that?"

"A looney toon. That's who," Detective Pitt said sarcastically.

His sarcasm was expected, so I ignored it. I couldn't stop thinking about Alva and why she would go to so much trouble for a few paintings that no one seemed to care much about. Detective Pitt wasn't the most supportive person in my life, which was probably why I was talking to him and not Frank or my grandmother. He challenged me. He challenged my ideas, and my sanity. I didn't need support. I needed a nemesis.

I needed someone who would make my little gray cells work harder to prove my point. I told him everything, and because I knew Detective Pitt needed to have his ego stroked, I asked for his advice. I didn't need to see him to know he was rubbing his hand over his face and puffing out his cheeks.

"Look, if you think this woman was murdered, I suggest you call the police."

"As a member of the North Harbor Police Department, do you think they'll take me seriously?"

His silence spoke volumes.

"I didn't think so."

He sighed.

"Bradley, dear," Camilia said in the background.

Dear? Yucky yuck.

"We both know you're just giving Sam a hard time. You're too kindhearted not to help," Camilia said softly.

Kindhearted? Are we talking about the same man? I'd known Stinky Pitt a lot longer than Camilia, and I would bet one of my poodles that his reasons for helping me in the past were in no way attributable to his "kind heart." Fear of failure in front of his peers? Yes. A desire to look good in the media? Yes. Clueless? Yes. Kind heart? Not so much.

"There's one guy that might be able to help. He knows art and he doesn't have a history with you, so he probably won't blow you off." He sighed.

Gee, thanks.

"Special Agent Warren Brown is a good guy. He's young but has a good head on his shoulders. He's from Chicago. Been here working with a team of folks on an art-smuggling case."

"I read about that in the paper. Didn't they find that someone had been smuggling art between Chicago and Detroit and hiding it in caves and tunnels?"

"That's it," Detective Pitt said.

"Didn't they find some of it in New Bison?" I asked.

"Yeah. They think they caught the head rat who was behind it all, but they're still rounding up all of the other rats."

"If he's working art, would he help me with a murder?" I asked.

"Didn't you ask why she would go to that much trouble for some paintings?"

"Yes," I said reluctantly. *Holy cow. He actually listened.*

"And you wanted someone who wouldn't blow you off and that's what I gave you. Brown doesn't know you and your band of crazy old ladies, so he might just take your blinking-SOS,-toilet-paper murder seriously. No guarantees. That's all I got. Take it or leave it."

"I'll take it." I was grateful that I was on the phone and not in person so that Detective Pitt didn't see me stick my tongue out at the phone. It was childish, but I couldn't help myself.

He grunted and then rattled off a number. Before I finished writing it down, he had handed the phone back to Camilia.

"Sam, please be careful," Camilia said. "Give Frank my love and tell him to call his mother sometime."

I reassured her that I would be extra careful and then we said our goodbyes. I immediately called the number he'd given me before I had time to think and talk myself out of it.

"Special Agent Brown."

"My name is Samantha Washington. I was hoping you—"

"Washington? You wouldn't happen to be the Samantha Washington who owns Market Street Mysteries, would you?" he asked.

I paused for a beat before I answered. "I am."

"Love your bookstore, but I have a complaint."

I braced myself. "I'm sorry to hear that. Please tell me what happened."

"The last time I was in your bookstore, you only had one copy of *Dark Reservations* by John Fortunato. John's a member of the FBI and a good friend. Plus, as a fellow Michigander, I think it's important to support our local writers."

I walked over to a shelf with Michigan authors and saw at least six copies of *Dark Reservations*. "I'm sorry there weren't more copies when you were here, but it's been hard to keep them in stock. However, I just got a new shipment and I'm looking at six copies right now."

"Good, but I do have one other complaint."

"More low stock?" I asked.

"Yes. You were out of snickerdoodles," he chuckled.

"If you'd be willing to come by the bookstore tomorrow, I will make sure that there are plenty of cookies. In fact, I'll even send you home with a dozen for your own personal stash."

"Now, that's an offer I can't refuse." He laughed. "Now, what can I help you with?"

"I'm looking for some guidance. Normally, I would reach out to Stinky—I mean, Detective Bradley Pitt. He's a detective with the North Harbor Police, but he's on vacation. He gave me your number." I waited anxiously, hoping he wouldn't make me explain about Alva over the phone.

Special Agent Warren Brown hesitated a few moments. "Would tomorrow at nine work?"

"Perfect."

I hung up and rushed upstairs. I needed to bake cookies tonight.

Chapter 12

My assistant, Dawson Alexander, wasn't just a star on Michigan Southwest University's football team. Dawson was also an excellent baker who lived in the studio apartment over my garage. His kitchen was small, so he often baked in my kitchen, which meant that my freezer probably had leftover cookie dough, or his recipe was likely in the pantry.

I lucked out and found both. Snickerdoodles were basically a sugar-cookie dough rolled in cinnamon and sugar. Some variations included cream of tartar, which gave the cookies a bit of a bite. I baked the cookies in the freezer and then mixed up another batch using the recipe I found in the pantry. I glanced at the handwritten notes and adjustments Dawson had added to the side of the recipe.

Maybe we should consider a Market Street Mysteries Cookbook. Hmm. Or perhaps, Dawson would consider doing baking classes if I followed through and added the courses I'd been thinking about. I'll bet Frank would consider hosting the baking classes. I had an old Espresso Book Printer that cranked out print-on-demand books. I could use it to print the cookbooks, or any other books. Even though the manufacturer went out of business, the machine still worked. If I offered a four-week short story writing course, then the students could print the collection at the end of the four weeks. I could even sell the book in the store. The possibilities were endless. But would anyone pay to take a course? It was a lot to think about, but there was only one way to know for sure.

I baked and thought through the pros and cons. When I was done, the apartment smelled delicious, and I had plenty of cookies for bribing an FBI agent and sharing with patrons. I was also 95 percent sure I was going to give the class a try. I'd run the idea by Frank and Dawson and see what they thought. After all, the Espresso Printer was in my office. It might as well get some use before it gave up the ghost.

Baking was how Dawson worked through problems. He said it relaxed his mind. However, baking simply left me with more questions. *Was Alva murdered? If so, how? Did Carl kill her? Was Bethany in on the murder? Was Alva's money the motive? Why was it so important to Alva to give her paintings away that she wrote the addendum on toilet paper?* Carl didn't value the paintings and would have gladly given them away.

When the cookies were done and I'd eaten more than I should, I let the poodles out and decided to sort through the mountain of questions in my own way. Baking may have helped Dawson and even Frank sort through problems, but the only way I sorted through problems was by writing.

⚜

A well-trained butler never let his emotions show. Yet even Thompkins was shocked by Lady Elizabeth's revelation. "The prime minister suspects there may be a traitor in his inner circle?" the butler asked.

"Good Lawd." Mrs. McDuffie gasped.

Lady Elizabeth nodded. "There are some things that I need to share, but they are strictly confidential."

Thompkins held himself even more rigid and upright. "You can, of course, count on my discretion."

Mrs. McDuffie nodded. "Mine too."

Lady Elizabeth's shoulders relaxed, and she nodded. "It goes without saying that I trust you both completely, but this isn't my secret to share. However, we're going to need both of your assistance to carry this off."

Thompkins and Mrs. McDuffie both nodded.

"Prime Minister Chamberlain's attempts to avoid war with Germany have left his reputation in shreds," Lady Elizabeth said.

"Pshaw!" Mrs. McDuffie snorted. "They should have listened. Mr. Churchill saw what 'Itler and the Nazis were up to. Saw right through all the fancy speeches and agreements that weren't even worth the paper they were written on."

"I hate to say it, but Mrs. McDuffie's right." Thompkins frowned.

It wasn't often that the Marshes' housekeeper and butler were aligned, but on this the two senior members of the staff were in complete agreement.

"The very idea of another war after the devastation of the last one was so utterly unthinkable, that I'm sure Mr. Chamberlain was willing to try anything to avoid that." Lady Elizabeth shook her head. "But we can't sit back and do nothing while the Nazis take over sovereign nations. If the Germans can waltz in and take over Czechoslovakia and Poland it's just a matter of time before they'll try to take over France and England."

Mrs. McDuffie shuddered.

Thompkins gave a discreet cough. "Joseph is Jewish, and he keeps in touch with relatives in Germany and throughout Europe. There are reports of abductions, murders, and all manner of evil inflicted against men, women, and even children," Thompkins said softly.

Mrs. McDuffie gasped "All because they're Jewish?"

Joseph Mueller was a Jewish scientist who was married to Thompkins's daughter, Mary. He also spoke German and Polish fluently and was helping the Marshes with the three children they had received from the Kindertransport.

"According to Winston, it isn't just Jewish people being hurt," Lady Elizabeth said.

"You're right. The Nazis are certainly targeting the Jews, but according to Joseph's sources, it's wider than that. They're brutalizing the Romas, Poles, the disabled, and homosexuals," Thompkins said.

"Lawd have mercy," Mrs. McDuffie said.

"Hatred like that shouldn't be allowed to spread." Thompkins frowned.

"The prime minister isn't a bad man. I think he's a man of honor and he just couldn't imagine the hatred that could permit hurting innocent men, women, and children simply because of their religion, nationality, or disability." Lady Elizabeth huffed. "Britain isn't the most tolerant nation and still has some archaic laws about sexual persuasion, but Hitler has taken things too far. It's taken a toll on the prime minister."

"I listened to him on the wireless and he sounds broken." Mrs. McDuffie sniffed.

"He's half the man he was a month ago. The press hasn't been kind, and it's come to the point where Mr. Chamberlain has become a detriment to the party."

Thompkins gawked. "Are you saying he has plans to step aside?"

Lady Elizabeth nodded. "I believe that's the plan. James—Lord Browning seemed to think it was just a matter of time."

Lord James Browning, the 15th Duke of Kingsfordshire, was married to Lady Elizabeth's niece, Lady Daphne Marsh. He was also a member of MI5, the British secret service, and was closely involved with the inner workings of the government.

"Is that a good idea? Now that we're at war, who'll lead the nation?" Mrs. McDuffie asked.

"The House of Commons doesn't seem to have much confidence in the prime minister right now," Thompkins said.

Lady Elizabeth nodded. "If the war ends quickly, he may stand a chance of holding onto his position, but most people can see the writing on the wall. Plus, he's ill. He's not telling people, but the pressure is only making things worse. James believes the prime minister will resign and Winston will be appointed. Which is why this dinner is so important."

Mrs. McDuffie and Thompkins shook off the shock and waited for Lady Elizabeth to elaborate.

"Britain doesn't stand a chance against the Nazis if there's someone in the prime minister's War Cabinet feeding information to the enemy. They have to get rid of the spy, not only to secure the war effort, but to eliminate any negative concerns about Winston stepping in as the next prime minister," Lady Elizabeth said. "Which is why we are going to help set a trap and catch the traitor."

Chapter 13

I was up early for my meeting with Special Agent Warren Brown. Despite having assisted Stinky Pitt in solving a number of murders in the past, I was nervous. Detective Pitt was a member of the North Harbor Police, but he wasn't in the same league as an FBI agent. My palms were so sweaty I had to keep wiping them on the leg of my jeans. My heart was beating out a merengue rhythm while I tried to calm myself by performing the combat breathing routine Frank had taught me.

Inhale through my nose while counting to four . . . or was it seven . . . ? I tried seven but nearly passed out from the lack of oxygen and decided it must have been four. One more time. Inhale for four. Hold for four. Exhale through my mouth for four.

I didn't feel calmer, but my heart had settled into a cha-cha. I considered that progress. I repeated the process until my heart rate abandoned the Latin rhythms for an old-fashioned waltz. Definitely progress.

"Samantha, what are you doing?" Nana Jo asked.

I hadn't realized that I had been nodding to the imaginary beat until Nana Jo spoke. "Nothing."

"You're wound tighter than a two-dollar watch."

I stared at my grandmother. "What?"

"It means you're nervous. Now, what's wrong? I know you're meeting that FBI guy, but that doesn't explain why you're so uptight. You've helped Stinky Pitt solve plenty of murders."

"I know, but this is different. The FBI isn't like talking to a local cop, and even with the local police, Detective Bradley Pitt isn't exactly the Columbo of law enforcement officers."

"Columbo?" Nana Jo snorted. "Stinky Pitt isn't even the Inspector Clouseau of law enforcement."

I chuckled, but the comparison between Detective Pitt and the inept and incompetent police detective of the French Sûreté, Inspector Jacques Clouseau, from the Pink Panther films, was shockingly appropriate. "Stinky Pitt doesn't dress nearly as dapper as Inspector Clouseau, and his ego is somewhat lower."

"I agree with you on the attire. Peter Sellers was incredibly handsome, especially with that mustache. But when it comes to ego . . . well, that might be a tie."

"I don't want to come across like a complete idiot," I said.

"You won't. Just be open and honest. It'll be fine." Nana Jo patted my back.

There was a knock at the door, and I went to unlock it.

Special Agent Warren Brown was about the same height as my fiancé, Frank Patterson. He was about forty with short brown hair, brown eyes, and a friendly smile. He held a wallet with his shield and identification up to the door for me to read.

I unlocked the door and ushered him inside. "I'm sorry. I meant to unlock that sooner. I got distracted talking to my grandmother."

"No worries." Special Agent Warren Brown extended his

hand. "I'm glad to meet you. It's not often that I come face-to-face and meet an author." He surprised me by reaching into his pocket and pulling out a copy of my book, *Murder at Wickfield Lodge.* "I'm hoping that you will sign that for me."

I tried to fight the grin that was forcing my lips upward, but there was no fighting it. I wasn't used to people asking for my autograph, but I didn't think the warmth that spread through my body would ever get old. "Of course I'll sign it."

I grabbed a pen and turned to ask how he wanted the book addressed but found he'd wandered off to a shelf of new releases. "Looking for anything in particular?"

He shook his head. "Just enjoying the moment."

I must have looked puzzled because he quickly added, "I feel like a kid in a candy store. It's not often that an avid reader of detective stories finds himself alone in a mystery bookstore."

"I know the feeling." I laughed. "Take your time looking. I'll be in the back with a plate of snickerdoodles when you're ready."

"You got me at snickerdoodles." Special Agent Brown followed me to the back.

I introduced Nana Jo, who brought him a cup of coffee to wash down the cookies.

Warren Brown ate. No, he savored four cookies before he sipped his coffee. "Hmm. These are amazing." After a few moments, he looked at me and smiled. "Now, how can I help you?"

I wasn't sure how to approach the conversation, but I decided to dive in with both feet. I told the FBI agent everything I knew. He asked a few clarifying questions but sat patiently while I talked. When I finished, he sipped his coffee and then asked, "What do you need from me?"

That was the problem. I didn't know what I needed. "Normally, if there were a murder, I would talk to Detective Pitt, but he's not here. Most of the other detectives that I've met aren't too keen on an amateur meddling in police matters."

Special Agent Brown nodded. "I can imagine. It's dangerous."

"Besides the fact that I'm not even sure there *is* a murder,"
I said.

"Of course she was murdered," Nana Jo said. "We just
need to get someone to prove it before that sleazeball nephew
and his bleached-blond wife have a chance to have her cremated so no tests can be performed."

"They want to have her cremated?" Warren Brown asked.

I shrugged and turned to Nana Jo.

"All right, maybe I got swept away, but if they did kill Alva,
you can't expect them to sit back and wait for someone to figure it out, can you?" Nana Jo asked.

"What do you want from me?" Special Agent Brown
asked.

"Can you get an autopsy?" I asked.

"Not without a good reason. Chances are, her body has already been taken to the mortuary, and she may already have
been embalmed. It'll be virtually impossible to find anything
once that happens."

"I was afraid of that," I said.

"What else are you afraid of?" he asked. "What's really bothering you?"

"I feel like I'm missing something." I took a deep breath
and told him about the art.

"Are you sure this Alva Tarkington wasn't some Rembrandt in hiding?" Special Agent Brown asked.

"Fairly sure. I'm not a professional, but the one painting I
saw hanging at the house didn't look very good." I shrugged.
"Besides, her nephew, Carl, didn't seem to think her paintings
were worth the canvas they were painted on." I hesitated. "But
then Carl probably knows less about art than I do."

"It sounds suspicious that she would go to such lengths for
a few worthless paintings unless . . ."

"Unless?" I asked.

"Unless she either knew beyond a shadow of a doubt that the paintings had value. Or . . ." He looked sheepish.

"Or?" Nana Jo's gaze narrowed.

"Or if Alva wasn't playing with a full deck." He held up a hand to ward off the barrage that Nana Jo and I were revving up to unleash. "Hey, I'm not saying Alva was nuts, but you have to admit the blinking SOS and toilet-paper addendum are a bit far out." He paused and gave us both hard stares. When we didn't immediately assault him, he continued. "She may have been perfectly sane, but you asked for my opinion."

I heaved a sigh. "What do you suggest?"

"See if you can get a look at one of those paintings. Take it to an expert and get it appraised. Then you'll know if she was just a nutty old woman or an undercover Picasso."

Special Agent Warren Brown gave us the names of a few art appraisers in the area. Then he took the book I signed and his extra snickerdoodles and left.

Chapter 14

Nana Jo scoured the Internet for Alva's obituary and stumbled across a tiny notice in the River Bend Tribune. Alva Tarkington's memorial service was today. I hadn't planned on attending a memorial service today, but there was no way I was going to miss it. Even if it meant closing the bookstore. Fortunately, my assistant, Dawson, didn't have classes this afternoon and was able to cover, so I didn't have to close the store.

Nana Jo got the word out to everyone about the last-minute memorial service, while I dug out my *I'm going to a funeral* outfit: a simple black-sheath dress that I dressed up with a string of pearls and a multicolored jacket.

When Dawson arrived and Nana Jo and I were both dressed, we left. I drove to Shady Acres and picked up the rest of the crew. Under other circumstances and with advanced notice, Shady Acres would have provided a van to shuttle residents to the funeral home. Apparently, the notice of Alva's memorial had been as much of a surprise for the staff at Shady Acres as it had been to us. With a bigger car, I might have been able to take more people, but my SUV could only hold so many. I shook off the guilt that wasn't my burden to bear. I would pay my respects to Alva and do my best to avoid giving Carl a piece of my mind.

I drove to South Harbor Funeral Home and Crematorium, pulled up in front, and let my passengers out. Experience told me that they would scatter and get any information they could by the time I found a parking space.

Nana Jo and her friends were experts at getting people to talk. They were friendly, with faces that made people trust them with their secrets. Or maybe they looked harmless. Regardless of the reason, they had perfected a technique that almost always guaranteed results.

The lot next to the building wasn't full. I had no trouble finding a space nearby, which made me sad. I hadn't known Alva for a long time, but I liked her. I would have expected a bigger turnout, but Nana Jo had checked the newspaper for an obituary every day and only that morning decided to check the funeral home websites and the River Bend obituaries. I wanted to believe that was suspicious, but in all fairness, newspapers were slowly going the way of the dinosaurs. North and South Harbor were small towns with fewer than thirty thousand people combined. As far as newspapers go, the North Harbor *Herald* had never been Pulitzer caliber. Now, it was barely more than a supermarket tabloid. Over the past decade, the *Herald* had scaled back from a daily newspaper and was now only printed on weekends with more ads and coupons than actual news. Located less than thirty minutes from the Indiana state line and ninety miles from Chicago, North Harbor residents were more connected to its neighboring states than its own. Anyone wanting the news on weekdays bought papers from River Bend, Indiana, or Chicago, Illinois. The River Bend *Tribune* capitalized on this by including a section called "Michiana News," which included news from North and South Harbor.

Inside the funeral home was a small room with elevator music playing and a portrait of Alva Tarkington. Rather than going up front and paying condolences to Carl and Bethany, I found Nana Jo sitting next to Isabella, Alva's housekeeper. She was also the only person who was openly grieving.

Part of the technique that Nana Jo and the girls had mastered to get information at funerals involved the strategy of divide and conquer. People were more likely to talk to an individual than a group. They were also more likely to speak to an elderly person they underestimated and rarely saw as a threat. Big mistake.

I sat down and forced myself not to glare at Carl, who impatiently stood in a dark suit at the front of the room near Alva's picture.

"Isabella, I believe you know my granddaughter, Samantha Washington." Nana Jo squeezed the woman's shoulders.

Isabella took a moment and wiped her eyes. "I remember. Miss Alva liked you."

"I liked her too." I reached over and squeezed her hand.

"Isabella wasn't just Alva's cook and housekeeper, she was also her friend," Nana Jo said.

The young woman nodded vigorously.

I'd been to memorials before, but still this one felt awkward. I struggled to put my finger on what was missing. That's when it hit me. I leaned over and whispered to my grandmother. "We should have sent flowers." I glanced around at the room, which was devoid of the floral displays that were common symbols of caring and loss.

Nana Jo passed me a program and pointed to the bottom. Alva's family requested no flowers. In lieu of flowers, there was an account at a brokerage house listed where anyone wishing to send donations in Alva's memory could.

I raised a brow and glanced at my grandmother. "Isn't that the brokerage house that Carl works for?"

"It is." Isabella nodded. "It's shameful, and Miss Alva loved flowers. He's nothing but a greedy *hemar*."

Nana Jo and I stared at Isabella before asking. "What's a *hemar*?"

"Donkey." Isabella blushed.

"I haven't met him, but from what I've heard, he's at least the back end of a *hemar*." Nana Jo nodded.

The funeral director was a short, bald man with glasses. He walked to the front and cleared his throat. The music stopped, and the few guests in attendance found seats. The ceremony was impersonal, bland, and short. He read a poem and the obituary from the program, and then we were all asked to spend two minutes in silent reflection about Alva. After two minutes, which felt like two hours, he expressed his condolences to Carl and Bethany and then dismissed us. That was it. From start to finish, the entire thing was less than fifteen minutes.

Nana Jo and the girls were stunned. More than stunned, they were angry. Nana Jo looked like she was ready to bite the head off nails. She pulled out her phone and fired off a series of text messages.

"What a pile of—"

"Irma!" everyone said.

Irma coughed.

"I agree with Irma." Ruby Mae frowned. "That was an insult. Alva wasn't some nameless person that no one knew. She was warm and loving. She had friends and family. She deserved better than that."

After a quick glance at her phone, Nana Jo stood. "It was a slap in the face and I'm not going to stand by and let them get away with it." Nana Jo marched to the front of the room.

I was so shocked it took a few seconds for the paralysis to fade enough so that I was able to move. When I did, I grabbed my purse and hurried after my grandmother. She was a woman of action, although I didn't think she would cause a scene. At least I hoped not.

"Excuse me," Nana Jo said loudly as she stood next to the funeral director.

Everyone stopped what they were doing and turned to face her.

"I want to thank Mr. Isaacs for his kind words." She turned to the funeral director, who forced his lips up into a smile. "Alva Tarkington was a beloved resident of Shady Acres Retirement Village, and we would like to invite all of her friends"— Nana Jo paused and took a deep swallow—"and, of course, any family members interested in remembering and celebrating the life of our dear friend to join us for a small reception in the Shady Acres Community room."

Molten lava rose up Carl Tarkington's neck. His face was beet red. He huffed and looked as though the top of his head was going to blow off.

Nana Jo turned and faced him. Tall and straight, she pushed her shoulders back and lifted her head. She had at least a half foot on Carl Tarkington. Yet, at that moment, she towered over him like an Amazon warrior looking down on a petulant child.

Their gazes locked. In that instant, Carl Tarkington must have gotten a revelation. He must have realized what it felt like moments before a grizzly took down a deer. He must have realized in this situation he was Bambi. His chest heaved, but he lowered his gaze in a sign of submission and then walked away.

Nana Jo marched full steam ahead toward the lobby.

"What was that about?" I asked when I finally caught up to my grandmother.

The steam that drove her through the funeral home dissipated. Like a balloon with a leak, her shoulders relaxed, and she came to a stop. "Alva deserved better. She was a person. A warm, caring person. She lived. She created beauty through her art. She deserved to be remembered. She deserved to have someone speak her name." Nana Jo shook her head. "I can't explain it, but listening to that watered-down, milquetoast ceremony just set my teeth on edge."

"In Egyptian culture, a person's name was believed to be essential to their very being. It was such a vital part of who they were, that they had to preserve their names and their identities by inscribing them on monuments and tombs so that it would be spoken aloud. They needed this to survive in the afterlife as much as they needed their mummies. The greatest insult was to be forgotten and not have your name spoken aloud. As a form of punishment, names were even chiseled away from monuments. In Latin, it was called '*damnatio memoriae*,'" Isabella said. "The condemnation of memory."

I hadn't heard Isabella's approach until she spoke.

"You know a lot about Egyptian history," I said.

"Sorry, I didn't mean to interrupt, but I was born in Cairo. It's my history." Isabella turned to Nana Jo. "That was really nice. Miss Alva would have appreciated you."

"I had to do something," Nana Jo said.

"How did you arrange it so quickly?" I asked.

"I sent a text to the recreation director at Shady Acres and told her to make sure there were cookies and punch in the lobby," Nana Jo said. "The least we could do would be to say goodbye to our friend properly."

I squeezed my grandmother's shoulders. "I'm pretty sure Dawson has some cookies, and Frank might have a pie that we could bring." I reached for my phone.

"Both have sweets waiting, and Jenna is going to pick them up on her way to Shady Acres." Nana Jo held up her phone and grinned. "Fastest thumbs in the West."

"May I come?" Isabella asked.

Chapter 15

The drive to Shady Acres was quick. I dropped off Isabella—who had taken a cab to the funeral home—Nana Jo, and the girls at the entrance and parked. As I was making my way inside, I saw Jenna pull into a parking spot nearby. I helped her carry in a cake and two boxes of cookies.

Inside, people were gathering in the reception area. The seating had been rearranged from the last time I was there when everyone was gathered around the television watching the MISU Tigers clobber a conference rival. A table was set up with paper plates, napkins, boxed cookies, cheese, and crackers. Jenna and I placed our contributions on the table and stepped back while Isabella and the residential manager worked their magic to make everything look pretty. One of the kitchen staff wheeled out a cart with coffee, hot water for tea, and all of the essentials. Many of the residents wandered down. Before long, the room was full of people. Some of them might have only come for the treats, but that was fine. At least they were there.

When everything was arranged, Nana Jo stepped in front of the fireplace and cleared her throat. "Look, I'm not going to waste your time reading to you when Alva was born and when she died. Y'all can read that in the obituary." She waved the program she'd picked up at the memorial. "We're here to celebrate the life of Alva Tarkington. I met Alva in art class." Nana Jo shared a couple of funny stories about the wine-and-painting class and then the wine-and-sculpture classes that she had taken with Alva. Apparently, the wine had made everyone a lot less inhibited, including the young man who they convinced to serve as a figure model for the group.

I leaned close to Jenna. "Do I want to know what a figure model is?"

Jenna shook her head.

Isabella overheard my question and snickered. She mouthed. *Nude.*

Yep. That's what I thought.

After Nana Jo's stories, several other residents shared touching stories about Alva. The atmosphere was subdued but not melancholy. When everyone finished, we raised our glasses in a toast to Alva Tarkington.

Jenna and I sat on a sofa next to Isabella, who dabbed at her eyes with a tissue. "Miss Alva would have liked that."

"Had you known Alva long?" I asked.

"No. I only met Miss Alva when she moved back to the United States from Cairo."

"I thought . . . I'm sorry. I assumed . . ." I stumbled over the awkward apology. I took a deep breath. "I'm truly sorry. You know what they say about assuming."

Isabella tilted her head and gave me a puzzled look.

"It makes an ass of u and me," I said.

"But it wasn't a bad assumption." Isabella laughed. "I am from Cairo. My mother was Oliver Tarkington's secretary. It's my mother who knew Alva and Oliver Tarkington. If I ever met her, I was too young to remember. When I was older, my mother sent me away to boarding school in England. Then I attended college in the United States. My mother died a year ago and I decided to take some time off before graduate school. Alva reached out and offered me a job. It wasn't a great job, but it was pocket money and a roof over my head. Alva spoke Arabic. She understood Egyptian culture. She knew my mother." Isabella shrugged. "It was a job with someone who reminded me of home."

I squeezed her hand.

Isabella told us about her mother, her life in Egypt, and what she remembered about Alva and Oliver Tarkington, which wasn't much. She'd been a small child, although she had fond memories of being on an excavation site with Oliver and pulled out a gold necklace that she wore around her neck. At the end of the chain was an amulet.

Jenna and I leaned close. Initially, I thought the pendant was stone, but closer inspection showed it to be metal-tinged with green in a teardrop shape with engraved images.

"Is that bronze?" I asked.

Isabella nodded. "Oliver Tarkington discovered it at a dig site years ago."

"Is that Greek?" Jenna asked.

"May I?" I asked.

Isabella nodded and Jenna and I leaned even closer and examined the amulet.

"It looks like someone riding a horse," I said.

"One side shows a rider on a galloping horse," Isabella explained.

"What's that circle?" Jenna pointed to a round circle around the rider's head.

"A halo."

"It looks like the rider is about to kill someone, a woman lying on the ground. That can't be good," I said.

"The rider is overpowering the evil spirit of Gello, a demon that threatened women and children. A Greek inscription engraved above the rider's head reads, 'The One God Who Conquers Evil.' The letters spell the Jewish name for God. It was believed that females wore this for protection."

"Protection from who?" I asked.

"The evil eye." Isabella flipped the amulet over. "Here you see the evil eye being vanquished with an arrow and what looks like a pitchfork. The inscription here means, 'One God.' Egyptologists think young girls would have worn the amulet to protect against demons and the curse of the *evil eye*."

"What exactly is the evil eye?" Jenna asked. "Was that a pagan belief?"

Isabella fingered the amulet. "Lots of cultures believed in something called the evil eye. Greek. Roman. It was believed that Gello and even some powerful magicians could level a curse against someone by using a malevolent glance." She shrugged. "The evil eye was even listed in the Bible, the Koran, and Shakespeare."

"The Bible?" Jenna asked.

" 'Eat thou not the bread of him that hath an evil eye, neither desire thou his dainty meats.' Proverbs 23:6," Isabella quoted.

"This looks really old," I said.

"It is. It dates back to the Byzantine period, and it's more than fifteen hundred years old." She glanced down lovingly at the amulet. "At least, that's what I was told."

"This seems really valuable," Jenna said.

"I don't know about that. If it was really valuable it would have been catalogued and sent to the Cairo Museum as a national treasure. You can't just take artifacts for your personal use. Oliver Tarkington gave this to me." Isabella took one last look at the amulet before putting it back in her shirt. "It was a gift, so it's valuable to me."

"Alva must have really loved you to go to so much trouble to make sure you got those paintings. Have you thought about having them appraised? I have the names of some art appraisers and I'd be more than happy to help you get them appraised." I thought about my conversation with Special Agent Warren Brown. "You'll want to get them insured if nothing else."

"That's very kind, but I don't think insurance will be necessary. I cared very much for Miss Alva, but she wasn't a great painter." Isabella laughed.

"Why do you think she went to so much trouble to make sure you got her paintings?" Jenna asked.

"I have no idea, but maybe she knew that I wouldn't burn them like Carl." She frowned.

"Surely he wouldn't. I mean, they may not have been valuable, but Alva was family. He could have given them to a museum or taken them to the Goodwill." I paused. "One man's trash is another man's treasure."

"Ha! He didn't care about Miss Alva. The only thing he cares about is himself. If he could make money from the paintings, then he would sell them." She blinked back a tear. "He didn't love her. I don't think Carl loved anyone, including his wife."

"What do you mean?" Jenna asked.

"Was Carl having an affair?" I asked.

"Not Carl." Isabella clamped her lips closed.

"Bethany?" Jenna and I exchanged a glance.

"I don't suppose you know who?" I asked.

Isabella shook her head. "No, but I overheard her whispering to someone on the phone. She was saying things that you would only say to your lover and Carl was home."

Interesting, but that isn't a reason to kill Alva.

"Carl isn't a good man. Miss Alva knew it. He would have burned those paintings just because he could. Carl Tarkington is an evil man with an evil eye." Isabella pulled the amulet out and held it up. "He's the evil that needs to be vanquished with a spear."

Chapter 16

Before she left, I made arrangements with Isabella to take her paintings to an art appraiser. When the reception was over, we went to Nana Jo's villa to talk. Instead of having our meeting at Frank's restaurant, we sat in Nana Jo's sunroom and ate chicken salad sandwiches, homemade chips, and cookies that Frank sent with Jenna when she picked up the cake for Alva's memorial.

Nana Jo's villa was a single-family residence with magnificent views of Lake Michigan. Property with lake views generally was outrageously expensive, but Nana Jo had bought into the retirement village when it was still farmland and sand. After my grandfather died, Nana Jo was among the first to see the benefits of selling the large house where she and my grandfather had lived and buying a home in a new retirement village. The original house was a large country farmhouse with acres of land that backed up to the St. Thomas River. The house was old with all the charm and the problems of an older home. It had been in my grandfather's family for generations and was perfect for raising the large family my grandparents wanted. Unfortunately, they only had one daughter. The property had been too much for a small family of three and way too much for one. With her daughter grown, married, and on her own, and my grandfather gone, Nana Jo made the difficult decision to sell. She spent most of the week with me at the bookstore, but she kept her home with its views of Lake Michigan.

When everyone was full, Jenna and I relayed our conversation with Isabella with the group.

"That was a weird thing for Isabella to say," Nana Jo said.

"That 'evil-eye' business gives me the shivers," Ruby Mae said.

"Yeah, that 'destroyed by fire' stuff was really creepy," Dorothy said. "Do you think she's dangerous?"

"If Carl had been the one killed, I might think she had something to do with it, but Isabella seemed to genuinely care for Alva," Jenna said.

Nana Jo pulled her iPad out and started taking notes. "So, Isabella knew Alva and Oliver Tarkington in Egypt."

"That's what she said, although . . ." I searched for the right words. "There's something odd about that."

"Why?" Dorothy asked. "If her mother worked for Oliver Tarkington in Cairo, then it would make sense that Alva would seek her out."

"Why now? She didn't remember Alva from Cairo and barely remembered Oliver, except for the necklace he gave her," I said. "Which is also weird."

"Maybe he was just an old man who wanted to show off for a young kid?" Nana Jo said. "She was just a kid."

"She must have been fairly young. She said she was sent to boarding school in England and college in the United States," Jenna said.

"Sounds expensive. What did her mom do, again?" Ruby Mae asked.

"Secretary," I said.

"Some countries pay their clerical staff well, but that doesn't usually cover the costs of boarding schools in other countries," Nana Jo said.

"Maybe Frank can look into who paid for Isabella's education," I said.

Nana Jo nodded.

"Have any of you met Margery Brooks?" Dorothy asked.

"She was at the reading of the will, but we weren't formally introduced," Jenna said.

I had forgotten about the mousy woman who sat next to Ethan Linton.

"She must have been the plain woman I saw making goo-goo eyes at that pompous museum director," Ruby Mae said.

"Goo-goo eyes?" I asked.

"She stared at him like he was the last piece of pizza in the box, and she was starving." Ruby Mae tilted her head and glanced down her nose.

"She was at that travesty that Carl and Bethany passed off as a memorial. I ran into her in the restroom," Nana Jo said.

"I assumed she was Alva's nurse," I said.

"There you go *assuming* again," Jenna said with a smile in her voice.

I resisted the urge to stick out my tongue at my sister, but just barely.

"I don't think she was a registered nurse, but she might have been a licensed nurse practitioner. She was hired to look after Alva," Nana Jo said. "Help with bathing, light housekeeping . . . and I suspect spying."

"Spying?" Jenna sat up and stared. "She told you that?"

"She didn't say it in words, but I could read between the lines." Nana Jo waved away any objections to her assessment. "She talked about Alva as though she was a few fries short of a happy meal. Then, she went into a long lecture on how important it was to watch out for vulnerable elderly people who were easy prey for manipulative young women."

"Manipulative young women . . . like Isabella?" I asked.

"If I had to guess, that's who I'd pick. She didn't come flat out and accuse Isabella of manipulating Alva, but she came awfully close," Nana Jo said.

"But Isabella genuinely cared for Alva," I said.

Nana Jo barely made eye contact.

"She did. You could see it on her face. She was completely torn up." I turned to my sister. "You saw. You talked to her."

Jenna paused for several beats and then shrugged.

Nana Jo reached a hand across the table and squeezed my hand. "If she really cared, then she would have behaved exactly like she did." She paused and swallowed hard. "But if she was faking and only wanted people to *think* she cared, she would have behaved the exact same way."

I shook my head. "I don't believe it."

Nana Jo took a deep breath. "According to Margery, when she first started working there, Alva got along well with her family. It was actually Alva's idea to have Carl and Bethany move in with her. She knew she didn't have a lot of time left. Then Isabella showed up, and everything changed. Isabella ingratiated herself into Alva's life," Nana Jo said.

"How?" I asked.

"She planted seeds of doubt into Alva's head. Margery used to prepare Alva's meals. One day, she made soup and Alva got violently ill later that night. Margery swears there was nothing wrong with the soup. She'd eaten some herself. But Margery thinks that Isabella convinced Alva that someone must have tried to poison her because after that, Isabella cooked all of Alva's meals. After Isabella arrived, Alva became paranoid and didn't trust her family or Margery. Isabella was the only one she trusted. The only one she confided in." Nana Jo turned to me. "Sam, I like Isabella too but we need to keep an open mind."

"There are lots of people out there who take advantage of the elderly," Dorothy said softly.

I didn't want to believe that Isabella was one of them, but I had to acknowledge that maybe I'd been wrong. "But she seemed so sincere," I said weakly.

"A good con man or woman has no conscience. They prey on the elderly," Dorothy said.

"Daryl told me that the police are getting so many calls about criminals using artificial intelligence to dupe unsuspecting seniors, that they don't have enough manpower to even follow up on all of the accusations. He got a grant from the state to pay for a few more detectives. He's going to have some of them come to Shady Acres to talk to us about avoiding these scammers." Ruby Mae pulled out her knitting and stabbed a ball of yarn with vigor.

"I saw something about that on one of those morning shows," Irma said. "They found recordings of one of the reporter's children and created a recording that made it sound as if they had been kidnapped."

"I saw one where they called a woman and told her that her grandson had been arrested for drunk driving, and she needed to send money to keep him out of jail. It was horrible. The poor woman was sobbing." I shivered.

"It's horrible. I've had to create safe words for the twins," Jenna said.

"I know about safe words. I use those when things get a little too . . . intense during—"

"Irma!"

Irma broke into a coughing fit.

Jenna shook her head. "This is a safe word so that if something happens and the boys need to get in touch with Tony or me, then they have a secret word that they can use so we know it's really them and not some AI scam."

"It's a shame that you have to do that. It's gotten to the

point where I'm afraid to open links in email. I don't trust anything I see on social media, and now they're making it so you can't even trust your own hearing." Ruby Mae clucked her tongue.

"When did all this craziness start? I don't remember worrying about phishing emails and fake phone calls," Dorothy said.

Nana Jo shook her head. "Con artists aren't new. They've been around since the serpent slithered into the Garden of Eden. The problem is that modern technology has made deceiving others much easier than ever."

Could Nana Jo be right? Did Isabella infiltrate her way into Alva's life so she could take advantage of a dying woman? Steal from her? "Okay, I don't want to believe it, but it's possible that Isabella isn't the caring person she comes across to be. But that doesn't mean she killed Alva." I sighed. "What else did Margery say? Did she have any proof that Isabella was preying on Alva?"

"Nothing concrete, just suspicions," Nana Jo said. "But we should check into it anyway."

Everyone agreed.

"If she was conning Alva, then she wasn't very successful," I said.

"What do you mean?" Nana Jo asked.

"All she got for her effort was five thousand dollars and some of Alva's paintings that probably aren't worth much," Jenna said.

"Maybe." A thought flitted through my mind, but it was gone before I could grab it. Experience told me that the more I tried to catch hold of the thought, the more elusive it would be. So, I pushed it aside for now. Still, I couldn't shake the feeling that maybe Isabella hadn't been as unsuccessful as she first appeared.

Chapter 17

I shared my conversation with Special Agent Warren Brown and his recommendation that we get the paintings appraised.

"Do you think Isabella will agree?" Ruby Mae asked.

"Isabella is letting me take the paintings tomorrow to one of the art appraisers that Special Agent Brown gave me. I convinced her she should do it for insurance purposes. I doubt that Ethan Linton will get his own paintings appraised." I turned to Jenna. "Is there any way to make him do it from a legal perspective?"

"I suppose Carl and Bethany could request it. Technically, those paintings are part of Alva's estate." Jenna shrugged. "But Carl isn't interested in them, and I get the feeling he isn't going to do anything that could delay his ability to get his hands on Alva's money. Your best bet would be to suggest he get the paintings appraised for insurance purposes too."

"Maybe Ethan Linton can help," Dorothy said. "He owns an art museum. If anyone should have a clue about the paintings worth, it should be him."

"I don't like that vampire." Nana Jo shuddered.

Jenna spit out the tea she'd just sipped. "Vampire? Where did that come from?"

"He's too handsome and well-preserved to be human—"

"And pale," Irma interrupted.

Nana Jo didn't like being interrupted, but considering it was Irma, it could have been worse. She waited a beat before continuing. "He's probably a couple of hundred years old with a coffin in his basement."

"He's still cute and I hear vampires are virile, so he can suck my blood anytime." Irma patted her beehive.

Nana Jo mumbled something that sounded like "dingbat," but I couldn't be sure.

"Well, Clarence and I had a lovely evening," Irma said.

"Did he know Carl?" I asked before she could go into every intimate detail about her time with the accountant.

"According to Clarence, Carl's firm is in financial trouble. In fact, word in financial circles is that Carl might actually be arrested." Irma pulled out her lipstick and used her spoon as a mirror as she reapplied.

"Irma! Focus," Nana Jo said. "Why was Carl going to be arrested?"

"Embezzling." Irma smacked her lips together and used a napkin to blot the excess. Then she looked over her shoulders and leaned forward as if she was afraid of being overheard, even though no one was here to overhear. "Some of Carl's clients moved to other firms and complained about their investments being mismanaged and transactions they never authorized. Clarence said the firm's being investigated, and no financial institution wants to take the risk that word will get out that someone was doing anything shady with the money. Clarence thinks they'll toss Carl to the wolves."

"Did he have any idea how much money Carl is accused of embezzling?" Jenna asked.

"Clarence thinks millions," Irma said.

A stunned silence settled on the room.

"I wonder if that's why Carl was so anxious to get his hands on Alva's money," I said.

"If he's embezzled money or even just mismanaged client accounts, I don't see how Alva's money can save him," Nana Jo said.

"Maybe he planned to use Alva's money to replace the money he took," Ruby Mae said.

Jenna shook her head. "I'm not a financial expert, but there would be a paper trail. If auditors are involved, it's too late. He can't just replace the money and pretend like all is well."

"I'm sure a savvy embezzler who'd managed to bilk investors of millions of dollars could figure out a way to cover his assets so that somebody else took the fall," Dorothy said.

"That's the key," Nana Jo said. "Carl isn't savvy. The man's an idiot."

"He may be an idiot, but the real question is, is he also a murderer?" I asked.

Chapter 18

We spent another hour talking in circles, but we still hadn't come up with any solutions. Eventually, I needed to get back to the bookstore and Jenna had to get back to work. Everyone agreed to keep digging. We arranged to meet again tomorrow morning.

When I got back to the bookstore, Dawson had things under control. Everything was running smoothly, but he had football practice and homework.

Nana Jo took care of the few customers who came by while I cleaned.

"Sam, you've been sweeping the same spot for the last twenty minutes." Nana Jo took the broom from my hand.

"Sorry, my mind was wandering."

"Why don't you go upstairs and write for a while. I've got this." I started to protest, but she stopped me. "I'll call you if we suddenly get an influx of customers."

Reluctantly, I agreed. Maybe writing would help me sort through the muddle of things racing through my mind.

The dinner party had gone off without a glitch. Despite the short notice, Mrs. Anderson had outdone herself with the food. Now, the party had retired to enjoy brandy and conversation in the drawing room in front of the fireplace.

Lady Elizabeth sat in her favorite seat on the sofa near the fireplace. She opened the bag with her yarn that was always nearby. The heat and the glow from the fire enveloped her like a comfortable blanket. She sat quietly and listened to the hum of conversation around her. Smoke curled up around Lord William's head as he gripped his pipe between his teeth. Lady Elizabeth looked lovingly at her husband. Over the decades since she first came to Wickfield Lodge as a blushing bride, many things had changed. Lord William, the eighth Duke of Hunsford, had aged well. The dark-haired man she'd married was now almost completely gray. His waist had expanded by several inches, and the lines that once only appeared on the sides of his eyes and mouth when he laughed were permanently etched on his face. Still, it was a good, kind face. Lady Elizabeth loved every line. The creases, extra pounds, and gray hairs reflected the years of love, hard work, and dedication the duke had provided to his country and his family. It all came together to create the man the duke had become and the life they had created together. Lord William's eyes flashed with passion as he waved his pipe, flinging tobacco in the process, as he emphasized a point he was making as he argued with their cousin, First Lord of the Admiralty, Winston Churchill.

Across from Lady Elizabeth sat her nieces, Lady Daphne Browning and Lady Penelope Carlston. On the surface, the two sisters were nothing alike. Lady Daphne was petite with fair skin, blond hair, and blue eyes, much like their father, Lord Peregrine Marsh. Her sister inherited the dark hair and dark eyes of their mother, Lady Henrietta Pringle. Lady Elizabeth and Lord William had not been blessed with children of their own, but when Lord William's brother and his wife were both killed in a car accident not long after the birth of their youngest daughter, Daphne, they had raised the two girls as their own.

Lady Daphne chatted with former barrister Sir Bentley Gardener. While Lady Penelope was engaged in a deep conversation with the portly Home Secretary, Major Horatio Templeton. Meanwhile, the two newer and younger members of the House of Commons, Lord Cecil Scott and Stanley Tate, talked quietly in a corner.

Nelson Wilmington, curator of the National Museum, stood alone. He sipped brandy and watched. His thin face and large beak-like nose reminded Lady Elizabeth of a hawk.

"Thank you, again for your hospitality in allowing us to descend on your home." The prime minister pointed to the seat next to Lady Elizabeth. "May I?"

"Of course." Lady Elizabeth moved her yarn and turned her body slightly, so she faced the P.M.

Prime Minister Chamberlain sat down and smiled. "I hope we haven't been too disruptive to the peace and tranquility of your home."

Lady Elizabeth smiled. "Not at all. In times of war, it's the duty of every citizen to do what we can. This is a small contribution and we're happy to do whatever we can."

"Thank you." The prime minister dipped his head.

Lady Elizabeth noted the lines that creased his forehead, and the dark circles under his eyes. "Arthur, how bad are things, really?"

The prime minister gave a wry smile. "I feel like a schoolboy who's been called on the carpet. No one but my governess has called me Arthur in over fifty years." After a few moments, he sipped his brandy and winced. "Germany is a fierce opponent. They've been preparing for war a lot longer than anyone realized. Well, almost anyone." He glanced up at Winston. "I should have realized."

Lady Elizabeth reached across and patted his hand. "I don't think very many people expected this."

He paused for several beats and then took a deep breath. "The British economy hasn't fully recovered from the last war. Poland and France are overrun, underfunded, and outmanned. After the economic devastation of the last war, most leaders believed . . . hoped that it would never get to this point again. We didn't want to believe it. I didn't want to believe it." He took a deep breath. "We're in trouble."

"But we defeated Germany once. Surely . . ." Lady Elizabeth put her hand to her throat.

"We nearly didn't, and we can't count on our allies as we did before. Mussolini is in bed with Hitler, which means Italy will side with Germany."

"What about the United States?" Lady Elizabeth asked.

"The United States is dealing with its own internal battles. On top of the same economic issues and lack of preparedness for another war that the rest of us are facing, the U.S. is also fighting appeals for isolationism." He paused. "There are far too many people who believe this war doesn't have anything to do with them."

"But it does. It's about right and wrong."

"Ah, but when you're cold and hungry you can't afford the idealism of right versus wrong. Besides, why should their men be sent overseas to die on the battlefields of Europe again?"

"But the battlefield won't stay in Europe," Winston said, joining the conversation. "Like the Black Plague that traveled across seas and continents. It was no respecter of person. It was a disease that destroyed rich and poor, men, women, and children. Hate is the same. It's a disease that eats away at the heart like a plague. That's what the Nazis are, a plague. The hatred and destruction they carry won't be contained within the borders of Czechoslovakia, Poland, or France. The poison of hatred will spread from nation to nation. It will pollute the hearts of all people and make its way to the shores of Britain, Canada, and the United States."

Silence settled over the room.

Prime Minister Chamberlain heaved a heavy sigh and nodded.

The door to the drawing room opened and Joseph Mueller entered. Mueller glanced at the crowd and halted. "I'm sorry, I didn't realize—"

"Please come in." Lady Elizabeth waved for the young man to join them. "This is Joseph Mueller, a close friend of our family."

Joseph Mueller glanced around the room and his eyes landed on Nelson Wilmington, who rushed forward. "Hi, Joseph. Remember me?" Wilmington stuck out a hand.

"Nelson?" Joseph stuttered.

"Yes." Wilmington's eyes bore a hole into Joseph Mueller, who eventually snapped out of his stupor long enough to shake.

"We went to school together," Joseph stared. "It is Nelson, right?"

Nelson Wilmington chuckled. "Yes, Nelson. You got the right brother."

"Mueller? That sounds Jewish," Sir Bentley Gardener said.

"It is Jewish." Joseph's head snapped around. "Is that a problem?"

All eyes moved to Gardener.

"Not for me, although it might be for others." Gardener's lips curled upward.

"Should anyone have a problem with the guests that I invite into my home, then they are more than welcome to leave," Lord William said sharply.

Silence crackled like electricity.

Sir Bentley Gardener frowned, but said nothing else.

Joseph's eyes drifted back to Nelson Wilmington, but he likewise said nothing.

Lady Elizabeth extended her hand. "Joseph, have you met the prime minister?"

Joseph Mueller hesitated but quickly walked over to Lady Elizabeth and shook hands with Chamberlain as introductions were made.

"Joseph has been a great asset to us," Lady Elizabeth said.

"An asset?" the prime minister asked.

"He's shared his culture with us. Educated us and the children. He's been invaluable," Lady Elizabeth said.

Joseph Mueller's cheeks flushed at the compliments.

"Children?" Stanley Tate glanced around as though he were expecting them to leap out at any moment.

"The Kindertransport children," Lady Daphne said.

It was hard to believe that nearly a year had passed since the start of the Kindertransport, a program developed to rescue children from Nazi-occupied territories. The Marsh family had taken in three children; Johan, Josiah, and Rivka were some of the first children rescued.

"It's a pleasure to meet you. My cousin considers you a lifesaver and believes that you can help us," Winston said.

Joseph Mueller's eyes reflected his confusion. "I'll be happy to help, but I don't know what I can do."

"We must be prepared for the German attack. We need to evacuate our most vulnerable citizens out of the path of danger," Winston said.

"Operation Pied Piper, indeed." Stanley Tate snorted. "Frankly, I think you're overreacting."

"Leading the women and children out of London to the countryside, hiding the nation's treasures in caves and cellars across the empire." Lord Cecil Scott shook his head. "It's basically admitting defeat. We're showing the enemy that we can't defend our cities. If we can't even protect our women and children, how are we going to handle anything else the Nazis send our way? We're telling the Nazis we have more faith in the power of their Luftwaffe than we do in our Royal Air Force."

"The Luftwaffe decimated the Polish Air Force in less than two weeks," Neville Chamberlain said.

"Well, the Royal Air Force is on a completely different level from the Poles'." Stanley Tate chuckled.

"Winston, I would have thought that you and Hitler would have gotten along better, seeing as you both fancy yourselves as artists," Lord Scott said.

Nelson Wilmington snorted. "Hitler is a no-talent hack who only wants to control art and artists."

"Hitler has confiscated or stolen art from Jews throughout Europe to build his dream of some great German National Gallery in which to house it all," Joseph Mueller said.

"Perhaps that is why Hitler and I don't get along. I want to create art, and Hitler wants to control it." Winston refilled his glass and took a sip. He turned to face Stanley Tate. "Art is valuable, but our most valuable treasure are the women and children that will be the future of this great country. They are worth protecting at all costs."

Lady Penelope clapped. "Agreed."

"That's just one of the reasons we love you, Cousin Winnie." Lady Daphne walked over to her cousin. She wrapped her arms around him and squeezed and then kissed him on the cheek. "You come across as a growly lion, but you're really just a big cuddly teddy bear."

Winston wrestled with his lips to keep them from curling upward into a smile. "Don't let that out, my dear. Men don't mind poking a bear, but rarely do you find anyone brave enough to poke a lion."

The prime minister listened quietly. Occasionally, Lady Elizabeth noticed he took a drink and winced as if in pain.

"Are you all right?" Lady Elizabeth asked.

"After all of these years, it turns out that I don't have the stomach for politics like I once did." Neville Chamberlain frowned. "But I do appreciate all that you've done to advance the war effort."

"I don't know that I've done much." Lady Elizabeth frowned. "Nothing compared to the sacrifices that our men and women who are going off to fight have done."

"Don't underestimate your contributions.

You're housing the art from the National Gallery, which could be dangerous if our enemies were to discover it. You've taken in three Polish orphans. You're lending your home to us by feeding and housing the war cabinet. All of these things enable us to do our jobs. You deserve a reward and when this is over—"

Lady Elizabeth was shaking her head before he could finish. "Please, I don't want any recognition. I want to help."

"You are helping. More than you know." Prime Minister Chamberlain glanced around to make sure that no one was nearby. He leaned forward and whispered, "One of the members of my war cabinet is a traitor. Information is being leaked back to the Germans. It sickens me to think that someone close to me . . . someone close to Britain . . . a member of our government would betray our nation." The prime minister's knuckles turned pale as the grip on his glass tightened. "I intend to find out who. With your help, I plan to trap the traitor."

I was jolted out of 1939 and back into the twenty-first century when my cell phone rang. One glance at the screen showed my sister's face. I swiped, but before I could speak, Jenna said, "Carl Tarkington is dead. He was murdered."

Chapter 19

"Murdered? When?"

"No idea," Jenna said.

"Bethany?" I wasn't even sure what I was asking. Was Bethany dead? Did she kill Carl? I wasn't sure, but it really didn't matter.

"All I know is that the call came in about Carl while I was at the police station. I'll see what information I can find out." Jenna hung up.

I went in search of Nana Jo and found her closing up the bookstore. When I told her, she was as stunned as me.

"That's a bummer," Nana Jo said.

"That's an understatement. Murder is certainly a bummer, but I didn't think you liked Carl."

"I don't. Didn't. But he was a great suspect for Alva's murder. I doubt very seriously that Carl killed Alva and then committed suicide out of remorse," Nana Jo said.

"Carl didn't strike me as the remorseful type."

"He liked himself too much to have committed suicide," Nana Jo agreed.

"Besides, Jenna said 'murder,'" I said.

Nana Jo sent a text update to the girls while I closed up the bookstore. Together, it didn't take long to get everything cleaned and ready for tomorrow. When we finished, my phone rang again. I smiled when I saw Frank's picture on the screen.

"Hey, Beautiful. Are we still on for dinner?"

I gasped. *OMG! It was date night.* "Sure."

Frank chuckled. "Now, why do I get the feeling that you forgot?"

"I have no idea. Maybe because you know me so well." I chuckled. "Actually, I did forget, but that doesn't mean I don't want to go."

"If you're tired, we can—"

"Who says I'm tired?"

Frank laughed. "Okay, if you're sure."

"I'm sure. Give me fifteen minutes to change."

It took twenty minutes, but Frank didn't seem to mind. When I was ready and came into the living area, he was sitting on the sofa. Snickers was in his lap flat on her back while he scratched her tummy with one hand. With his other hand, he held onto a stuffed duck that had seen better days, while playing tug-of-war with Oreo.

"Looks like you've got your hands full." I laughed.

"I'm a man of many talents. I'm good at multitasking." Frank got the upper hand on the duck and tossed it across the room.

Oreo jumped up and chased the sagging animal before pouncing on it. He shook it in his mouth for good measure before trotting back so Frank could wrestle it away from him again.

"Ready?" Frank put Snickers on the floor and stood.

Snickers didn't like losing her personal belly scratcher, but at eight pounds, she didn't have much say in the matter.

"Your grandmother filled me in on Carl. I can't say that I'm surprised."

My face must have reflected my surprise. "You expected him to be killed?"

"Carl was an arrogant, egotistical jerk. Frankly, I'm surprised nobody killed him sooner. I spent less than thirty minutes with him, and I wanted to strangle him. I have no idea how Bethany managed to live with him as long as she did."

"I would have smothered him with a pillow in his sleep," Nana Jo said from the breakfast bar.

Frank chuckled. "You never would have been crazy enough to have married him in the first place."

"Truth." Nana Jo looked down at Snickers, who was now clawing at her pants in an effort to get picked up. "You only want me now because Frank is leaving."

Snickers didn't deny it.

Nana Jo picked her up and cradled her like a baby as she scratched her tummy. "You're spoiled. You know that?"

Snickers used her paw to adjust Nana Jo's hand so she was being scratched in the place that made her tongue hang out of the side of her mouth and her eyes roll back into her head.

I shook my head at the sight. When I first got Snickers almost fifteen years ago, I never dreamed how she would wiggle her way into the family. She had been a handful as a puppy, full of energy and mischief. As an adult she provided entertainment, love, and support. After Leon's death, Snickers had cuddled and licked away many tears. Her muzzle was full of gray, showing her age. She wasn't as energetic or playful as she had once been. And a few years ago, the vet diagnosed her with heart disease. I spoiled her, but I had no regrets. She was a good dog, and I loved her. She had earned her cushy life, and all the belly scratches she could get.

Date night with Frank was always a great culinary adventure. He liked to sample and experience different cuisines that I might normally never have tried. Frank's restaurant wasn't just a job. He loved good food. He was a foodie and loved to try new restaurants. Tonight, we tried a new Ethiopian place. I'd never had Ethiopian food before, but I trusted Frank. Having traveled the world, he had tried just about every type of food there was. He knew me and knew what I'd like, and he was rarely wrong. The food was good. The atmosphere was warm, cozy, and romantic.

Finished eating, I was sated and content. We sat in a companionable silence sipping coffee.

I sighed.

"Penny for them," Frank said.

"I was thinking about Alva."

Frank reached across the table and squeezed my hand. "You know there was nothing you could have done, right?"

It took a moment, but I conceded. "I know, but it still hurts."

"Wanna talk?" he asked.

I wasn't sure that talking would change anything, but I told Frank about both memorial services and the information we'd found. I also shared my conversations with Special Agent Warren Brown.

"Getting the paintings appraised is a good idea," Frank said. "Cooper left the anonymous tip and now that Carl's dead too, I think the police will be willing to delve a little deeper into Alva's death."

"You don't think it's too late?" I sighed.

"Honestly, it might be. A lot will depend on how she was killed. But at least if the police are asking questions and looking around, then it should make the murderer nervous. If he or she is nervous, then they may make mistakes."

I sighed.

"That's three sighs in less than five minutes. What's wrong?" Frank asked.

"Nothing, I just can't shake the feeling that I'm missing something." I shook my head. "Whenever I think I figured it out, then it slips further and further away."

"Then don't think about it. Let's just enjoy the evening. You are all meeting at my restaurant tomorrow. Maybe you'll find that missing piece by then."

Frank was right. I needed to stop trying so hard to remember and just enjoy the moments together. So, that's what I did.

Frank brought me home and was doing a great job distracting me from all thoughts of Alva and Carl until he got a call. There was an emergency at the restaurant. Snickers and Oreo followed him downstairs and went outside one last time. Frank let them back inside and made sure everything was locked up before he left.

In the quiet of the evening, I allowed my brain to wander once again. No matter how many times I thought through the situation, I couldn't see past Isabella and the evil eye. Eventually, I decided to stop wandering aimlessly and sat down to write.

Thompkins refreshed the trays with bacon, sausage, eggs, and toast in the dining room. Making sure that the coffee and tea were both full and hot, he stood nearby. From a quiet corner, Thompkins kept a watchful eye on the buffet set up in the Marsh dining room for breakfast. Thompkins was vigilant, but still his mind drifted back in time. In the butler's grandfather's reign as butler to the Marsh Family, breakfast would have been as formal of an affair as dinner with multiple courses served by an army of servants. During Thompkins's father's service, breakfast was much more relaxed with a buffet that was tended by footmen. Thompkins didn't like change. He took great pride in serving the Marsh Family, but as the father of two girls, neither of whom chose a life of domestic service, he was happy that his daughters had choices. His oldest, Mary, was happily married to Joseph Mueller, while the youngest, Eleanor, had declared a desire to study nursing. It was a career that she was well suited to. Now that England was at war, Eleanor would be in demand. Thompkins was proud of his girls, but he couldn't help but worry.

The world was changing for all of them. Even here at Wickfield Lodge, change was in the air. With all the footmen off to war, it was now Thompkins's responsibility to do many tasks he would have once seen as falling beneath his station. Yet Thompkins would do his duty to the family, just as his father and his grandfather had.

Many of the great Families had collapsed. Fortunes were lost through poor management, gambling, or taxation. Yet the Marshes had weathered the storms of war and economic depression. They'd adapted. Even Thompkins had adapted— not only in his domestic duties, but through the services he provided to the government. He wondered what his wife or his children would say if they knew the role that he'd played in helping not only Scotland Yard, but King George, to catch murderers.

"Psst."

Thompkins watched Flossie, the day maid, nervously enter the dining room. She made her way to the butler's side.

"I'm sorry, Mr. Thompkins, sir, but Mrs. McDuffie needs you," Flossie whispered.

Thompkins nodded. "Thank you. Tell Mrs. McDuffie I'll be there shortly."

Flossie hesitated for a moment, clearly wanting to say more, but she merely gave a brief curtsy before rushing from the room.

Lady Elizabeth caught the eye of the butler and gave a silent nod.

Thompkins left the dining room. In the servants dining hall, he found Mrs. McDuffie, Flossie, and his son-in-law, Joseph.

Joseph was pale while Mrs. McDuffie's cheeks were flushed. Millie sat at the table clutching a cup of tea. Flossie huddled against the wall.

"What's going on?" Thompkins looked around the room.

"I didn't want to bother you, but we didn't know what else to do." Mrs. McDuffie wrung her hands.

"Do about what?" Thompkins asked.

"It's happened again," Mrs. McDuffie said.

"What's happened?" Thompkins asked.

Mrs. Anderson stuck her head around the corner. "I'm making a sauce and asked Mr. Joseph if he'd go down to the cellar and get me a bottle of red wine."

All eyes turned to Joseph.

Joseph Mueller looked up at his father-in-law and swallowed hard. "I went to the cellar. It was dark. I tripped over something and fell on my knees."

Thompkins noticed Joseph's clothes were stained.

"That's where I found him. On the floor of the cellar." Joseph closed his eyes and swallowed again. "He was dead."

"Found who? Who's dead?" Thompkins asked.

"Wilmington." Joseph Mueller gazed at the butler. "He'd been stabbed."

Chapter 20

The next morning, we all met at Frank's restaurant for breakfast. Frank brought a large pot of coffee and a tray of pastries. "If it's okay, I'd like to go first."

Everyone nodded.

"I got a bit of information, but I don't know if it will be helpful."

"Anything is better than what we have right now, which is nothing," I said.

"Okay." Frank pulled his phone from his pocket. He swiped a few screens and then found what he was looking for and read. "Alva and her sister, Zelda Charleston, were identical twins. They were extremely close. The sisters were both talented artists. Alva's specialty was sculpture, while Zelda was a painter. Zelda never married, choosing instead to travel the world and pursue her painting. She spent many years in Russia."

"Russia?" Dorothy frowned.

"Why the surprised look?" Nana Jo said. "What's wrong with Russia?"

"Nothing." Dorothy shook her head and relaxed her brow.

"Usually, when I think of artists, I think of Paris, Italy, Amsterdam, Vienna . . ." Dorothy waved her hand.

"Do you think there was something sinister about her spending time in Russia?" I asked.

"No. Russia has great art too. It's just not the first place I think of an artist spending years," Dorothy said.

My brain buzzed. "I thought Alva was the painter."

"Maybe they both painted, but my sources swore that Zelda was the painter." Frank hesitated but then went on. "Anyway, neither was exceptionally talented, but they were passionate."

"Do you remember the painting over the fireplace at Alva's house?"

Frank nodded.

"That was Alva's or Zelda's?" I shook my head. "One of them painted it."

"It didn't look valuable, but maybe . . . Anyway, Alva married the love of her life, Oliver Tarkington. Oliver was an archaeologist who spent decades teaching at Cairo University and searching for the tomb of Cleopatra. Everything we've found on Oliver indicates he was well respected in his field. He and Alva never had children. Both were from small families with only one sibling. Oliver died—"

"How did Oliver die?" I asked.

"He was out at an excavation and a tunnel collapsed. He was buried under tons of sand and rock."

"Yikes. That sounds like a horrible way to go," Dorothy said.

"I don't know. It sounds like he died doing what he loved." Frank took another sip of coffee before continuing. "He was well-respected and successful. He left Alva well taken care of financially. After Oliver's death, Zelda moved to Egypt with her sister."

"What happened to Zelda?" I asked.

"Died."

"How did she . . . ?"

"Heart attack."

I must have looked disappointed because Frank chuckled. "Not every death is murder."

"I know. It's just . . ."

"It's just that you write murder mysteries, so you have a tendency to believe that everyone is bumping off their relatives?" Frank joked.

"I do not." I gave him a playful swat.

"Sure, but in this case, no one had a reason to kill Zelda. She didn't have any money. Alva was the wealthy one. Well, she was wealthy after Oliver's death."

"Was Oliver's brother wealthy too?" Ruby Mae asked.

"No. Apparently, they were night and day. Whatever Oliver touched turned to gold. Whatever his brother Henry touched, well . . . it turned to dust. If Oliver bought a gold mine, it struck gold. If Henry bought the gold mine next to it, then it dried up."

"That must have made Henry jealous." Nana Jo looked hopeful.

"If he was, there's nothing to show it. Everything I can find indicates the brothers were tight. Henry joked about his bad luck and never showed any resentment toward his brother."

"Wow! Henry must have been a paragon of virtue," I said.

"Why? They were brothers. Maybe he was just happy for his brother's success," Frank said.

"Spoken like an only child," I said.

"So, if Jenna hit the lottery, you'd be jealous?" Frank asked.

I thought for a few minutes. "Depends on timing. When I was younger, I would have been jealous and expected her to share the wealth." I glanced at Jenna who stuck out her tongue.

I paused for a few minutes. "Now, if she hit the lottery, I'd be super excited and wouldn't expect anything from her."

"What changed?" Frank asked.

"I grew up?" I laughed. "If Jenna hits the lottery, then good for her. It's her life, her money, and I'd be happy for her."

"Amen!" Jenna raised her glass in salute.

"I guess Carl Tarkington never grew up. He certainly felt that his aunt Alva wasn't entitled to his uncle's money," Nana Jo said.

"What else did you find out?" I asked.

Frank looked at his phone. "After Zelda died, Alva spent several years traveling and enjoying life abroad. A couple of years ago, Alva started having health problems. Carl started pressuring Alva to come back to the United States. Eventually, she did. Carl and his wife, Bethany, moved in. Alva's health had started to decline. Carl took over the management of his late uncle's estate and that's when the problems started."

"So, Carl really did embezzle funds and steal from investors?" I asked.

"Looks that way. If Carl hadn't been killed, he would be facing criminal charges and years behind bars." Frank looked up at me. "Any chance Carl killed Alva and then took his own life?"

"Nope. Nada. No way." I shook my head. "Carl Tarkington was an arrogant jerk. He thought too highly of himself to consider taking his life."

"Agreed," Frank said. "But it sure solves one problem."

I tilted my head and waited.

"Carl's firm is off the hook." Frank saw me prepared to object and raised his hand. "I'm not saying Carl didn't embezzle and steal the money. I firmly believe he did. In fact, my sources are 99.995 percent sure that Carl and only Carl was guilty. But now with Carl dead, the company can throw him under the bus and save their own skins, whether they deserve to be saved or not."

"You mean, maybe Carl wasn't the only person guilty, but

now that he's gone . . . his accomplice, if he had one, gets away free and clear?"

Frank nodded. "There's no proof that he had help, but . . ."

"But?" I asked.

"But to steal a line from your grandmother, Carl wasn't the sharpest knife in the drawer. So, there may have been someone else involved, but now we may never know because he or she can make Carl the fall guy for *everything*." Frank gave me a pointed look.

"Everything. Including Alva's murder."

Jenna's phone chimed. She glanced down and her lips pursed.

"What?" I asked.

She held up her phone. There was a text message. It was one word. **Stabbed**. No other words were needed. I knew exactly who she was referring to.

"Carl?" Frank asked.

Jenna nodded.

My mind kept drifting back to Isabella's comments about Carl and the "evil eye." Had she wielded the spear that vanquished Carl? I didn't want to believe it. I liked Isabella. But if she thought he was evil and was responsible for Alva's death, then maybe she saw herself as an avenging angel.

Chapter 21

After breakfast, Nana Jo and I walked home. I wasn't an early morning person, but today I'd woken up early to leave for our meeting. When I got home, Snickers was curled up in my bed. She wasn't a morning dog and hadn't gotten the memo that today was going to be different.

"Hey, sleepyhead. Time to get up." I shook her.

At eight pounds, it didn't take much shaking. She rolled over on her back so I could scratch her tummy.

"Look, you need to get up and go outside," I said while I scratched. When I saw her eyes roll back into her head, I knew more drastic measures were needed. So, I picked her up.

Oreo had stuck his head out of his crate at the noise and was completing his morning stretches.

"Let's go." I tapped my leg and walked to the stairs. The sound of toenails on the hardwood floors told me that Oreo was behind me.

At the stairs, I put Snickers down and we all walked downstairs.

When they finished taking care of business, we went upstairs. Nana Jo was in the kitchen drinking coffee and reading the morning paper.

I took a deep breath and allowed the aroma to seep into my brain. Then I took a sip. I closed my eyes as the warmth spread throughout my body and the caffeine gave my heart a jolt.

"I feel like I shouldn't be watching." Nana Jo chuckled.

"What?"

"You are the only person I know who treats a cup of coffee like a sensual experience."

"Mmm. It *is* a sensual experience." I took another sip. When I finished the cup and refilled, I remembered that Nana Jo had asked a question. "Did you ask me something?"

"I asked where you were going."

"I got a text from Isabella. She's moving out today. I had offered to take the paintings and have them appraised. She said I could swing by and get them."

My phone vibrated. "It's from Frank. He made two coffee cakes in case I want to take one to Bethany."

"He's a good man."

Frank *is* a good man. I sent him my thanks. "He's going to have one of the waiters drop them off."

"How was your date last night?"

"It was good, but he had to leave. His new stove was installed yesterday and there was a problem with the gas connection."

The doorbell rang and I was about to go when Nana Jo stopped me. "I need to stretch my legs. You stay there and have a few minutes alone with your coffee and I'll get these."

Moments later, Nana Jo and the aroma of cinnamon and sugar wafted up with her.

"That smells fantastic."

"And it's still warm," Nana Jo said.

We got plates and took big slices of the cinnamon coffee cake. It was the delicious complement to go along with the coffee. We both took an extra slice for the road and then I left Nana Jo and the poodles.

I drove to Alva's house at Shady Acres. Unlike last time, there were no cars parked in the driveway.

I rang the bell.

Isabella opened the door and I was surprised to see her eyes were red as though she'd been crying. Isabella had made no secret of her feelings for Carl. She didn't seem like the type to cry at the drop of a hat, but then I barely knew her. Maybe she was the overly emotional type.

"Are you okay?" I asked.

Isabella hugged me. "No. They think I killed Carl."

"Who? Who thinks that?" I asked.

"The police. They're going to arrest me."

Chapter 22

When the shock of Isabella's words wore off, I rushed her inside. The last thing we needed was to put on a show for the neighbors.

I closed the door without dropping my coffee cake. "Isabella let's go sit down. I'm sure things aren't as bad as you think."

"Oh, it's you." Margery Brooks came down the steps. She carried a suitcase and had a smug look on her face. "I assumed it was the police."

Isabella spat a few words in a language I assumed was Arabic.

Margery smiled and headed for the door.

"Did the police approve leaving the scene?" I asked as innocently as I could. "I didn't think they allowed people to leave a crime scene with . . . evidence." I made a pointed glance at the suitcase.

Molten lava rose up Margery's neck and erupted on her face. "Are you implying that I had something to do with Carl's murder?"

I passed the coffee cake to Isabella and held up both hands

in a sign of surrender. "I'm not accusing you or anyone of anything. I'm simply stating that when there has been a murder, the police don't usually permit people to remove anything from the scene until they've had a chance to check it."

"The police have spent all night going through every inch of the house." Bethany came into the hall and folded her hands across her chest.

"I wanted to come and extend my condolences on your loss—"

Bethany snorted. "And did you bring me another pie?"

"Coffee cake." I pointed to the box Isabella held.

Bethany's stomach growled. She unfolded her arms. "I'm sorry. The lemon meringue pie was the best pie I ever tasted, and I'm starving." She took a deep breath. "Perhaps you'd like to join me."

"I'd love to." Okay, *love* was an exaggeration, but I wanted to hear Bethany's side of this story.

Isabella was hesitant, but I gave her a gentle push. As we headed after Bethany, I noticed that Margery wasn't coming. I stopped and extended an arm in her direction. "It's really good coffee cake."

Margery glanced at her phone and then shrugged, placed her suitcase by the front door, and followed us.

In the kitchen, Isabella went to work making a pot of coffee while Bethany got plates and silverware. Margery sat and watched, arms folded.

When everything was finished, we all sat down to coffee cake and coffee. Initially, I planned to skip the cake, but changed my mind. Nana Jo wasn't here to tell that I'd already had two servings.

"Hmm. This is so good." Bethany closed her eyes and savored the flavors. When she opened her eyes and saw we were all staring at her, she chuckled. "What?"

"Nothing. I'll have to tell Frank how much you enjoyed it," I said.

"Your fiancé really made this?" Isabella asked.

I nodded. "He loves to cook, which is a blessing and a curse."

"How so?" Margery asked.

"I can see the blessing, but where's the curse?" Bethany asked.

"It's a blessing because he loves to cook and he's good at it. The curse comes from the fact that I'm afraid I'll be four hundred pounds before the wedding." I laughed. "My assistant at the bookstore, Dawson, is an excellent baker too."

"What a rough life. You've got two amazing men who just want to bake for you. I'm so jealous. Carl couldn't boil water," Bethany said.

"I would kill for a man who could bake like this."

Silence descended on the room at Isabella's comment. Her hand froze halfway to her mouth and the blood drained from her face. Realizing what she said, she dropped her fork. "I'm sorry . . . I didn't mean . . . I—"

Bethany reached over and patted her hand. "It's okay. We know you were joking."

"Do we?" Margery put down her fork and glared across the table at Isabella.

"What is that supposed to mean?" Isabella asked.

"Enough." Bethany looked from Margery to Isabella. "Carl's death, while unfortunate, is no one's fault."

" 'No one's fault'? He was stabbed. Which means that it was absolutely someone's fault." Margery scowled.

I hated to admit it, but Margery had a valid point. Still, I didn't need a catfight between Isabella and Margery.

"I meant his death wasn't the fault of anyone here," Bethany said.

"Do the police know who killed him? Where was he killed?" Normally, I wouldn't ask a new widow such tough questions, but Bethany didn't seem to be in mourning and, based on her previous comments to Jenna and me, she wasn't too broken up over his death.

"Carl's body was found down on the beach," Bethany said.

"Really?" I don't know what I expected, but that wasn't it. Lake Michigan created the shoreline that stretched through South Harbor and North Harbor. While the lake was visible from Shady Acres, access was limited. The terrain was sloped, creating bluffs that overlooked the lake, but without beach-front access. If Carl was killed on the beach, he must have been near Silver Beach Park, which was in downtown South Harbor.

"Carl loved walking on the beach. He said watching the waves crash against the pier to the lighthouse helped him think." Bethany shrugged.

That explained why the police hadn't cordoned off the house and why Margery would be allowed to leave with lug-gage. It also meant that Carl's murder could have been com-mitted by anyone. The beaches, especially in South Harbor, were considered safe, although that wasn't always the case. Un-like most areas where beachfront property was highly valued, South Harbor's beachfront had a bit of a troubled past. The area now known as Silver Beach was first opened as a resort in 1891. Over time, the area expanded from merely cottages with a pavilion to include an amusement park with roller coasters, a roller rink, dance halls, and even a boxing arena. The area thrived until crime and civil unrest from the 1960s forced its closure in 1970. The structures were demolished, and the property was bought by a local corporation and later sold to the county. A revitalization meant that the area now thrived and was considered safe. Still, no matter how safe an area was, things happened. Even on the pristine beaches of a tourist town, crime could rear its ugly head. Carl's killer didn't have to be one of the three women sitting at the table with me. It could have been a disgruntled colleague or client. Or it could have been a stranger he met on the beach in a mugging gone terribly wrong. Carl's killer could be anyone.

Chapter 23

"Do the police have any suspects?" I asked.

Margery looked pointedly at Isabella, who slammed down her coffee mug, spilling coffee onto the table, and shook with anger.

"I did not kill him. I did not kill anyone." Isabella fumed.

"I didn't say you did." Margery smirked.

I went to the counter and got a paper towel to wipe up the spillage.

"What are you saying?" Bethany asked.

Margery sipped her coffee slowly. After a few moments, she sat her mug down and glared at Isabella. "I never bought into that poor, helpless orphan routine. I saw through you. You wheedled yourself in between Alva and her family. You planted seeds of doubt so that poor, old woman didn't trust anyone but you. But I saw through your Little Miss Innocent act. And I told them . . . I told Carl and—"

Margery suddenly clamped her lips shut as her neck and cheeks flushed red.

"Who else did you tell?" I asked. "Carl and who?"

Margery fidgeted. I could see the wheels in her brain turning. Should she come clean and tell us? Or should she keep her secret? A long sigh signaled her decision. She leaned back in her seat and shrugged. "It's no big secret. I told Ethan."

Bethany slammed her own mug down on the table. "Ethan? Ethan Linton?"

Margery huffed. "Yes. He's a nice man. And Oliver Tarkington promised he'd support the museum, but Alva never followed through. She should have honored her late husband's wishes, but she didn't. Then Isabella came around, flaunting her stolen necklace."

"I did not steal anything." Isabella shook with anger.

"Ethan said that necklace was an antiquity and there was no way the Egyptian Ministry of Tourism and Antiquities would have allowed someone to remove a valuable necklace like that from an excavation." Margery smirked.

The blood left Isabella's face as she fingered her amulet. "It was a gift."

Margery snorted.

"What does Isabella's necklace have to do with Ethan Linton or Carl?" Bethany glared at Margery, who squirmed in her seat.

"It shows what kind of person she is." Margery glared at Isabella. "Anyone who would stoop so low as to steal from a tomb, would have no hesitation about stealing from an elderly woman."

"I did not steal this necklace." Isabella punctuated each word with a finger jab in Margery's direction.

Margery rolled her eyes.

"So, you've been spying on us?" Bethany asked.

Margery frowned. "I wasn't spying. I was helping the family. Carl explained that the money belonged to his uncle Oliver."

"Alva was his wife. She was entitled to the money," Isabella said.

"While she was alive, but when Alva died, it was only right that the money went to the family and to the people that *Oliver* would have wanted to have it without some . . . some . . . con woman manipulating an addle-minded old woman." Margery glared at Isabella.

"Conwoman!" Isabella stood so rapidly, she knocked over her chair. "Why you . . . *ya gazma!*"

I righted the chair and pulled Isabella back down.

"What did you call me?" Margery scowled.

Isabella refused to answer, in a flash Margery pulled out her cell phone and Googled the insult. After a few moments, she paused and frowned. After a moment, she looked up. "You called me a shoe?"

Isabella's chest heaved with anger, but she folded her arms across her chest and kept her lips sealed.

Margery slammed her phone on the table, folded her arms across her chest, and scowled back at Isabella.

Isabella and Margery glared at each other like prizefighters sizing each other up before a bout.

I glanced across at Bethany, wondering if she would be able to intervene if the two women suddenly got into a catfight. Instead of instilling confidence, Bethany looked as though she might join the fray, although I wasn't sure which woman she would be fighting. This was not good. I wasn't prepared for this. I wasn't a fighter. Nana Jo and Jenna were the fighters. They were the dominant predators—the alphas. I was a peacemaker. *Where is Nana Jo when I need her?* She wasn't here, of course, and there was no way she could get me out of this mess. I was on my own.

What would Nana Jo do? I smiled as several options passed through my mind—everything from taking her "peacemaker" out of her purse and pistol-whipping all three women, to using her aikido skills to take them down like a bad habit.

"What are you grinning about?" Bethany asked.

"Nothing. I was just thinking about my grandmother." I forced my lips to behave and plastered on my most serious expression.

Bethany stood up. "Well, this has been most enlightening, but I think I'd like for all of you to leave."

Margery was the first to get up. "Gladly."

A few moments later, the front door slammed.

"I was leaving today anyway." Isabella marched out of the room.

Bethany turned to me. "I'm sure you can see yourself out." Then she turned and walked out of the room, leaving me alone.

I walked out the front door and sat in my car for a few minutes as I tried to process what just happened. Eventually, I chuckled. *Not exactly how Nana Jo would have done it, but I managed to clear the room.*

Before I pulled away from the curb, the front door opened. Isabella ran outside with two paintings.

I turned off the car and got out.

Isabella handed me the paintings. "I almost forgot. You promised to take these to get them appraised."

I took the paintings and put them on the back seat on the car. With the paintings carefully stowed, I turned to look at Isabella. "Are you okay?"

She nodded. "Yes. It's better this way. I was leaving anyway."

"Where will you go?" I asked.

Isabella shrugged. "I'll probably spend a couple of nights at a hotel, then I'll go stay with a friend in Chicago."

"You're welcome to stay with me for a few days."

"I don't know . . . I don't want to impose."

"You won't be imposing." I put my arm around her shoulder and gave her a squeeze.

Isabella hesitated for a few seconds, but then nodded. "That would be perfect. If you're sure."

I nodded.

She ran back to the house.

I sent a text to Nana Jo. She offered to stay at her house and give Isabella her room. Before I could respond, there were bubbles that showed Nana Jo was sending another message. When the bubbles stopped, she responded that Dawson was going out of town for a football game and offered Isabella his apartment over the garage. I thanked both of them. Before I could type more, Isabella returned with two suitcases.

We wrestled them into the back of my SUV, and got inside. Before I pulled away, I glanced at Alva's house and saw Bethany Tarkington watching us.

Chapter 24

A fence connected the back of my building to the detached garage, creating a courtyard. I pulled my SUV into the garage. By the time I had turned off the engine, Nana Jo had come through the side door and was waiting with Snickers and Oreo.

The poodles barked, pounced, and welcomed Isabella with open paws.

"I thought you could check out the apartment while we're here. Then you can decide if you want privacy or if you want to hang out inside." Nana Jo led the way up the stairs inside the garage.

At the top was a large open area. When I bought the building, this space had been covered in dust and cobwebs. The previous owners must have planned to use it for a rental because they had squeezed in a toilet and shower, and the beginnings of a small kitchenette. After a thorough cleaning, some repairs by Andrew—the same Amish craftsman who built the bookshelves in the bookstore—and lots of paint, the small apartment had been converted from a storage space into a habitable apartment. Andrew added a skylight and stairs for an external fire escape, so the apartment was bright and up to code. Furnished with mostly thrift-store finds and excess furniture from Jenna's and Nana Jo's attics, Dawson had created a cozy space that gave him a break from campus and an escape from his often drunk, sometimes violent father.

Isabella stood in the middle of the floor and looked around the apartment.

I looked around. "It's small, but—"

"It's lovely." Isabella beamed. "But I don't want to inconvenience anyone. I don't want your assistant to have to find someplace else to stay."

"Pshaw." Nana Jo waved away Isabella's protests. "MISU has an away game and he's out for the next four days, so no one is inconvenienced."

"But if you'd rather be inside with us, that's fine too. Let's take a look and then you can decide which space you prefer." I smiled and led the way into the house.

"I think we should have some tea and more of that coffee cake," Nana Jo said.

Inside, I showed Isabella around the bookstore and then we went upstairs. Compared to the studio over the garage, my apartment over the bookstore felt massive. The space over the bookstore was over two thousand square feet, but unlike houses that had multiple levels with nooks, crannies, and lots of private spaces, my home was much more open. The living room, dining room, and kitchen were one big open space. There were two bedrooms and two bathrooms, so the tour didn't take long.

Nana Jo went back to the bookstore while Isabella and I had tea at the back of the store.

"This is nice." Isabella sipped her tea.

"It's a new blend. My assistant's girlfriend, Jillian Clark, spent the summer in New York and stopped at the Brooklyn Tea shop. This is one of my favorite blends."

Isabella smiled. "The tea is nice, but I meant this." She waved her hand around the store.

"This was my dream and sometimes, I still pinch myself." I smiled.

"I would love to have a store like this one day."

"What would you sell?" I asked.

She lowered her gaze, and her cheeks flushed. After a few moments, she took a deep breath. "I would love a small spice shop. Attareen—spice sellers—are such wonderful places. You can learn so much by spending time talking to them." Isabella sat up taller when she started to talk. "It's not like in the United States where you can go online and order whatever spices you want. I'm talking about the shops where you can buy bulk spices. Did you know there are some spices that must be harvested at night? And others that should only be plucked during a full moon?"

"I had no idea."

"It's fascinating and there's a science to it. Some plants should be ground using a marble mortar and pestle and others that need brass," Isabella said.

"You really know a lot about spices. Is that what you studied in college?" I asked.

"No, but . . . I met Ahsan in college. His family owns one of the oldest spice shops in Cairo. His father, Ahmed, inherited it from his father before him. For over one hundred years, his family has sold spices and one day, Ahsan will inherit the shop."

"And you like Ahsan?" I asked.

Isabella nodded. "Yes. I like Ahsan a lot."

I reached across the table and squeezed her hand. "That's wonderful."

"It is, but . . ."

"But?" I asked.

"My aunt doesn't want me to marry Ahsan and run a spice shop."

"Your aunt doesn't like Ahsan?"

"No. It's just that she wants me to do something . . . bigger. My mom was her sister. She sent me away to boarding school and college to learn. My mom always hoped that I would be a doctor or someone important." She sighed.

"She loves you and I'm sure she wants you to be happy." I patted her hand. "What does your father want?"

She shrugged. "I didn't know my father."

"I never had children, but I think most parents just want their kids to be healthy and happy. If Ahsan makes you happy, then I'm sure your aunt will adjust to the idea."

"My aunt loves me, and she doesn't want me to struggle like my mom did. A lot has changed in my country, but some things are slow to change." Isabella sipped her tea.

Isabella decided to stay in Dawson's apartment, so Nana Jo helped her pick out a culinary cozy mystery from Leslie Budewitz's Spice Shop Mystery series and the first book in the Amelia Peabody Mystery series by Elizabeth Peters, which is set in Cairo. We took her bags up to the apartment where she settled in with a plate of cookies and a pot of tea, and left her with Snickers and Oreo for company.

After a call to William Merkel, owner of South Harbor Art and Framing, I left Nana Jo at the bookstore. William said business was slow and he could take a look at the paintings right away, so I got directions and headed out to South Harbor.

South Harbor Art and Framing was a small storefront downtown. Despite the fact that North and South Harbors were sister cities, they were both extremely different. North

Harbor had a number of older buildings that were abandoned and boarded up. In contrast, South Harbor had a bustling downtown with picturesque cobblestone streets and brick storefronts that sold everything from fudge and truffles to overpriced coffee. It was a tourist's paradise with quaint shops.

I lucked out and found a parking space a couple of doors away from the store, grabbed the paintings, and made my way inside.

The front of the store showcased framed paintings in a variety of sizes on the walls with small signs indicating prices that ranged from a few hundred dollars all the way to upper five figures. I tried to mask my shock at a painting that was about the size of a paperback book, with a price tag that was more than I'd paid for my bookstore.

"Lovely, isn't it?"

I turned to see a short man with curly brown hair and hazel eyes. He had an infectious smile and a bubbly personality.

"Yes, but . . . is that price right?" I whispered.

"Oh yes, that is an original Turner." I must have looked confused because he went into his teaching persona. "Joseph Mallord William Turner was a brilliant English painter. He was known for his use of color. And his landscapes . . . were so magnificent, they elevated landscape art to an entirely different level. Like Mozart, Turner was a child prodigy—a genius. At fourteen he enrolled at the Royal Academy of Arts, and exhibited his first work at fifteen. He was a prolific painter. When he died at age seventy-six, he left over five hundred oil paintings, two thousand watercolors, and thirty thousand works on paper."

"Wow!"

"I'm sorry, I could talk about art all day. I apologize. I'm William Merkel. How may I help you?" He smiled.

"I'm Samantha Washington. I called and—"

"Yes. Yes, of course. Mrs. Washington, come in. Come in." Mr. Merkel waved me toward the back of the store.

He directed me to a table in the back corner where I placed the two paintings.

"Please, have a seat." He pulled out a chair and I sat.

Mr. Merkel took a pair of white gloves from his pocket and put them on before picking up the paintings to examine them. He stared at them for several minutes. When he finished with one, he picked up the other one and gave it the same level of scrutiny. After a few minutes he put the paintings down on the table and turned to face me. "These are both signed paintings by Alva Tarkington, who I believe is recently deceased."

I nodded.

"What would you like to know?" he asked.

"Alva Tarkington left these two paintings to a friend. I suggested she get them appraised for insurance purposes."

Mr. Merkel gave a sad smile. "Does your friend have documentation to prove ownership?"

"They were specifically mentioned in an addendum to Alva's will." I avoided mentioning that the addendum was written on toilet paper. That probably wouldn't bode well for pricing unless paintings by eccentric artists were more valuable.

"Does your friend want to sell them?" he asked.

"No. They were a gift, and she was very fond of Alva."

He nodded. "Still, your friend should get paperwork showing the transfer of ownership, you never know when a work may turn out to be valuable. Although . . . I don't believe that these paintings will garner more than a couple of hundred dollars. However, I will be more than happy to do some research and provide a report."

"That would be lovely."

Mr. Merkel glanced at one of the paintings, of a man wearing a green tie, and frowned. He had removed his gloves, but he put them back on and held the painting up to the light. He frowned. "May I remove them from the frames? I'd like to look more closely," he asked.

"It won't damage the paintings, will it?"

"Absolutely not."

"Then I'm sure my friend won't mind."

William Merkel carefully removed the paintings from their frames and examined them closely from all angles.

After what felt like an eternity, I asked, "Is anything wrong?"

"No. Nothing's wrong, it's just . . . do you know if Alva Tarkington was in the habit of painting over her old canvases?"

"I have no idea. Is that common?" I asked.

"Actually, more than you would think. It's called pentimento. Many of the experts—da Vinci, van Eyck, Vermeer, and Cézanne . . . all of the greats did it."

"Why would an artist paint over their work?" I asked.

"There are a multitude of reasons. Mostly, money. Many artists couldn't afford new canvases and took older paintings and simply painted over them. That is the most common reason." He gazed down at the paintings again.

Something in his eyes indicated there was more he wasn't saying. "I don't think money was an issue for Alva Tarkington," I said. "Her husband, Oliver, left her a wealthy woman. She could afford new canvases."

"Perhaps she didn't like the original painting." He forced a smile. "Some artists are perfectionist."

I looked carefully at Alva's paintings. She wasn't a great artist, and these didn't look like the work of a perfectionist. "Is there another reason?"

"Artists have painted over works to hide what's underneath," William Merkel said cautiously.

"Why would an artist deliberately ruin a painting by painting over it?" I frowned.

"Pentimento doesn't mean what's underneath is ruined. It

could be that the artists weren't satisfied with the positioning or the colors. He or she may have simply decided to make alterations. There is a famous painting of Jacques de Norvins, Napoleon's chief of police in Rome. The painting by Ingres shows him sitting in front of a red curtain which is draped behind him." Mr. Merkel shuffled back to the counter and came back with a large book. He opened it and flipped until he found what he was looking for. He pointed at a portrait of a young man sitting in a chair wearing black with his left hand tucked inside his jacket in a pose that even an art novice like me recognized as Napoleon-esq.

William Merkel passed me a magnifying glass and pointed at the drapes.

I leaned over the book and stared. I gasped when I noticed the faint impression of a head that I originally took for a shadow against the curtains.

William Merkel nodded. "You see?"

"It's a head."

"X-rays and modern technology show that in the original painting there was a bust of a boy's head on top of a column. Experts assume the bust was of Napoleon's son, who was known as the 'King of Rome,' Napoleon II. We assume the bust was overpainted with the curtain after the fall of Napoleon. The overpainting could have been the work of Ingres or another artist." He shrugged.

"But why? I mean, the painting was a moment in time. I mean . . . why bother? Okay, Jacques de Norvins was the chief of police. He was appointed by Napoleon. That's a fact. It's history. Whether you like Napoleon or not, it doesn't change the facts, so why bother painting over a bust of Napoleon's son?"

Mr. Merkel smiled. "That my dear, we may never know. Ingres may have been afraid. Or maybe the new regime wanted to wipe out all connections to Napoleon and all references to his son. It was common to scratch out the names of leaders who were deemed unfavorable." He shrugged. "Of course, there could be a very simple explanation."

"Like what?" I asked.

"Maybe that side of the painting was damaged. The owner may have felt that the bust was a minor detail. In order to save the greater work, the decision was made to paint over the bust." He rushed to the back of his studio and came back with another book that he opened. "I looked up Alva Tarkington after you called. Her husband, Oliver, was an Egyptologist and she spent many years in Egypt."

I nodded.

"It was common to attempt to remove the names and images of unfavorable leaders. Akhenaten or Amenhotep IV, was nearly lost to history."

"I've heard of him. Wasn't he King Tut's father?"

William Merkel nodded. "We don't know for sure, but he is believed to be the father of Tutankhamun. Amenhotep tried to change the Egyptian culture away from their polytheism to a more monotheistic religion worshipping the 'Aten.' He even tried to move the capital to Amarna. His predecessors tried to erase him from history, so we don't know for sure, but the practice of trying to change history has been going on for thousands of years."

"Is there a way to see what's underneath without ruining the paintings?" I asked.

"Like I said, modern technology may be the safest bet. We can take X-rays, which shouldn't cause any damage at all. If the X-rays reveal that there are paintings underneath and they want to see them, then the owner can take more drastic steps."

"Drastic? How drastic?"

"Very drastic." He stared. "First, I would recommend a conservator. They can test the paint and mix a special solvent. Then they would slowly and very carefully remove the overpaint. The top layer of paint will be completely removed, but with extreme care and a delicate hand, the original painting should be undamaged."

"That *is* drastic."

William Merkel motioned for calm. "I would not recommend that unless there was a significant reason to do so." He stared at the green-tie painting again. "However, there are some things that don't make sense."

"Really? Because I can't think of a good reason to destroy Alva's paintings."

William Merkel frowned, took his magnifying glass, and studied the back of the painting. "The canvas is older—much older."

"How much older?" I asked.

"Hard to tell, but if I were to guess, I'd say at least a hundred years. It's cotton canvas, but it may have been sized with animal glue." His face was mere inches from the canvas as he examined it with the magnifying glass. "This overpaint layer covers what is underneath, but . . . it isn't how a professional would cover the painting." He scratched a small glob of paint from the edge with his fingernail. "It's a mystery."

I left the paintings in the capable hands of Mr. Merkel. He was intrigued and planned to ask a friend at MISU to X-ray the canvas. He swore no harm would occur to the paintings.

William Merkel called it a mystery. What kind of mystery? What is so important about these two paintings that Alva wrote an addendum to her will on toilet paper to leave them to Isabella? Why paint over another painting?

All of those questions rattled around in my head as I left downtown South Harbor and headed home. I stopped at Frank's and picked up lunch. We flirted for a few minutes while I waited, but lunchtime was a busy time for the restaurant, so I made my visit short and headed back to the bookstore.

When I pulled into the garage, I sent a text to Isabella, letting her know that I had soup and a sandwich with her name on it, literally.

She came down and thanked me for the food. She was enjoying her books and went back upstairs.

I took over the bookstore duties so Nana Jo could eat. There was enough traffic to keep my mind from wandering too far. Eventually, Nana Jo returned, and I went upstairs to eat.

Alone, my brain wandered back to the question of the paintings. Was Alva just a frugal artist who painted over her failures? If so, why use old canvases? Why not use the right paint to properly cover the work if she was ashamed of them? So many questions. Writing might help steady my mind, so I took a mental trip back in time and across the ocean.

Lady Elizabeth sat on the sofa near the fireplace in the drawing room. Lady Daphne sat next to her aunt while her sister, Lady Penelope, paced in front of the fireplace. Lord William sat in his favorite chair with Cuddles, his Cavalier King Charles Spaniel, curled up at his feet. Her cousin Winston puffed on his cigar in a chair. Lady Elizabeth could almost believe it was a normal family gathering if it weren't for the prime minister and a Scotland Yard detective sipping tea while the latter balanced a saucer and a notepad on his lap while constables roamed the cellar.

When the Marsh Family had stumbled across criminal situations in the past, they had been fortunate to have the assistance of Detective

Inspector Peter Covington. Peter was shrewd, tactful, and trustworthy. Lady Elizabeth smiled at the way the detective inspector had not only handled murderers, but had won the trust and the heart of Lady Clara Trewellen-Harper and the entire family, including King George. Now that Peter and Clara were married, he was a trusted member of the family. However, with Peter enlisted and on leave from Scotland Yard, the family was now in the capable hands of Detective Waterstone.

"All right, let's hear your story." Detective Waterstone sipped his tea.

"He called himself Nelson Wilmington," Joseph Mueller said.

"What do you mean 'he called himself Nelson Wilmington'?" Waterstone asked.

The Marsh Family first met Detective Waterstone a few months earlier. Waterstone was a short, squat, ruddy-faced man who had cultivated the persona of a dumb copper. With a cheap suit and wrinkled trench coat, Waterstone maintained a blank expression that belied the intelligence that existed behind his dark eyes.

Joseph rubbed the back of his neck. "I met Nelson and his brother, Noah Wilmington, years ago at university."

Thompkins stood near the door. Rigid and serious, even if a bit pale.

"How awful to lose a sibling." Lady Daphne's eyes filled with tears as she glanced at her older sister, Lady Penelope. "Were they close?"

"Very close." Joseph nodded. "Nelson and Noah were twins."

"Twins?" Detective Waterstone asked.

"Identical. I've never seen two people who were more alike, at least physically," Joseph said.

"What do you mean?" Lady Elizabeth asked.

"Physically, they were identical. Same height. Same build. Same . . . everything. They used to joke that even their mum couldn't tell them apart. Of course, they liked to play practical jokes and switch places." Joseph shook his head at the memory. "It used to be quite aggravating sometimes because they would inevitably want to get you in trouble, talking about the other one and then spill the beans that you were actually bad-mouthing the other twin."

"How horrible." Lady Daphne shivered. "And cruel."

"It was until one of my mates finally figured out a way to tell them apart. But you didn't need to know the trick if you got them talking. The two were virtually inseparable. I was surprised to see Nelson here alone. I've never seen one without the other, but . . . that was several years ago. I had heard things had changed and they weren't as close as they once were." Joseph shrugged.

Lady Elizabeth picked up her knitting from the bag she kept near her seat and sat quietly for several moments. "Was Noah into art like his brother?"

"Nelson was definitely into art. Nelson was a painter. Noah was more athletic. He preferred cricket and rugby." Joseph paused and then shook his head. "Or maybe it was the other way 'round. Maybe Noah was the painter and Nelson was the athlete. I can't remember. It's been years since I've seen either of them."

"It sounds like you didn't like them very much," Lady Elizabeth said.

"You're as perceptive as ever." Joseph rubbed his neck. "Actually, I liked Nelson just fine. Noah was always the crueler of the two. At least, I think it was Noah."

"Why don't you tell us how you just happened to be here," Detective Waterstone said.

"Joseph has every right to be here. He is a trusted friend and member of this family." Lady Penelope folded her arms across her chest and stared down at the Scotland Yard detective.

"That's right. If anyone didn't belong, it's Wilmington." Lady Daphne frowned at the detective.

The perfect butler never allows his feelings to be seen, and Thompkins was the perfect butler. Only someone who knew him well would be able to notice the vein on the side of his head that pulsed and the way he clinched his jaw to contain his emotions.

"That's right. As far as we're concerned, Joseph Mueller is beyond suspicion, but this Noah or Nelson or whoever he claimed to be is the one you should be looking into." Lord William clamped down on his pipe and scowled.

Heat infused Joseph Mueller's cheeks as he glanced around the room.

Detective Waterstone might have enjoyed playing the part of the bumbling detective, but he was no fool. He glanced around the drawing room. He didn't often find himself in the country manor house of the landed gentry. A duke, an MP, the prime minister, and three women who were married to aristocrats and cousins to the king. He tugged at his collar, which suddenly felt tight, and then held up both hands to ward off any further attacks. If he was going to get to the bottom of this murder, and salvage his career, he was going to need to gain the family's support. "Now, hold on. No one is accusing anyone of anything. I'm just trying to get the facts." He glanced around the room.

Lady Penelope unfolded her arms and resumed her pacing. Lady Daphne's shoulders dropped a quarter of an inch and the frown that had plastered her brow smoothed. Winston chomped on his cigar and leaned back in his seat while the prime minister sat back and crossed his leg in a much more relaxed attitude. Even the butler was no longer vibrating with contained rage.

"Nelson Wilmington was the curator of the National Gallery," Lady Elizabeth said. "None of us had ever met him before yesterday." She glanced around and everyone shook their heads.

"Why was he here if no one knew him?" Detective Waterstone asked.

Lady Elizabeth glanced at the prime minister, who sighed.

"This is confidential. A matter of national security." The prime minister stared at the detective, who nodded. "Now that the country is at war, we have to protect our nation's treasures from the Nazis. We have reason to believe that

Hitler will either bomb or loot our galleries. Most of the artwork has been removed to . . . secret hiding place across the commonwealth. There were a few items that we hadn't been able to secure, and Lord William and Lady Elizabeth were kind enough to allow us to store them here temporarily until we can make arrangements to have them shipped . . . elsewhere."

"Ah, I see." Detective Waterstone nodded. "So, Nelson Wilmington brought the art here for safekeeping, and ran into an old friend." Detective Waterstone turned his attention back to Joseph Mueller.

Joseph frowned. "That's just it. We weren't friends and—"

Thompkins gave a discrete cough. "I don't think you should continue without a solicitor."

"But I didn't—"

"Thompkins is right." Lady Elizabeth extended a hand to Joseph. "We need to get you a solicitor. Then we can—"

The door opened and Mrs. McDuffie's head pushed through the gap. After a brief word to Thompkins, both of them left.

A few moments later, Thompkins returned with one of the constables who had arrived with Detective Waterstone.

Thompkins was pale, but still maintained his demeanor. He gave another discrete cough. "There's a gentleman here who claims to be Nelson Wilmington."

"*What?*"

"That's impossible."

The constable rushed to the side of the Scotland Yard detective and hurriedly whispered in his ear.

Detective Waterstone's face registered shock, but then he quickly cleared his expression. He turned to look at the anxious faces that were all directed at him. "That's not all," Detective Waterstone said. "It also appears that someone has managed to steal two of the paintings."

Chapter 25

"Samantha, are you ready?" Nana Jo asked.

I shook my head like one of the poodles to clear my head, bringing myself back into the twenty-first century. I glanced at the time and realized that I only had about fifteen minutes before our meeting. So, I closed my laptop and took the poodles out to take care of business.

When they were done, I saw that Nana Jo had already prepared their special treats. The treats they only got when we left. Two hollow rubber Kong dog toys were each filled with a half of a hot dog, cooked and cut into small pieces, with a dog biscuit plugging the hole to extend the time it took to get to the good stuff. When they saw their treats, both dogs raced to my bedroom. Their eagerness always brought a smile to my face.

Nana Jo placed the Kongs in their crate and then hurried out of the bedroom and closed the door.

"What are you smiling about?" I asked.

"Those dogs have such unique personalities. Did you know Oreo bites the top off of his dog biscuit and works to get to the hot dog? While Snickers tosses hers in the air until the biscuit pops out. Then she eats the hot dog first."

I chuckled. "I had no idea."

"I caught them and couldn't help laughing. Those two are alike in so many ways, but their personalities are so different."

Something about Nana Jo's comments brought a thought to my mind, but just as quickly as it came, it left.

"What?" Nana Jo asked.

I grasped around in my head for the thought, but it was just out of reach. After a few moments, I gave up. "Nothing. Something you said triggered a memory, but then it was gone."

"Well, no point trying to find it now. It'll come when you least expect it. Let's eat." Nana Jo grabbed her purse and headed to the stairs.

"What about Isabella?" I asked. "I hate leaving her here, but she's a suspect."

"I invited her, but she said she was going to stay in." Nana Jo shrugged. "I promised we'd bring her dinner, but she just wanted to read and rest."

"If you're sure."

"I think she's exhausted. I know after your grandfather died, I was an emotional wreck, but I couldn't fall apart."

"I remember after Leon died, I felt like I was on autopilot for months. There were a thousand different things that I had to do, so I put one foot in front of the other and did what needed to be done. I think it was at least a month later before I allowed myself to grieve."

Nana Jo rubbed my back, and I knew she understood. "She'll be fine. Just like you were. Everyone grieves in their own way.

"We'll bring her dinner anyway, but we have things to discuss. And you're right. She's still a suspect." Nana Jo held up a hand to stop the disagreement she saw coming. "I'm not saying she killed Alva or Carl, but we have to be fair."

I nodded and we headed to Frank's restaurant.

He was behind the bar when we arrived. When he saw us, he smiled and joined us.

"Hey, Beautiful," he whispered in my ear as he kissed my neck.

"Is everyone upstairs?" Nana Jo asked.

"The gang's already upstairs waiting," Frank said.

"I hope you found a female server," Nana Jo said.

"One day, Irma is going to meet her match." Frank chuckled. "And I did get a female server."

"Good." Nana Jo walked upstairs, leaving Frank and me to follow.

"Are you going to be able to join us?" I asked.

"I should be able to. I have some intel that I need to pass along, but I'm waiting for a call from a contact in Cairo." Frank's cell rang and he stopped. He glanced at the number. "This is it." He kissed me and then made his way to the small office he'd made at the back of the kitchen.

I glanced at his retreating back and then made my way upstairs. He would join us when he could.

Nana Jo took her seat at the head of the table and I sat nearby, between her and Jenna.

A server I didn't recognize brought a glass of Moscato and a pitcher of water with lemon upstairs. She placed the Moscato in front of Jenna and poured me a glass of lemon water. She flashed a bright smile and asked if she could get me anything else.

I returned the smile and let her know I was fine.

One of the things I loved about Frank was his thoughtfulness. He knew water with lemon was my beverage of choice and Moscato was my sister's.

She sipped her Moscato, which we both knew wasn't a brand he typically served in the restaurant, but was from his own private collection.

The server took everyone else's orders and then hurried downstairs.

Dinner was delicious and when it was over, Nana Jo pulled out her iPad and we got down to business.

Irma raised her hand. "I have a hot date, so is it okay if I go first?"

No one objected.

"Clarence said that Carl's firm is just about to make an announcement. Word on the financial streets is they not only plan to throw Carl under the bus, but they plan to run that bus back and forth and squash him like a bug." Irma sipped her whiskey.

"What do you mean?" I asked.

"They had an internal audit done and got a preliminary report that would have made the firm look really bad. Now they can blame everything on Carl. They'll apologize to their clients, and give them a discount on brokerage fees for two years."

"Now that Carl's dead, he can't really defend himself." Jenna sipped her wine. "If there's anything to defend."

"So, they're going to come out publicly and announce that Carl stole from their clients?" I asked. "Won't that still make them look bad?"

Irma shrugged. "Clarence says it depends on how they spin it."

" 'Spin it'?" Ruby Mae asked.

"You know, the publicity spin." Irma waved her hand around in a circle. "They'll paint a picture of Carl as some lone wolf who betrayed all of them."

"Sadly, it'll probably work." Nana Jo pursed her lips.

"It's probably the truth," Irma said.

"Probably, but whether he was or not, it won't matter. By the time the publicity folks are done, Carl will have been to blame for every theft for the last century and the investment company will be the innocent victims."

"Well, I spent a very boring afternoon interviewing Ethan Linton," Dorothy said.

"Did you learn anything?" I asked.

"I learned the man has an incredibly high opinion of himself." Dorothy rolled her eyes.

"Well, for someone his age, he's sort of attractive in a pale, vampiric sort of way," Nana Jo said.

"He gives me the creeps," I shuddered. "He's just so . . . I don't know . . . handsome. It's freaky."

"I don't know if I should be happy or sad by that comment." Frank came upstairs carrying a chocolate cake and plates.

"It wasn't directed at you, although I do think you're handsome." I smiled.

"I bought this from a bakery in New Bison, Michigan. It's called Chocolate Soul Cake and its divine." Frank placed the cake on the table and sliced pieces for all of us.

I took one bite and moaned. It was so good. I heard a chuckle and opened my eyes to see that Frank was indeed laughing at me. "What?" I licked my fork.

"That reaction was amazing." He grinned and looked around the table.

The room had suddenly gone quiet. Everyone ate cake and the conversation stopped while we all savored the experience.

"I need a cigarette. That cake is better than se—"

"Irma!"

Irma coughed.

Our server came upstairs with coffee, which was the perfect finish.

"I've got to go. Don't wait up." Irma stood, wiggled her hips, and took a tug at her skirt, which was too short and too tight. Then she gave her blouse a tug so that her breasts pushed up. Irma winked and hurried downstairs.

Nana Jo shook her head and mumbled something that sounded like "smut," but I might have misunderstood.

"Dorothy, what else did you get from the vampire?" Nana Jo asked.

"He spent an hour telling me about his illustrious family. But I don't think the museum is doing as great as he would have us believe. When you look below the surface, the carpet is threadbare, the wallpaper is peeling in the restrooms, and wasn't there more staff?" Dorothy glanced around.

"There used to be tour guides and someone selling tickets and gifts," Jenna said.

"And a security guard," I added.

"That's what I remember too. Now, it's just Ethan Linton doing everything. He was running around like a headless chicken. When I asked about it, he gave me a condescending smile and mumbled something about good help being hard to find." Dorothy shook her head.

"Especially when you can't pay them," Ruby Mae said.

We turned our attention to her.

"Do you know something?" Nana Jo asked.

"I don't want to interrupt," Ruby Mae said.

"Please, go on. I think your information is much more interesting that mine." Dorothy waved Ruby Mae on.

"If you're sure." Ruby Mae glanced at Dorothy, who nodded. Seeing no other objections, she pulled out her knitting and started working on a baby blanket. "Well, y'all know my daughter Stephanie owns a cleaning company. Her company had a contract to clean the museum five days per week for years. I used to clean his grandmother Charlotte Linton's house years ago. When I retired, Stephanie took a lot of the contracts and Charlotte liked Stephanie and signed her to do the museum." Ruby Mae allowed pride to wash over her face for a few moments before she pushed the look away. "Then Linton reduced the contract from five days per week to three days. He claimed the museum was getting a lot less foot traffic, so he didn't need five days, which made sense. Although I think if the business is open five days, then he should have at least had the restrooms cleaned, but that was none of my business." Ruby Mae pursed her lips.

We all agreed with her assessment, and I made a mental note to never use the restrooms at LIMA.

"Then Linton reduced the contract from three days per week to once per week, and the last check he sent bounced."

"That must have hurt his ego," Dorothy said.

"He blamed the bank, but Stephanie doesn't play when it comes to payment. She believes in paying her workers on time." Ruby Mae took a moment to bind off her knitting before continuing.

"Banks can make mistakes. Did Stephanie believe him?" Nana Jo asked.

Ruby Mae shook her head. "Nope. Plus, my nephew's grandson was a security guard there for a hot minute and said the staff that were there complained about not getting their checks on time. So, she isn't cleaning LIMA anymore."

"It didn't look like anyone was cleaning from the layer of dust on the furniture," Dorothy said.

"Maybe things will improve now that he's gotten the legacy from Alva's estate." I looked at Jenna.

"Possibly, but like I mentioned to Bethany at the seminar, it can take years to get settlement from wills. Even if she had a trust, now that Carl's dead . . ." She shrugged. "It will depend on the police."

"Well, I have something about that too," Ruby Mae said. "I talked to Daryl. He said the North Harbor Police Department got several anonymous calls about Alva's death being suspicious. Then, when Carl was murdered, he was able to get an order to have Alva's body exhumed and they'll run an au-topsy on her."

"That's great news," I said.

"Daryl doesn't know if it'll do any good. He thinks if she was poisoned, that it's not likely that they'll find out what was used." Ruby Mae took a moment to count stitches before continuing. "Plus, it'll take time. North Harbor doesn't have the facilities to do the type of testing, so he's going to have her autopsy done by the River Bend police."

"It's a bigger town and they have a lot more resources," Jenna said.

"At least someone will be looking into it. That's good news," Nana Jo said.

We spent a few minutes discussing the challenges solving crime in a small town presented, but then moved on.

"The police investigation should put a halt on Alva's will paying out. If Alva was murdered, the court will want to make sure she wasn't killed for her money," Jenna said.

I shared the information from this morning. *Was it only this morning that I went to Bethany's house?*

"Are you sure having Isabella in your garage is a good idea?" Frank asked.

"She's in the garage, not the house. I'm being careful." I squeezed his leg under the table. "Plus, Nana Jo's there."

"And you better believe I've got my peacemaker at the ready," Nana Jo said. "Nobody messes with my granddaughters."

Frank fought back a grin and whispered, "When we're married, please tell me that I won't have to fight your grand-mother for the right to protect you."

I kissed Frank's cheek. "I'm fully capable of protecting my-self, but you're too much of a gentleman to hit a lady. So, if you did have to fight, my money's on Nana Jo."

Frank had taken a sip of wine and nearly choked.

Chapter 26

"Dorothy, did you finish your report?" Nana Jo asked.

Dorothy was a million miles away, but snapped back to the present at Nana Jo's question. "Yes. I was just thinking about something Ethan Linton said." She paused for a few moments. "He knew Oliver Tarkington. Apparently, Oliver Tarkington came into town eons ago. He did a speech at MISU and then held an exhibit. Ethan swears that Oliver Tarkington made arrangements with Charlotte Linton, to leave a large bequest to the museum."

"Alva did leave a bequest to the museum," I said.

"I think Ethan Linton had expectations that were a lot higher than twenty thousand dollars and a couple of worthless paintings," Jenna said.

"Maybe the paintings aren't worthless," I said.

Frank got a call and got up and walked downstairs to take it. I watched his back retreat. He worked hard, too hard. Maybe we should take a vacation. Our wedding was in two months and he'd been working extra hard to get his house ready to sell, and to keep the restaurant going. Just as owning a mystery bookshop had been my dream with Leon, Frank dreamed of having his own restaurant. Even though Leon didn't live long enough to see the dream come to reality, I had been blessed to have my family to help me. Frank's mom was a surgeon. While I had no doubt she could whip the restaurant's vendors, contractors, and waitstaff into shape, she wasn't interested in a career change. At least, I didn't think so, but maybe now that she was . . . dating Stinky Pitt, she might want to move to North Harbor. No way, though. She's a surgeon. If anything, Stinky Pitt would move closer to her, right?

"Sam!" Jenna elbowed me in the ribs.

"Sorry," I said.

"Daydreaming?" Nana Jo asked.

"No, I was just thinking." I didn't need a mirror to know that I was blushing. I could feel the blood rushing to my head. "Sorry, what did I miss?"

"Did you learn something at that appraiser you talked to today?" Nana Jo asked.

"Like is Alva some forgotten artist whose works are now worth millions?" Dorothy chuckled.

"Obviously you haven't seen Alva's paintings," Jenna mumbled as she sipped her coffee.

"I've heard that after an artist dies, their paintings increase in value," Ruby Mae said.

"No. William Merkel estimated that Alva's paintings probably weren't worth more than a few hundred dollars, but . . ." I said.

"But you don't believe him?" Nana Jo asked.

"I do believe him. Alva was a really nice lady, but she wasn't talented. Those two paintings that she left to Isabella weren't very good." I sighed and tried to collect my thoughts. "It makes me sad to think that Carl might have been right when he said the paintings weren't worth the canvas they were painted on. Mr. Merkel looked at the paintings with a magnifying glass and it looks like Alva painted over a previous painting."

"Why would she do that?" Nana Jo asked. "Was she trying to save money?"

I shrugged. "No idea. But it makes me wonder why she went to so much trouble to make sure that Isabella got the paintings."

"Maybe she imagined that after she died, her paintings would be worth a lot more money. You know, Vincent van Gogh never sold many paintings during his lifetime, and he left all of his paintings to his brother, Theo. Sadly, Theo died about six months after Vincent and his wife, Johanna, inherited them. Theo was an art dealer who always believed in his brother's talent, and Johanna believed in Theo. It was Johanna's efforts that brought recognition to Vincent years after his death," Dorothy said.

"How do you know so much about Van Gogh?" Nana Jo asked.

"Google." Dorothy waved her phone. "I've been researching art for this article. Plus, I spent an incredibly long day with Ethan Linton at the museum. They have a Van Gogh display. I had to keep myself from falling asleep somehow."

"LIMA has a Van Gogh?" I scraped my brain to recall if I remembered seeing any when we took field trips in elementary school. Although I don't think I would have known who Van Gogh was back then.

"Are you joking? That museum couldn't afford a real Van Gogh. They just set up some books with pictures of his sunflower paintings and used a laptop to display the pictures," Dorothy said. "I think it was Van Gogh's birthday or something. He didn't even splurge for real sunflowers. He had a vase with fake flowers he must have bought at the dollar store." Dorothy shook her head. "Although he did put the art that Alva bequeathed him on a display promoting local artists."

"Hard to talk about Alva in the same breath as Van Gogh.

Alva Tarkington's works don't even seem to be in the same universe as Vincent Van Gogh." Something tugged at the back of my mind. "Still, Alva took a lot of risks to write that addendum to her will on toilet paper. If we accept that she wasn't batty." I glanced around the table and received nods confirming that we were all still in agreement. "Then, why? Why take those two paintings and leave them to Isabella? Why risk getting caught altering her will? I mean, Carl had zero respect for Alva's art. If she just told him she wanted to leave those paintings to Isabella, I would think Carl would have gladly given them to her."

"You're right." Jenna frowned. "He certainly didn't seem sentimentally attached to the paintings at all."

"Maybe Carl didn't realize the paintings were valuable. He wasn't exactly the sharpest knife in the drawer," Nana Jo said.

"First off, Alva's paintings aren't valuable." Jenna twirled her Moscato in her glass and stared at the pale pink liquid as if in a trance. After a few moments, she continued. "No, Sam's right. If Carl thought those paintings were worth anything, I have no doubt that he would have contested the addendum based on the way he exploded when Andy mentioned it. He was ready to fight tooth and nail if Alva had left her money to someone else. Once he found out what the addendum entailed, he immediately dropped it."

"Anything else?" Nana Jo turned to Dorothy.

Dorothy frowned. "Nothing. But there was something about one of Alva's paintings that seemed odd to me."

"Which painting?" I asked.

"It was the painting with the two sisters together. I can't put my finger on it. It bothered me, so I took a picture with my phone." Dorothy pulled out her cell and swiped through her photos until she found the photo she wanted. She sent it to each of us.

Moments later, all of our phones pinged as we received the picture. Then we all stared at our screens, trying to figure out what had captured Dorothy's attention.

"I stared at that painting and tried to figure out what about it bothered me, but . . . I don't know. It just struck me as odd." I pinched the image on my screen and expanded it.

"I don't see anything that leaps out at me, but there is something strange. Do we know which one is which?" Nana Jo asked.

"Look at the lockets," Dorothy said. "I found a picture of Alva and Oliver Tarkington at the British National Gallery exhibit. It's at least fifty years old, but Alva is wearing a locket just like the one in the painting. And the locket has an A. Zelda's locket has a Z." She sent us the link to the article.

When we compared the two photos we could see that both girls in Alva's painting were wearing lockets. The girl on the left had a locket with an A while the girl on the right wore a locket with a Z.

"Even knowing which girl is which, I can't tell them apart," Ruby Mae said.

"I have no idea what it is about the painting that seems off, but there's something odd. I just can't see it." Dorothy shook her head in frustration. "Darned twins."

"I know what you mean," Jenna tilted her head to the side. "Alva and Zelda were identical twins, but even with identical twins there is usually something different about them. There's something that makes them different."

"Well, you had twins, so you should know," Ruby Mae said.

"My boys are fraternal twins, not identical, but I've talked to lots of parents of twins, especially when the boys were babies. And they all had similar stories," Jenna said. "There's usually something that distinguishes one twin from the other. Whether it's a birthmark, dominant writing hand, head shape, or freckles, there's usually something that the parents latch onto to tell their kids apart."

"I heard of a lady who painted her babies' toenails different colors so she could tell them apart, but of course when they got older, their personalities made it easier," Nana Jo said.

"I wonder if Alva or Zelda had a distinguishing feature," I said.

Dorothy and Jenna were both hit by the same lightning bolt. "That's it."

"What?" we all asked.

"Alva did have a distinguishing feature," Dorothy said. "She had a mole near her right ear."

We all stared at the picture on our phones. After several moments, Nana Jo broke the silence. "That is odd," she said. "If the lockets are on the right daughters, then why is Zelda the one with the mole?"

"What does that mean?" Dorothy asked. "The woman we knew as Alva definitely had a mole."

Nana Jo said, "So, either Alva grew a mole over her ear that exactly matches the one her sister Zelda had. Or . . ."

"Or the woman we knew as Alva was really Zelda," I said.

Chapter 27

"How is that possible?" "Why?" "That's crazy."

Everyone started talking at once. I held up a hand to stop the questions. "They were identical twins. Alva's husband, Oliver, was already dead. If they didn't have any other close relatives, then who would be able to tell which sister died?"

"But surely someone would notice. How did Zelda . . . Alva die?" Ruby Mae asked.

"Heart attack," Frank said.

I hadn't noticed his return until he spoke.

"I just got a call from . . . a friend. When the sisters were young, one of them, Alva, got rheumatic fever, which caused heart problems," Frank said.

"I haven't heard of rheumatic fever in decades," Nana Jo said.

"Me either. I thought it had been wiped out like polio," Ruby Mae said.

"What is rheumatic fever?" I asked.

"Let's find out." Frank pulled out his phone and dialed. After a few moments, she picked up. "Hey, Mom, I have a medical question . . . No, I'm fine. I . . . Sam's fine too." He rolled his eyes. He opened his mouth several times, but closed it and mumbled agreement. When he got to a break in the conversation, he hurriedly said, "Mom, I'm going to put you on speaker. I'm here with Sam, Nana Jo, Dorothy, Jenna, and Ruby Mae."

"Hello, everyone," Dr. Camilia Patterson said. "Don't tell me there's been another murder."

"There's been at least one, but maybe two," Nana Jo said. "Camilia, this is Josephine. What can you tell us about rheumatic fever?"

"Rheumatic fever?" Camilia paused. "Wow, I haven't heard of any cases of that in decades. At least not in this country."

"When I was a kid in Alabama, one of my cousins got it. The doctors thought she would die. It was awful. I thought they wiped that scourge off the face of the earth." Ruby Mae shook her head.

"Rheumatic fever isn't common in developed nations. Sadly, it's still around. Mostly, it's more prevalent in sub-Saharan Africa, the Middle East, Central and South Asia, and the South Pacific. We don't hear of it much here in the States," Camilia said.

"What is it?" Jenna asked. "Is it a virus?"

"No. It's not a virus. It's an autoimmune disease," Camilia said. "It's an inflammatory disease that comes from the group A streptococcus bacteria."

"Streptococcus, like strep throat?" I asked.

"Strep throat or scarlet fever are streptococcus group. A bacteria. Generally, what we see is if those aren't treated properly, rheumatic fever can develop."

"How is it treated?" I asked.

"Antibiotics," Camilia said.

"If someone had rheumatic fever as a child, does it cause problems as an adult?" I asked.

"Rheumatic fever can permanently damage the heart valves and causes rheumatic heart disease. So, the answer is yes. If someone contracted rheumatic fever as a child, it could cause problems later in life," Camilia said.

We asked a few additional questions. When the questions slowed to a trickle, Frank ended the call.

"So, after Oliver died, Zelda went to live with her sister, Alva," Nana Jo said.

"They were identical twins with no close family nearby to notice any differences," Jenna said.

"That still seems hard to pull off," Dorothy said. "I mean, do you think Alva was in on it? Or did Zelda just decide to take her sister's place?"

"I'll bet Alva was aware of it. They were close." I shrugged. "We don't have any reason to believe otherwise. Alva . . . I mean, Zelda—"

"I think we should continue calling the woman we knew 'Alva.' It's too confusing to switch now." Nana Jo glanced around. Everyone nodded agreement.

"Why do you think she did it?" Dorothy asked. "When Oliver died, Alva—the real Alva—would have inherited the money. Why not just make her sister her beneficiary?"

"I can answer that," Jenna said. "I talked to Andy Martin, Alva's attorney. Oliver's will provided access to Alva for her lifetime, but then was written in a way that granted access to descendants and family."

"So, when Alva—the real Alva—died, then the money would have gone to Carl's descendants and family?" Ruby Mae asked.

Jenna and I weren't twins, but I knew my sister and there was something bothering her.

"What?" I asked.

"It's just the wording that's odd." Jenna frowned. "Alva and Oliver didn't have any descendants, but Andy had notes from his grandfather, who wrote up the original will. Oliver was adamant about the wording."

We spent a few minutes picking Jenna's brain about wills, even though we knew she didn't have a crystal ball that would let her look back in time and figure out what Oliver meant or why. Jenna's phone rang, which put a stop to the questions.

"It's Bethany." Jenna scowled at the phone for a moment before taking a deep breath and answering. "Hello."

We could only hear one side of the conversation, but Jenna's body language and facial expressions filled in the parts that we couldn't hear. "Bethany, the police have the authority to freeze assets under certain conditions." Jenna tapped her fingers on the table. *Impatience.* "Carl was murdered and was under an investigation . . ." Jenna sighed. *Frustration.* "Bethany, I'm not your lawyer. I think you should contact your attorney, Andrew Martin, for advice." Jenna frowned. *Anger.* "Bethany, I'm going to end this call so you can call your attorney. He's familiar with your finances and will be the best person to advise you. Goodbye and good luck." Jenna ended the call, closed her eyes, and took several deep breaths.

"Can the police really freeze their assets? I mean, Carl's dead," Ruby Mae said. "It's not like he can hop on a plane and run to some country with his ill-gotten gains."

"Frankly, I'm surprised it took them as long as it did to freeze their assets, but if Carl has defrauded his clients, then the last thing they want is for Bethany to get away with the evidence. Plus, they can't rule out Bethany as an accessory." Jenna rolled her shoulders. *Weariness.*

"An accessory? Surely the police don't think she was involved. Do they?" I asked.

"Why not? Just because they weren't happily married doesn't mean that Bethany didn't know what Carl was doing and that she wasn't involved," Jenna said. "It turns out Carl's clients weren't the only ones defrauded."

"What do you mean?" Nana Jo asked.

"Carl and Bethany had access to Alva's bank account and have taken every dime. Carl's been liquidating all of Alva's assets along with everyone else's. Alva Tarkington was broke," Jenna said. "Bethany's frozen accounts are the least of her worries."

Chapter 28

After that depressing bombshell, we were all shocked. We agreed to meet again tomorrow evening, but right now our heads were spinning.

After saying goodbye to Frank, Nana Jo and I grabbed the takeout for Isabella and walked home. I went upstairs to take care of Snickers and Oreo while Nana Jo dropped off Isabella's food.

My brain was swimming. *Alva wasn't Alva. Zelda was Alva? Alva was broke. Did Carl kill Alva? Did Bethany kill Carl? Holy cow. This is too much.* I sat down at my laptop and tried to sift through the muck by spending time in the British countryside.

"Nelson Wilmington?" Detective Waterstone's cheeks pushed out and a tidal wave of red heat started at his neck and spread across his face.

"Show the gentleman in," Lady Elizabeth said.

If Joseph hadn't just told them that Nelson Wilmington had a twin, they would have thought they were looking at a ghost.

"Remarkable," the prime minister said.

The gentleman entered and looked around the room. Shock crossed his face at the sight of the prime minister, but he collected himself and walked to Waterstone. "Detective?"

Waterstone collected himself as he gazed at the man who was the spitting image of the corpse in the Marshes' cellar. "Who are you?"

"My name is Nelson Wilmington." He extended his hand.

Detective Waterstone shook. "I'd say we have a bit of a problem. There's a dead man in the cellar who said *he* was Nelson Wilmington."

Nelson's face crumbled and his legs buckled.

Thompkins was quick and prevented the man from falling.

"Bring him by the fire," Lady Elizabeth directed the butler.

Once he was seated, Lady Elizabeth poured a cup of tea and added several spoonfuls of sugar. She shoved the cup at the man, who'd gone quite pale. "Drink this. It'll help with the shock."

The man claiming to be Nelson Wilmington shook his head. "No. I'll be fine."

"Young man, I suggest you do as you're told. My cousin can be a formidable force when she wants to be." Winston chomped on his cigar.

Nelson Wilmington took the cup and sipped. "Thank you." He winced at the sweet, syrupy beverage, but took another sip before setting down his cup. "Thank you. I feel better."

"You don't look better." Lady Elizabeth turned to the butler. "Thompkins, perhaps you should bring something a bit stronger."

The young man started to object, but no one listened. Thompkins left and returned with a decanter and a glass with an amber liquid.

Winston smacked his lips. "Good idea. Seeing this man, who is the spitting image of the dead man, has been a shock to all of us."

Lady Elizabeth nodded to Thompkins, who poured glasses and offered them around. All of the men accepted except Prime Minister Chamberlain.

"Now, perhaps you can explain who you are and who is in the cellar?" Detective Waterstone asked.

"I haven't been in the cellar, but if the man looks like me, then I am sure that's my twin brother, Noah." Nelson Wilmington took a handkerchief and wiped his eyes.

"I don't mean to sound insensitive, but do you have any identification? The man in the cellar claimed to be Nelson Wilmington," Detective Waterstone asked.

Nelson reached into his pocket and pulled out his national registry along with his passport.

Detective Waterstone examined the documents. "You'll understand if I hang on to these. I need to check these out. They could be forged. The other gentleman had similar documents proclaiming him to be Nelson Wilmington too."

Nelson shook his head. "Noah was always a bit . . . unstable."

"What brings you here?" Detective Waterstone asked.

"I got a call from my brother last night saying he was in some trouble and asking me to meet him here. When I arrived, I saw the police and I knew I was too late." Nelson Wilmington broke down in tears.

"Perhaps this could wait until Mr. Wilmington has a bit of a rest." Lady Elizabeth turned to Thompkins. "Could you see Mr. Wilmington to a room, please."

Thompkins nodded and helped the young man to his feet and out of the room.

"Now, don't that beat all. I feel like we're playing that kids' game, Button, Button, Who's Got the Button." Detective Waterson ran a hand through his hair.

Lady Elizabeth put down her tea and picked up her knitting.

Lady Penelope and Lady Daphne exchanged looks while their aunt knitted. After a few minutes, Lady Penelope touched her aunt's sleeve. "I can't take it anymore. You've got that look in your eyes that says you're figuring things out."

"I was just thinking. Knitting helps me sort through the things in my mind so I can keep everything straight." Lady Elizabeth smiled fondly at her niece.

Detective Waterstone returned to his chair. "Maybe I should take up knitting. This case is a muddled mess and I have no idea how to determine which of the men is Nelson Wilmington and which one is Noah Wilmington."

"I think we'll be able to figure that out easy enough." If Lady Elizabeth noticed the silence that settled in the room after her statement, she didn't show it.

"Easy? You think that will be easy?" Detective Waterstone asked.

"There's bound to be a way to tell them apart." Lady Elizabeth looked at Joseph.

"It's been years since I saw either one of them. If I knew, then I've forgotten it," Joseph Mueller said.

"Convenient," Detective Waterstone mumbled. "For all I know, you're involved in all of this, too."

Joseph Mueller was flushed, but he didn't say anything.

Winston Churchill walked over to his cousin and stared into her eyes. "I've known you your entire life and I know that look too. Now, if the identity of the corpse isn't the problem, then what is? What's bothering you?"

"Too many coincidences." Lady Elizabeth frowned. "I don't believe it's a coincidence that Nelson Wilmington arrived at the same time that the prime minister is here with his war cabinet. And at the same time . . ."

"That the paintings from the gallery are in the cellar," Lady Daphne said.

"And when two of those paintings are now missing," Lady Penelope added.

Lady Elizabeth nodded. "Exactly."

"You think someone in my cabinet is involved in theft and murder?" Prime Minister Chamberlain asked.

"Whoever did this is guilty of more than just theft and murder," Lady Elizabeth said.

The prime minister stared for several beats before shaking himself and asking, "What could possibly be worse than that?"

"I think what my dear cousin is trying to avoid saying," Winston said, "is that whoever committed these dastardly deeds is also guilty of treason."

Mrs. McDuffie's cheeks were flushed. She rushed through the servants' hall, barely noticing the cook seated at the large table.

"Matilda, you are going to run yourself ragged. Now sit down and have a proper cup of tea," Mrs. Anderson said.

"I suppose a few minutes won't hurt." The housekeeper looked a bit frazzled, but she flopped down in a seat. She took a sip of the hot tea and allowed her shoulders to relax. "That's good. Thank you."

"You've been running around like a crazy woman since dawn." Mrs. Anderson placed a generous piece of bread on a plate and pushed it in front of the housekeeper. "Now eat. You have to keep your strength up."

Mrs. McDuffie knew the cook had been playing around with various recipes to use up the excess courgettes, but she wasn't sure about having them for tea. Still, the cook wouldn't serve anything that wasn't top quality. She took a small forkful and her face burst into a smile. "Sybil, that's delicious. Don't tell me this is courgettes?"

Mrs. Anderson fought to keep her lips in a neutral position, but her shoulders relaxed at the praise. "It is. I have to say, I was worried when I first tried the recipe, but the courgettes have a lot of water and keep the bread moist. I added a bit of lemon to give it more flavor."

"Well, this is fantastic." Mrs. McDuffie hastily finished off the slice and didn't put up any opposition when Mrs. Anderson gave her another.

"I don't think I'll have any trouble getting Johan and Josiah to eat green vegetables." Mrs. Anderson chuckled. "I think both boys will eat a bushel."

The two servants spent a few moments indulgently talking about the three children who had come to stay at Wickfield Lodge from the Kindertransport.

"How are you holding up?" Mrs. Anderson asked.

"I should be asking you." Mrs. McDuffie stared at the cook. "You're the one that's 'ad to feed a 'ouse full on a moment's notice."

Mrs. Anderson waved her hand. "I'm fine."

"In addition to the family and staff, you've also got to feed the prime minister, four members of the war cabinet, and a 'ouseful of policemen," Mrs. McDuffie said.

"Pshaw. I'm not cooking for the coppers."

Mrs. Anderson huffed. "But I have to admit it's nice to have the house full again. With Frank and Jim off to war, and Lady Penelope and Lady Daphne married with families of their own, it was getting a bit . . . lonely."

Mrs. McDuffie smiled. "I agree. It's been tough not 'aving a full staff of maids to take care of the rooms, but it's nice to have a full 'ouse again."

Mrs. Anderson twisted a napkin in her hands as she worked up her nerve.

"Whatever is bothering you, just come out with it." Mrs. McDuffie reached over and patted the cook's hand.

Mrs. Anderson looked over her shoulder, leaned close to the housekeeper, and whispered, "Last night I couldn't remember if I'd taken out everything for today's meals, so I got up and came down to the kitchen." She hesitated. "I heard voices. Men's voices. Angry."

Mrs. McDuffie leaned close. "Could you make out what they were saying?"

Mrs. Anderson shook her head. "I don't want to get anyone in trouble. I'm sure it was nothing. I mean, there could be any number of reasons, but I just wondered if you think I should say anything. I don't like talking to the police. I mean, if it were Lady Clara's young man, that would be different. He's family, but I just don't know what I should do."

"You need to tell her ladyship, that's what. Lady Elizabeth will know what to do." Mrs. McDuffie patted the cook's hand.

Mrs. Anderson took a deep breath and nodded. "You're right. Her ladyship will know exactly what should be done. I just hate causing
trouble for a member of the household."

Mrs. McDuffie gasped. "A member of the
'ousehold? Who did you 'ear?"

"Joseph. He was arguing with that man that
got himself murdered."

Chapter 29

"You look like crap." Nana Jo passed me a cup of coffee the next morning.

"Thanks." I sipped my coffee and swallowed the snarky response that hovered in my mind.

Nana Jo waited until I'd finished two cups and was fully caffeinated before broaching the subject again. "Want to talk?"

Do I want to talk? I shook my head. "Not really. I just feel like I'm missing something."

"Something about Alva?"

"Or Zelda," I said. "Do you think anyone knew that the woman we all thought was Alva was really Zelda?"

"You think maybe somebody found out that Zelda was pretending to be Alva, and that was why she was killed?" Nana Jo thought for several moments. "I can't see why they would, but it's possible. What scenario are you thinking that would make someone want her dead?"

"No idea. We don't know anything about Zelda." I put treats out for Snickers and Oreo, and Nana Jo and I went down to the bookstore.

"Maybe we need to see what we can find, but if she's been pretending to be Alva for close to twenty years, I can't imagine someone waiting that long to kill her."

My phone rang. When I saw Frank's picture, I smiled. "Hey."

"Hey, Beautiful. Do you have a few minutes before the store opens?" Frank asked.

"I always have time for you."

Frank mentioned a couple of things that brought heat to my cheeks before hanging up and promising he would be down shortly.

I was curious, but didn't have to wait long. In just a few minutes, Frank was at the door with a package. I opened the door. "That was fast."

"Not usually what a man likes to hear, but in this case I'll take it as a compliment." Frank grinned.

Heat rushed up my neck and I turned away to hide my face from my grandmother as she came from the back of the store.

"Good morning, Frank." She took a deep breath. "That smells delicious. I'll get the plates and coffee while Sam pulls herself together."

Frank winked at me and followed Nana Jo to the back.

We sat at one of the bistro tables. Frank had a lemon loaf, which we sliced and ate while we drank coffee.

"Mmm. That tastes just like the lemon loaf from that coffee shop," Nana Jo said.

"I've been tweaking the recipe and I think I finally got it right," Frank said.

"You definitely got it right." I savored the mixture of lemon for a few moments.

"I'm guessing you didn't just come down here this morning to have us try out your new recipe, so you better get on with it," Nana Jo said.

Frank glanced around to make sure we were alone.

Nana Jo frowned. "Unless you need to talk to Sam alone."

Frank shook his head. "I got some information last night, but was waiting for confirmation from my source and he finally got back with me because of the time difference. He's about seven hours ahead of us."

I didn't even try to do the math to figure out what country was seven hours ahead. Instead, I scooped up the crumbs on my plate and waited.

"I asked my contact to find out what he could about Oliver Tarkington."

Out of all the people involved, I didn't expect that Frank would find out additional intel on Oliver.

"He heard a rumor, but didn't get confirmation until this morning. I don't know if it's important to the case, but . . ." Frank shrugged.

"Now you've really got my curiosity piqued." Nana Jo sipped her coffee.

"There was a rumor going around the university where Oliver Tarkington worked that he was having an affair with his secretary," Frank said.

"Isabella's mother," I said. "I suppose that says a lot about Oliver Tarkington's character, but I don't see—"

Frank nodded.

"What?" Nana Jo asked.

"I'm guessing Oliver Tarkington fathered a child with his secretary." I looked at Frank for confirmation.

"Yep." He nodded. "Three guesses as to the name of their love child, but I don't think you'll need them."

"Isabella is Oliver Tarkington's daughter," I whispered.

"Her mother, Aya Sadat, went on a sabbatical from the university and came back with a ring, and a story of marrying a soldier who was killed shortly afterward." Frank glanced through notes he'd taken on his phone.

"Likely story," Nana Jo said. "Although having a child out of wedlock is still frowned upon in some countries."

"True, but this isn't the Dark Ages. Babies are born out of wedlock all the time in this country," I said.

"But this wasn't just about Oliver. He was married to Alva," Nana Jo said quietly.

"Oliver Tarkington never acknowledged Isabella publicly." I looked to Frank, who shook his head.

"He never acknowledged her, but my friend is thorough, and he confirmed that Oliver Tarkington paid for Isabella's upkeep at expensive boarding schools, and college," Frank said.

"I guess that explains how a secretary could afford her daughter's pricey education," Nana Jo said.

"Isabella thinks she got scholarships," I said.

"That also explains why Oliver was so particular about the wording for his will," Nana Jo said.

"What exactly did Jenna say about the wording?" I asked Nana Jo.

Nana Jo pulled up her iPad and scrolled. "Oliver's will provided access to the money to Alva for her lifetime . . . and granted access to descendants and family."

"Oliver was trying to make sure that his daughter, Isabella, got the money. Not Carl," I said.

"This certainly gives Carl a reason to want Isabella dead. If it came to light that Isabella was Oliver's daughter, then he wouldn't have been entitled to anything. But Isabella wasn't killed, Carl was," Nana Jo said.

"Do we know for sure that Isabella didn't know Oliver was her father?" Frank asked.

Nana Jo and I exchanged glances.

"I don't suppose so. Why?" Nana Jo asked.

"Because if Isabella knew that Oliver was her father and

that Alva had withheld the money she was entitled to, she might have been resentful," Frank said.

"Resentful enough to want to kill Alva for remaining silent, and resentful to Carl for stealing her inheritance and squandering it." I swallowed the lump in my throat. "Which means Isabella had a reason for killing both Alva and Carl."

Chapter 30

"And she's living over your garage." Frank reached across and squeezed my hand. "I'd feel better if she found someplace else to stay."

"I can't kick her out. I told her she could stay a few days." I glanced at the back door to make sure that Isabella wasn't making an unannounced visit. "Besides, I don't think Isabella is a threat." I saw Frank revving up to argue. "I don't have anything to do with any of the things that Alva, Oliver, or Carl did to her."

"No, but if she figures out that you know she killed them, that makes you a threat," Frank said.

"Look, I may not have been in the military and did all kinds of John Wick crazy stuff, but I'm perfectly capable of taking care of myself." I folded my arms across my chest and put on the toughest stare I could muster.

Frank chuckled. "John Wick crazy?"

"You know what I mean," I said. "I'm not some helpless damsel who needs a man to rescue her."

Frank held up his hands. "I know you are an independent woman, capable of taking care of yourself, but if Isabella is the murderer, she's already killed twice. What's one or two more?" He looked from me to Nana Jo.

"Pshaw!" Nana Jo snorted. "I may not be young, but I've got experience. Don't you worry about Samantha. I'll keep my peacemaker handy, and I won't let her out of my sight."

"I don't need either of you to rescue me," I said. Before either Frank or Nana Jo could argue, I held up my hand. "Look, I appreciate that both of you want to protect me. I know you both care about me. I'll be careful. I promise, but I think having Isabella close is a good idea."

"What is that saying about keeping your enemies close?" Nana Jo asked.

"Sun Tzu," Frank said. "Keep your friends close; keep your enemies closer."

Chapter 31

Frank wasn't thrilled, but short of shutting down his restaurant and making himself my personal bodyguard, there wasn't much he could do. I promised not to be alone with Isabella, and Nana Jo promised to keep her peacemaker close. Although I don't think that brought Frank any comfort. Still, we had to open the bookstore, and he needed to take care of the restaurant. I might have even tried a bit of emotional guilt by suggesting that he didn't trust me to take care of myself. Outnumbered, he made a tactical retreat.

"What do you think we should do?" Nana Jo asked once Frank was gone.

"I think we should open the bookstore."

"Well, duh!" Nana Jo unlocked the front door and went behind the counter to prepare the register.

I didn't have any ideas beyond opening the store. Maybe something would come by going through the dull, mundane details of running the bookstore.

Isabella came in not long after we opened, just ahead of our first customer of the day.

"Good morning." Isabella smiled.

For two seconds, my brain went blank. My heart raced. My fingers forgot what they were doing and dropped the books I had been shelving. "I'm all thumbs this morning. How did you sleep?"

"I didn't."

I stood up with my armful of books. "I'm sorry. Was the bed not comfortable?"

"The bed was fine, but I stayed up reading." Isabella laughed and held up the books. "These were so good. The author described everything in such vivid detail, I could actually see the places."

I released a breath. "That's good, right?"

"I got so caught up in the setting and then the mystery, that I had to keep reading to find out Whodunit. I kept saying, I'm just going to read one more chapter. Before I knew it, the sun was coming up and I hadn't slept."

"That's the best. I'm glad you enjoyed them."

"I did enjoy them. In fact . . ." Isabella looked like a kid asking for a favor. "Can I buy more?"

"Of course." I chuckled.

There's nothing more gratifying than sharing my love of mysteries with new readers. I walked Isabella over to the shelf where I knew she would find more cozies. I noticed Nana Jo hovering one aisle over.

"I will be more than happy to help Isabella find more books. Why don't you go and help that customer." Nana Jo shouldered herself in between me and Isabella.

I gave my grandmother a wide-eyed stare that I hoped sent the message, *What are you doing?* However, if Nana Jo picked up my facial expression message, she didn't acknowledge it. I thought about blinking the message in Morse code. SOS was easy, but *Back off* was a lot more complicated for a novice. It would take too long to figure out what to say and there was no assurance that Nana Jo would listen, even if she did know what

I wanted. My respect for Alva increased a hundredfold as I realized the skill needed to blink a message in Morse code.

It was easier to simply comply than argue with Nana Jo, so I did. I glanced back at her and Isabella and tried not to notice that my grandmother kept a hand in the pocket of her jacket. Nana Jo was an excellent shot. She'd won several contests when she was young. However, I wasn't interested in testing her skills inside my bookstore.

It didn't take long for Isabella to pick up more books in the two series she had started and she and Nana Jo were at the counter. I offered to give her the books, but she refused.

"Absolutely not. You have been so kind to let me stay here. The very least I can do is to pay for these books." She handed over a credit card.

"Are you going to keep reading?" Nana Jo asked.

"I think I'll take a nap first. If I start reading now, then I'll spend all day reading and won't get anything done." Isabella laughed.

"What do you need to do?" I asked before I realized how nosy I sounded. "I mean, maybe there's something I can do to help."

If Isabella thought I was sticking my nose where it didn't belong, she didn't let on. "After my nap, I'm going back to Alva's house to get the rest of my things. Then I'm going to figure out if I should go home or not."

Isabella's voice held a note of sadness that wasn't there before.

"Ahsan?" I asked.

Isabella sniffed. Her tired, red-rimmed eyes weren't completely due to lack of sleep. She'd been crying. "He hasn't called," she said softly.

"Maybe he has a lot going on. There's a big time difference, right?" I asked.

"Seven hours." She nodded.

Is it a coincidence that Frank's contact also has a seven-hour time difference? I think not. Although I knew Frank had traveled the world and had friends everywhere, I would bet my next royalty check that Egypt was where his call originated.

"Ahsan used to call every day, but it's been nearly three days since I've heard from him. I'm starting to think that maybe he doesn't care about me after all. Maybe his family convinced him to marry Layla, the girl whose family makes rugs."

I went around the counter and gave her a hug. Isabella yawned, and I released her so she could go take a nap.

When Isabella had left, Nana Jo and I worked side by side for a couple of hours. There wasn't a lot of foot traffic, so Nana Jo suggested that I go upstairs and write, and I decided to take her up on the offer. Maybe a little time in the British countryside would help me figure things out.

Lady Elizabeth sat in the parlor, enjoying a brief moment of peace. The moment was quickly interrupted by a knock on the door. "Come in."

Mrs. McDuffie entered, followed by a reluctant Mrs. Anderson. "Please come in. Is anything wrong?"

Mrs. McDuffie stepped forward. "Mrs. Anderson 'as something she needs to discuss with you."

"Certainly." Lady Elizabeth breathed a sigh of relief. Domestic problems were a lot easier to solve than murders. She almost welcomed the interruption. "Please take a seat."

Mrs. Anderson perched on the edge of the sofa.

"Is there a problem with the menu?" Lady Elizabeth hurriedly added. "Because you don't have to prepare anything elaborate. The prime minister doesn't want to cause trouble. He—"

"No, everything's fine. I've got a lovely roasted tomato basil soup, rack of lamb with mint sauce, creamed peas, mashed potatoes, and a spotted dick for dessert. It's not fancy, but Mr. Churchill told me how much he liked my good old English cooking when he was here before." The cook shrugged.

"It sounds delicious." Lady Elizabeth nodded her approval. "If it's not the menu, then what can I help you with?"

Mrs. Anderson took a deep breath, cast a side glance at Mrs. McDuffie, who gave her an encouraging nod, and gathered her courage. "It's just that I was telling Matilda about hearing that gentleman what was killed arguing with Joseph."

Whatever Lady Elizabeth expected, this wasn't it. "Joseph? Are you sure?"

"Yes, ma'am," Mrs. Anderson said.

"Did you tell the police?" Lady Elizabeth asked.

"No, ma'am. I don't like talking to police . . . Of course, that nice Mr. Covington doesn't count, but he's not here and Joseph is family. He may be Jewish, but he's part of this family, just like . . . well, those of us on staff may just work here, but still we're family—Matilda, Thompkins, all of us—and I would never say anything to hurt this family." Mrs. Anderson clenched her fists by her sides.

Lady Elizabeth took a handkerchief and wiped away a tear. "Thank you. You're right. We are all one family. Upstairs and downstairs, we are family." She gazed into the fire for several moments. "'Truth will come to light; murder cannot be hid long; a man's son may, but at the length *truth will out*.'"

"Excuse me?" Mrs. Anderson looked puzzled.

"It's just words of wisdom from *The Merchant of Venice*." The cook's puzzled expression brought a smile to Lady Elizabeth's lips. "Shakespeare."

"I don't know about any merchants, but I don't believe Joseph is a murderer," Mrs. Anderson said.

"Neither do I, but we have to tell the truth to the police," Lady Elizabeth said.

"What if they arrest Mr. Joseph?" Mrs. Anderson asked.

"We'll just need to make sure to find the real killer so that doesn't happen."

Chapter 32

My phone rang, transporting me out of 1939 and back to the present. "Hello."

"Mrs. Washington, it's William Merkel."

I recognized the voice, but there was an added level of excitement today that hadn't been there before. "Have you discovered something already? I know you said that it could take quite some time before you finished your report."

"Actually, yes. I had several other projects that I should have been working on, but in all honesty, I was intrigued by the paintings you brought in, and I really want to share what we found. Is there any chance you could come over?"

I glanced at the time. "I'm sure my grandmother can cover the bookstore. I'll be there in fifteen minutes."

I hurried downstairs, and Nana Jo confirmed that she had everything under control.

Twelve minutes later, I pulled up outside of South Harbor Art and Framing. As soon as I went inside, William Merkel was waiting.

"Mrs. Washington, I am so thrilled. Never could I imagine . . . I am beside myself." He vibrated with energy.

"Is something wrong?" I asked.

"Wrong? No. Yes. I don't know." He gave a nervous chuckle. "I hardly know what I'm doing."

Someone came to the door, but Mr. Merkel hurried to the newcomer. "Oh, I'm sorry, but we are closed." He apologized and shooed the customer out the door. Then he locked the door and flipped around a sign indicating that the store was indeed closed.

Nana Jo's warning flashed through my mind briefly, but I instinctively knew that this kind man wasn't a threat. "Mr. Merkel, what's going on?"

"William. You must call me William." He took a handkerchief from his pocket and wiped his forehead.

"William, what's wrong?" I asked.

He swallowed hard, took me by the arm, and escorted me to the back of the shop. This time we didn't stop at the table, but moved behind the counter and through a narrow doorway into a workroom.

The room was cluttered with frames of all different types and sizes. There was a large worktable where Isabella's paintings were displayed.

"Were you able to X-ray the paintings?"

Mr. Merkel shivered. "Yes. I have a friend at MISU. He owes me a small favor, so he took the paintings and ran them through one of their machines."

"And you saw the images of Alva's old paintings that she had painted over?" I asked.

"Yes. No. I mean, I saw a painting, but it wasn't anything Alva painted."

William Merkel's nervous energy was rubbing off on me. Rather than pushing him, I decided to wait and let him get to the point of what he'd found.

Mr. Merkel rummaged through some papers on the desk.

He studied them until he found what he was looking for, then handed them to me.

I studied the black-and-white images, but couldn't really make out what I was seeing. They reminded me of the ultrasound photos pregnant friends shared. No matter how much I squint, it still looks like clouds rather than a baby. "I'm sorry, but I don't know what I'm looking at."

He picked up a magnifying glass and held it up over the image. "This . . . I cannot believe, but this is Giovanni Bellini's masterpiece, *Madonna and Child*," William Merkel spoke reverently as he gazed at the painting.

"Mr. Merkel, I'm—"

"William."

"William, I'm not an art expert. I'm afraid I don't know Giovanni Bellini from Andy Warhol."

"Giovanni Bellini was an Italian Renaissance painter from the fifteenth century. He comes from a well-known and distinguished family of Venetian painters."

"And you believe this is his painting?" I asked.

"I cannot be sure. It must be examined, it must be validated. But the brush strokes, his unique technique . . . yes. I think this is a genuine Giovanni Bellini." He looked at me with wide, teary eyes. "Never did I think I would be able to see a Bellini, let alone touch one." He choked up.

"Okay, so it seems like this painting is very old, but is it valuable?"

"Valuable?" William Merkel sputtered. "This Bellini's *Madonna and Child* is priceless."

"Okay, but how would Alva Tarkington have gotten ahold of it, and why on earth would she have painted over it?"

"During World War II, Hitler and the Nazis stole many of the world's greatest works of art. Bellini's *Madonna and Child* was moved from the Berlin Museum to a Berlin-Friedrichshain flak tower, which was under the control of the Russians. Most of the objects mysteriously disappeared."

"Disappeared? You mean they were stolen?" I asked.

William Merkel shrugged. "Stolen? Destroyed? Who knows for sure."

"I can't believe Alva Tarkington stole this painting." *Although, how would I know? Technically, I never met Alva Tarkington, only Zelda. Maybe she was a thief.* I pulled out my cell phone and Googled Giovanni Bellini. "Wait, this says Bellini's *Madonna and Child* is at the National Gallery in London . . . Oh, wait. No, it's at the Metropolitan Museum of Art. How?"

"Bellini painted many different Madonna and Child paintings." William Merkel looked at the photo on my phone, and pinched the photo to expand. Then he slid a large book that was nearby closer. He flipped to the page he wanted and showed me.

"These don't look anything alike," I said.

" 'Madonna and Child' was a popular theme, especially during that period. Bellini painted many different versions, but *this* one . . ." He pointed to the book. "Notice the starred banner behind the Madonna. The curls on the baby Jesus."

"Wait, so Bellini was mass-producing these?" I said.

William Merkel chuckled. "Not in the sense that a painting is mass-produced today, but it was popular, and he painted a lot of them. Still, this particular painting is the one that's missing."

"You think this is a stolen painting?" I rubbed my forehead.

"I'm not accusing anyone of theft." William Merkel held up his hands. "First, we must confirm if this really is *the* Bellini's *Madonna and Child*. No one has seen the painting for over eighty years. It could have been purchased legally."

"How?"

"During his regime, Stalin sold off untold numbers of Russian treasures to finance the country's industrialization. Not only did the Politburo sell antiquities, but they sold art from the Hermitage to private collectors and museums around the world." He shook his head. "The wealth from centuries was distributed and sold after the murder of the Romanovs. From Lenin to Stalin and probably beyond, the nation's wealth was exported or sold."

"So, Alva Tarkington could have purchased the painting from the Russian government?" I tried to wrap my head around that, but I just couldn't fathom a nation selling off such valuable treasures.

William Merkel nodded. "Often for a fraction of its real value."

"But that doesn't explain Alva painting over it. I mean, she was an artist. There's no way she wouldn't recognize this, right?"

"Ah, but that's where the cleverness comes into play. Pentimento is generally done by artists to cover up a flaw or to make a subtle change. The artist's intention is not that what's underneath will ever see the light of day. However, that's not the case with this. I believe this painting was deliberately painted over to conceal what was underneath with the intention of removing the top painting."

"Wait. You think Alva intended to have her painting removed?"

"It's the only thing that makes sense." He waved a hand at the painting.

"Let's say this really is Bellini's *Madonna and Child*. What would you estimate the painting to be worth?"

"With art, it is always hard to place an exact dollar amount." William must have noticed I was prepared to push for a concrete response, because he held up a hand to halt me. "As an art appraiser, it's my job to try to put a value on a painting.

There are lots of factors that determine a painting's worth. In this case, first, is it really a Giovanni Bellini painting? What's the condition of the painting? Has there been damage? We won't know the answers until this top layer is removed. What is the provenance of the painting? If it's stolen art, then it should be returned to the original owner." He took a deep breath. "The last Giovanni Bellini Madonna painting that was sold at auction in London went for over a million euros."

"Holy guacamole!"

Chapter 33

Tilt. Tilt. Tilt. William Merkel's words rattled around inside my head like a pinball machine. *Stolen paintings. Pentimento. Giovanni Bellini. Zelda is really Alva. Alva is dead. Oliver is Isabella's father. One million euros.* I rubbed the back of my neck. None of this made sense.

I got in the car and headed home. En route, I passed by LIMA and made a last-minute decision. A couple of turns and I found myself in front of the Linton Museum of Art, the family estate of Ethan Linton.

For several moments, I sat in my car and stared up at the large Victorian building. I'd been to the museum many times on field trips as a kid. This was the first time I've visited as an adult. In my memory, the house was larger and grander, but that might have just been because as a child, I was a lot smaller. A careful look at the house showed that it had seen better days. The paint around the doors and windows was peeling. The foundation plantings were full of weeds where there were once bright displays of seasonal flowers; the beds were empty. Several of the stained-glass windows were broken and in need of repairs.

I got out of my car and walked up to the front door. It creaked as I opened it and entered the dimly lit foyer despite the chandeliers that hung from the vaulted ceiling. An odor of damp, musk, old wood, and neglect greeted me. A threadbare rug covered the intricate inlaid-wood floors, which creaked as I entered.

"Welcome to the Linton Museum of Art." Ethan Linton smiled from the hallway. In a black suit and tie, the museum curator reminded me of an undertaker, complete with a boutonniere.

Linton was as much of a relic as the objects displayed in this museum. I couldn't recall the last time I'd seen anyone wear a boutonniere. And it looked real.

"Thank you."

Linton tipped his head to the side. "Do I know you?"

"We've never been formally introduced, but I'm Samantha Washington." I extended my hand.

"You were at the reading of the will with that other lawyer." Linton's mask slipped for a moment, and he frowned, but it was quickly back in place. "To what do I owe the pleasure of this visit?"

"I was just downtown and when I passed your museum, I decided to stop by. I haven't been here since I was a kid. We used to come here on field trips." I shrugged. "I guess I was just curious."

"Ahh. Well, welcome. Would you like a guided tour? Or would you prefer to walk around on your own?"

"I think I'd like to walk around on my own, if that's okay." I looked around. "Do I need to pay for a ticket?"

"We do ask for a donation." Linton pointed to a sign on a pedestal near the door that listed a *suggested* donation amount that seemed a bit outrageous. I pulled out my wallet and shoved the money at him.

Linton tucked the money into his pocket. "I'll leave you to explore on your own." He pulled a stanchion in front of the staircase that led to the second floor. "The upstairs is my personal living space and off-limits. However, you are free to explore the first floor at your leisure."

Geez! I don't know if I would have paid the *suggested* donation amount if I had known I would only be able to see four or five rooms.

I nodded and forced my lips upward into what I hoped came across as a smile. "Thank you."

"My pleasure."

Once Ethan Linton left, I turned to the right and walked into a parlor. I was halfway through the first room when I stopped to ask myself why I was there. I didn't have an answer. Maybe walking through the museum, looking at the exhibits would inspire me.

The Linton Museum featured a diverse assortment of art. From art to antique furniture, books, and antique collections, the rooms were cluttered with so many objects, it was hard to know what to look at first. One wall had a display of Victorian era cooking items including an ice pick, a cherry pitter, and something called an egg coddler. There didn't seem to be any rhyme or reason to the displays as long as they fit into the particular eras. A large threadbare green rug covered the floor. Decades of stains, wear and tears had taken its toll. A rust ring encircled a stain that someone had tried to clean. I walked into the parlor. Between the dark green damask wallpaper, dark wood trim and furniture, and heavily draped windows, the room felt dark and ominous. Practically every inch of every wall was covered. The major feature of the room was a massive fireplace with a dark, elaborately carved mantel and an onyx surround.

Despite the sensory overload, I walked slowly around the

room. I strolled through the room and crossed the hall to another room. This one was similar to the green parlor, but instead of the green damask, these walls were covered in red. Something floated at the back of my mind. Unable to catch the fleeting thought, I continued to look at the objects. I had made it halfway through the room when something pulled me back to the parlor.

What is it about this room? I walked around again, but slower this time, and took the time to actually stop and read the cards underneath the paintings and propped by the antiques. There were items dated from various centuries. I couldn't help but think about my book. "I'll bet Wickfield Lodge would have some of these things," I muttered to myself. I was halfway through the room when I caught myself squinting at one of the cards. "This room wouldn't be so bad without that dark wallpaper."

That's when it hit me. In my research for my book, I'd stumbled across a picture of wallpaper that was identical to this. I pulled out my phone and took a picture. Since I was here with my phone out, I did a panoramic of the room.

"Do you have any questions that I can answer for you?"

I was so into my pictures I didn't hear Ethan Linton until he spoke.

"You startled me." I pressed my hand against my heart.

"I'm sorry." Linton forced a smile, but it never made it to his eyes. "You're taking pictures?"

I held up my phone. "I hope that's okay. I didn't see a sign prohibiting pictures."

Linton paused for several beats. "I guess that would depend on how you want to use the pictures."

"I write British historical mysteries and I was taking pictures for inspiration."

"You're a writer?"

I turned my phone around and showed him the custom iPhone case that had a picture of my book. My nephew, Christopher, had ordered the case along with bookmarks and a ton of other items he called "swag" that I could hand out at events and use for promotion. Phones were such a prominent part of our daily lives that I was pleasantly surprised by the number of people who noticed the case and asked about my books.

"You're a published author. How nice," Linton said.

"Sometimes when I'm writing, it helps to have a visual image that I can use to describe a room. I find a lot of pictures on Pinterest and create storyboards while I'm writing. It helps me remember details."

That explanation didn't cause the lines on Linton's forehead to relax.

"I could even include LIMA in the acknowledgments," I said.

Linton's eyes flashed and this time the smile was real. "Free advertisement is always welcome. Perhaps we could even include a couple copies of the book in the gift shop."

"Gift shop?" I looked around.

"It's more like a gift *case* than a shop at the moment." Linton chuckled. "But I hope to expand soon."

"I didn't realize you were expanding." I glanced around at the empty museum and wondered where he was getting the funds for an expansion.

"We have big plans. Big plans. Would you like to see?" Linton asked.

"Sure."

He rushed out of the room. Before I could decide if I was meant to follow him or not, he was back holding a long tube. He pulled the cap off the tube and pulled out a roll of paper. He unfurled the roll and I could see it was an architect drawing of the museum.

"Wow. That's impressive." I pointed at a pyramid-shaped building. "That looks like the one at the Louvre."

Linton could barely contain his excitement. "I will admit

it was inspired by the Louvre, but this will be a greenhouse." He rolled the plans back and returned them to the tube.

"Very impressive. I didn't realize the museum owned so much land."

Linton glanced around as if he expected someone to overhear. He winked, leaned close, and patted the side of his nose as though he was hiding a secret. "We don't. At least not yet, but I have high hopes that LIMA will soon be able to take its place as one of the greatest private museums, able to rival that of the Isabella Stewart Gardner Museum in Boston, Hildene in Vermont, and Willet-Holthuysen House in Amsterdam." Linton's gaze was fixed on something in the future.

"That sounds . . . amazing, and expensive."

Ethan Linton snapped back to the here and now. "Yes, well. We have been fortunate to have some dedicated patrons."

"Like Alva Tarkington?"

"Oliver Tarkington was a close friend of the Linton family. He always planned to include LIMA in his estate plan. Although he led us to believe it would be substantially larger." Oliver sniffed as though he had just gotten a whiff of something foul.

"Twenty thousand dollars is quite a large bequest," I said.

One corner of Linton's lip curled up. "Large is relative. Oliver Tarkington was worth millions. If Alva didn't squander the money, there should have been a hefty sum for organizations that Oliver supported."

Something about this cocky man made me angry and defensive. "If the money was squandered, I don't think Alva was the one who did the squandering."

Linton waved a hand as if saying *que sera sera*. "I suppose you're hinting about the rumors about Carl."

I didn't acknowledge the question and merely folded my arms across my chest.

Linton leaned forward. "Oliver Tarkington was worth millions. My sources tell me that the majority of the money was gone long before Alva moved here and Carl got his hands on it."

My mouth fell open of its own accord.

Linton nodded with a smirk. "Now that both Alva and Carl are dead we may never know who squandered the money—will we?"

Chapter 34

My anger propelled me out of the building and into my car like a steam locomotive. I checked my reflection in the rearview mirror. Steam wasn't coming out of my ears, but my neck and cheeks were red.

I drove back to the bookstore, sifting through the information that I'd accumulated. When I went inside, Nana Jo was alone, sitting at a bistro table drinking a cup of tea. I flopped down on the seat across from her.

"You look like you're ready to strangle someone." Nana Jo went to the counter and got another cup of tea and a sugar cookie and brought it back. "You also look like you could use a good strong cup of tea."

I sipped the tea and ate my cookie.

"Now, what happened?" Nana Jo asked.

I filled my grandmother in on my conversation with William Merkel.

"Wait, so Alva or Zelda got their hands on this expensive painting and painted over it?"

"That's what Mr. Merkel thinks." That's when the light bulb went off in my head. "That explains it."

"Explains what?" Nana Jo asked.

"Alva didn't squander Oliver's money. I mean, Zelda didn't squander—never mind, but if Alva used the money to buy art, that would explain why the fortune that Ethan Linton claims Oliver Tarkington left in his estate is now gone."

"What on earth does Ethan Linton have to do with any of this?"

I explained swinging by LIMA and my conversation with Linton. Nana Jo didn't take kindly to his suggestion that Alva mismanaged the funds before Carl got a chance to embezzle them.

"Didn't Frank say that Zelda spent some time in Russia?"

Nana Jo pulled out her iPhone and flipped through the notes that she'd emailed from our meetings. She swiped until she found what she was looking for. "After Oliver's death, Zelda and Alva traveled. They spent time in Russia."

"Mr. Merkel said that the Russian government needed money and sold the nation's treasures to private collectors. I'll bet Alva was one of those collectors."

"Maybe, but I doubt if the Russian government kept detailed records." I opened my mouth, and Nana Jo held up a hand to stop me. "And if they did, I doubt if they're going to share them with us."

"Probably not, but I'll bet Frank could find out."

Nana Jo and I exchanged a glance, and a smile slowly spread across her face.

"That fiancé of yours certainly has the connections."

I made a quick call to Frank, and he promised to see what he could find out. Based on the background noise, he was busy, so we didn't linger.

Customers trickled into the store but my mind was not fully engaged.

"Why don't you go upstairs and write. That always gets your little gray cells moving," Nana Jo said. "I can handle this."

"Are you sure?"

"I got this. You go upstairs and write."

Lady Elizabeth sat on the sofa in the parlor with her knitting on her lap. Lady Penelope paced in front of the fireplace. Lady Daphne sat next to her aunt, but Lady Elizabeth could see her nervously twisting her handkerchief in her lap. Lord William sat in his chair, puffing on his pipe, and Thompkins stood at the door. Joseph Mueller sat straight in a chair in a corner. The scene looked familiar. Whenever the Marshes had been called upon to help solve a mysterious incident, the family always pulled together. Lady Elizabeth looked at the rigid form of Thompkins near the door and Joseph in his seat and she smiled. Neither Joseph nor the butler was related to the Marsh Family by blood, but they were family.

"There's no way anyone in their right mind could possibly believe Joseph would kill anyone." Lady Penelope paced.

Joseph's head snapped up and his eyes filled with tears, but he feigned a coughing fit and pulled out a handkerchief to hide his emotions.

"The police don't know Joseph like we do," Lady Elizabeth said.

"Well, they bloody well should get to know someone before they think of arresting them." Lord William waved his pipe as he spoke, flinging bits of tobacco over the chair. The duke turned a sheepish look to his wife and nieces. "Sorry for the bad language."

Lady Elizabeth flashed a smile at her husband while making a mental note to look into getting the chair reupholstered. The fabric was showing signs of wear. She glanced around the room and took a closer look at the furnishings. The peacock blue wallpaper was showing signs of fading. When she moved to Wickfield Lodge as a newly married bride, she had redecorated, removing the dark green damask wallpaper she feared would make them all sick. More than two decades later, the peacock blue was showing its age. She had been thinking about updating the décor, but now that the nation was at war, it seemed frivolous.

There was a brief knock on the door before it was pushed open and Mrs. McDuffie entered pushing a cart. The housekeeper's face was red, but she also carried with her an air of determination.

"Come in, Mrs. McDuffie, and please take a seat." Lady Elizabeth waved a hand to a chair across from her.

The housekeeper cast a nervous glance at the butler. "I can stand."

"Nonsense." Lady Daphne rose, walked over to the housekeeper, put her arm around the woman's shoulders, and guided her to the seat. The housekeeper loved both Marsh girls, but she had always had a special place in her heart for Lady Daphne.

"Well, if you're sure." Mrs. McDuffie perched on the edge of the sofa.

Lady Elizabeth poured tea and passed it around. When everyone was served, she sat back and sipped from her cup. "Now, we need to get to the bottom of this, and I have an idea how we may be able to accomplish that, but I'm going to need everyone's help."

"What do you need us to do?" Mrs. McDuffie asked.

"I know you run a tight ship and would never allow the maids to gossip." Lady Elizabeth looked at the housekeeper.

"I don't tolerate gossip. If I found out a maid was gossiping, she'd get the sack and quick." Mrs. McDuffie nodded.

"Which is why I wanted to get your support. You see, in order for this plan to work, I need two maids to pass along a bit of gossip."

The housekeeper stared open-mouthed at Lady Elizabeth for several seconds. She swallowed hard and lifted her chin. "If that's what you need, then I'll make sure they do it." She hurriedly added, "This one time, only."

Lady Elizabeth nodded approval. "Thank you."

"What gossip do you want them to spread?" Lady Penelope worked to keep her lips neutral.

"I need our guests to believe that the art being stored in the basement is about to be moved."

"But I thought we weren't supposed to talk about the art?" Mrs. McDuffie exchanged a glance with Thompkins.

"We are baiting a hook." Lady Elizabeth sighed. "I'm taking a chance, but I don't believe the person who stole the two paintings had time to get away. I believe he was interrupted."

"What makes you think that?" Lady Penelope stopped pacing and looked at her aunt.

"Why else would someone kill Nelson Wilmington? I think Wilmington interrupted the thief and was murdered." Lady Elizabeth looked at the puzzled expressions and put down her knitting. "The two paintings that were taken weren't the most valuable. If you're looking at art that's worth millions of pounds and you're willing to risk prison, why take only two paintings that aren't that valuable?"

"Which two paintings are missing?" Lady Daphne asked.

"They took two by Turner. Don't get me wrong, I think Turner is an excellent artist, but the paintings taken weren't his best works. Why take those two and leave paintings by Gainsborough, Constable, Rembrandt, and Vermeer?" Lady Elizabeth shook her head. "No, I think our thief thought he would have more time."

"You think Wilmington interrupted the thief and he panicked?" Lady Daphne asked.

"It's the only thing that makes sense." Lady Elizabeth picked up her knitting.

"And you think one of our guests is a thief and a murderer?" Lord William gaped at his wife. "The prime minister and five members of the House of Commons, including your cousin, are the guests that you think stole and committed murder."

"That sums it up, and now we need to get our plan in place to make sure they don't get away with it." Lady Elizabeth stabbed her knitting needle into a ball of yarn to emphasize her point.

Chapter 35

When I got up to answer the call of nature, I heard Nana Jo moving around in the kitchen.

"I'm sorry. I didn't realize how late it was."

"Sorry for what?" Nana Jo filled the water dish for Snickers and Oreo and put it back in place.

"I know you said you could handle the store, but I planned to go back down and give you a break."

"I like being helpful. I like having something to do." Nana Jo took a moment to think. "I love meeting new people and old friends."

"You do an excellent job. I just don't want to take advantage of you."

"You're not. Besides, we both know that I would have no hesitation in telling you if you were." Nana Jo chuckled.

"I do know."

"Did you solve all the world's problems?" Nana Jo joked.

"Not yet, but I feel like things are starting to fall into place. Where are we meeting?"

"I figured we'd give Frank a break and go to Randy's Steakhouse."

"He doesn't mind. He doesn't use the upstairs, and I think he likes it when we meet at his restaurant. He's able to sneak upstairs and contribute without completely abandoning his business."

Nana Jo shrugged. "If you're sure. I don't want him to feel as though we're taking advantage of his love for you."

I chuckled. "I asked him the same question, but he assured me that he liked having us. He's getting accustomed to us paying for our meals."

"True, but he always does something extra, like the cake he brought the last time. I don't want him going bankrupt because of us."

"Honestly, I think he would be offended if we went somewhere else."

"Well, I don't want to offend him. Let me send a note to everyone letting them know the location changed." Nana Jo whipped out her cell phone. Before she finished her text, my cell vibrated.

Frank's face popped up on the screen. "Speak of the devil."

"You heard?"

"Heard what?"

Nana Jo paused her text.

"We had a pipe break and the restaurant flooded. I've got a plumber, and an emergency restoration crew here, who guarantee that the restaurant will be ready to open tomorrow, but I'm going to need to close for the night."

I pulled the phone away and repeated that the restaurant was closed tonight. I returned to Frank. "Is there anything I can do to help?"

Frank mentioned a few things that he would like me to do that caused the heat to rise up my neck. None of his suggestions involved helping with the flooding.

"I meant is there anything I can do to help with the plumbing problems? Extra towels? Buckets?"

"Nope. I'm paying a small fortune to this restoration company, and they swear to provide all the necessary supplies."

Frank's restaurant was a great location, but the mechanicals were old and all seemed to have failed recently, so he'd be in good shape soon.

Someone was yelling for Frank in the background, so we kept it short. I hung up and turned to face Nana Jo. "I guess we'll be eating at Randy's Steakhouse after all."

"The girls want to hit the casino. Between wedding planning, author events, and everything, we haven't had time to go and let our hair down."

Thoughts of the last time I'd been to the casino crossed my mind and I shuddered. Maybe it would be good to let off some steam. I nodded to Nana Jo, who finished her text.

My phone vibrated, but I didn't bother looking at it.

"I checked on Isabella. She's going to pick up the rest of her things. Apparently her young man called. He's on his way here."

"Here? As in here." I pointed to the floor.

Nana Jo nodded. "He doesn't care about his family or the rug merchant's daughter. He wants to marry Isabella, and she wants to marry him."

"I'll bet she's ecstatic." I grinned at the thought of young love.

"She's floating on air."

"I should help her get her stuff. I don't like the idea of her going back to that house alone."

"I don't like the idea of you going back to that house alone with Isabella." Nana Jo grabbed her purse from the counter. "That's why I told her that WE would take her first thing in the morning."

"You know I'm not a child, right? I'm a fully grown woman and I'm capable of taking care of myself."

"I know that, but I also know that someone has killed two

people, and I have no intention of there being a third. Now come on." Nana Jo walked down the stairs.

After a few moments, I followed. Resistance was futile.

By the time I left Snickers and Oreo treats and made my way to the garage, Isabella and Nana Jo were talking in the garage.

My grandmother was right, Isabella was so happy, she practically levitated around the car and squeezed me.

"Did Mrs. Josephine tell you my good news?" Isabella beamed.

"She did and I'm so happy for you."

Isabella spread her arms and turned in a circle like Julie Andrews at the beginning of *The Sound of Music*. "He loves me. He told his family he intended to marry me and they either needed to accept me and we live there . . . or he would move here."

"He sounds wonderful." I hugged her.

"And then I got a call from Ethan Linton."

"Really?" I couldn't hide the surprise in my voice, although I think I did a good job hiding the shock on my face.

"He offered to buy my paintings." Isabella beamed.

"Really?" I felt the creases in my forehead and smoothed them out. "That's odd. Did he say why he wanted to do that?"

"He said they weren't valuable, but since he owned the local museum, he could display them as a bit of local history."

"What did you tell him?"

"At first I said no. I know the paintings aren't good, but they hold a lot of sentimental value." Isabella sighed. "But then he told me that Alva's work deserved to be shared with everyone and that it would be selfish to keep them to myself."

"How much did he offer?"

"Five thousand dollars." Isabella clapped. "Honestly, I wasn't going to sell the paintings, but I mentioned it to Ahsan and he suggested that I do it. The money will come in handy with the wedding." She bounced up and down on the balls of her feet like an excited kid.

"Are you sure you don't want to wait until the appraisal comes back?" I asked.

"Mr. Linton said the paintings were only worth a couple hundred dollars, but he was willing to go up to five thousand dollars because he cared about Alva. I told her all about Ahsan. I think she would want me to be happy. I also think her paintings deserve to be seen. Besides, I don't want to schlep the paintings back to Cairo."

"Wait, you're leaving?" I asked.

"We're going to Cairo to talk to Ahsan's family. We'll have to get rid of most of my things. Ahsan says that we have to be practical. I cared for Miss Alva, but I was only keeping the paintings for sentimental reasons. Anyway, I told Mr. Linton that I would sell them. I have to think about my future with Ahsan."

"Of course."

"Ahsan is coming!" She hugged me. "I can't wait until he gets here. I'm going to go upstairs, pack, and finish reading my books. Then I will dream of Ahsan. We'll get the rest of my things and then he'll take me home to Cairo." Isabella jumped up and down and then hurried upstairs.

Nana Jo chuckled. "She's like a kid rushing to get to bed on Christmas Eve because the faster they get to sleep, the faster Santa will be there the next day."

Before long we were on our way to Shady Acres. Dorothy, Irma, and Ruby Mae were waiting at the entrance and piled into my SUV.

The drive to the Four Feathers Casino and Resort wasn't long. The casino was owned by the Pontolomas, a Native American tribe indigenous to the area. The casino was one part of the two hundred acres of land owned by the tribe. The approach to the casino and resort was impressive. I drove down a

path that wound through woods full of wildlife. The bro-
chures for the resort mentioned deer, pheasants, coyotes, and
black bears, so I took the drive slowly and watched for wildlife.
The resort included a hotel, event center, three bars, seven
restaurants, and retail shops. It was practically its own town.

Normally, I let Nana Jo and the girls out at the entrance
and parked in the covered garage attached to the casino. However, tonight, I decided to splurge and pulled up to the valet
parking area.

Ruby Mae's connections always came in handy when we
needed to secure a table at the casino. She has such a large extended family that there's usually a third cousin once removed
or a great-niece willing to use their influence to see that she
and her friends received seats and the best food. Tonight was
no different. After hugs from relatives, we were seated at a table
close to the buffets and plates of delicious items that were only
served in the high-roller dining rooms.

We helped ourselves to dinner and spent a few minutes
chatting. As the conversation wound down, Nana Jo got out
her iPad.

"One of our key suspects, Isabella, is going to leave the
country with her fiancé in the next two days, so we need to
get this party started." Nana Jo glanced around.

I didn't like thinking about Isabella as a suspect, but she
was. In fact, she was a good suspect. I told the group about
William Merkel's assumptions about Alva's paintings and my
visit with Ethan Linton at LIMA.

"Those paintings give Isabella a big motive for killing Alva,"
Dorothy said. "And if Isabella takes them out of the country,
then she could literally get away with murder. Does Egypt have
an extradition treaty with the United States?"

"But if she knows what the paintings are worth, then she
wouldn't sell them to Linton for a measly five thousand dollars," I said.

"We only have her word that she plans to sell the paintings to Linton. Maybe she just said that to throw you off her trail," Ruby Mae said.

"You make me sound like a bloodhound," I said.

Ruby Mae smiles.

"Besides, if she was afraid I was 'on her trail' going to a country that has an extradition agreement with the US would just get her sent back here to face justice," I said. "I wish Jenna was here."

"Jenna and Tony had dinner plans and couldn't make it, but I'm going to ask." Nana Jo pulled out her phone and dialed. "Jenna, does Egypt have an extradition treaty with the U.S.?"

We waited while Nana Jo listened. After a few moments, she thanked Jenna and hung up.

"The answer is yes, but that might not matter. According to Jenna, there are some countries that have extradition treaties, but have refused to extradite." Nana Jo frowned.

"Let me guess, Egypt is one of those countries," Ruby Mae said.

"BINGO," Nana Jo said. "So, there's a good chance that if Isabella made it to Egypt, she may never face justice."

"We don't know that Isabella is guilty," I said.

"True, but do we have other suspects?" Dorothy asked.

"I think Bethany would be a good suspect," Irma said.

"I don't like her either, but why?" I asked.

"Clarence said his sources are certain Carl had help, and they're really looking at Bethany." Irma shrugged.

"I don't know that I can see Bethany killing Alva, but I could absolutely imagine her killing Carl. Heck, I could totally see her taking out Carl," I said.

"Maybe they were in it together. Maybe Carl killed Alva and Bethany killed Carl." Ruby Mae pulled out her knitting. "There's no honor among thieves."

"I wish we knew how Irma was killed. We don't even

know for sure that Alva *was* killed. I never thought I'd miss Stinky Pitt, but—"

"Hold that thought." Nana Jo scrolled through her emails. "Jenna sent her updates via email, and I just glanced over it before I left and I remember something about the autopsy."

We waited for Nana Jo to find the email.

"Here it is. Jenna talked to the D.A.'s office and the coroner found something that makes them think Alva was killed." Nana Jo paused.

"What did they find?" Dorothy asked.

"Arsenic."

Chapter 36

"Arsenic?" Dorothy said.

"How? I thought Carl had her cremated," I said.

"He did, but they collected strands of her hair from her pillow and brush," Nana Jo said. "They'll need a forensic toxicology lab and North Harbor doesn't have one."

This triggered a memory. "I went to a workshop offered by the local chapter of Sisters in Crime."

"Sisters in Crime? Are you planning a crime?" Dorothy asked.

"No. It's a writing organization that was started in the 1980s to increase equity for women crime writers within the publishing industry."

"Sad that an organization like that is still needed in the twenty-first century," Nana Jo said.

"It's shocking. Anyway, I went to a workshop where the presenter was a woman referred to as the Poison Lady."

"The Poison Lady? Sounds like a serial killer," Nana Jo said.

"Nothing like that." I chuckled. "Luci Zahray is a retired pharmacist with a master's degree in toxicology. She's an expert on poisons. She shares her knowledge with crime writers to help us get the details right in our books. At the workshop I attended she talked about arsenic. It was fascinating. I had no idea that arsenic was everywhere. It's in the ground, the water, pretty much everywhere."

"We used to keep arsenic on the farm to kill rodents," Nana Jo said.

"I was shocked when she said arsenic is in the water. I knew it had been used in paint and other chemicals," I said.

"We're destroying our planet and killing ourselves with chemicals," Dorothy said.

"If arsenic is everywhere, then how could it have killed Alva?" Ruby Mae asked.

"It's the concentration of arsenic that's the issue. Trace amounts of arsenic are almost everywhere. Large doses of arsenic are the problem." I pulled out my phone and swiped through my album until I found the one I wanted. I sent it to everyone here. "That's a photo I took today at LIMA."

"Other than the wallpaper being ugly, what's the problem?" Irma asked.

"In Victorian times, arsenic was one of the ingredients used to create a vibrant color called Scheele's green. It was popular in paint and wallpaper, especially in nurseries."

"Wouldn't someone need to eat the wallpaper to poison themselves?" Dorothy asked.

"The ink could flake off the paper and be inhaled. They also believed moisture or heat could release toxic vapors." I shivered.

"This is LIMA. Do we know what type of wallpaper was in Alva's bedroom?" Nana Jo asked.

"When Frank and I first went to Alva's house, Carl made a point of saying that Bethany had wasted money redecorating Alva's bedroom with hideous green wallpaper. I don't know if it's the same wallpaper. Or that it has arsenic," I said.

"True, but where would Bethany get the wallpaper?" Ruby Mae asked. "Surely they don't make it anymore."

"Maybe she got it from Ethan Linton." I shared his plans for expansion and renovation.

"It wouldn't be unusual to buy extra wallpaper." Dorothy tapped her fingers on the table.

"I think you might have something there. The last time I went to LIMA, Bethany showed up. I got the feeling there might be something going on between the two of them," Dorothy said.

"At Alva's memorial, Isabella said Bethany was having an affair with someone, but she didn't know who," I said.

"Bethany might have been Carl's partner in the embezzling." I turned to Irma.

"We know Bethany redecorated Alva's bedroom with Victorian green wallpaper, but we don't know if the wallpaper had arsenic." Nana Jo typed. "But, regardless, she lived in the same house with Alva. She would have the opportunity to slip arsenic into Alva's food. She had the means to have killed Alva."

"Plus, she seemed to genuinely hate Carl, but wouldn't leave him because she wouldn't get any money he might inherit from Alva's death." I shook my head.

"What if she got tired of waiting for Alva to die and decided to speed things up?" Ruby Mae asked.

"Bethany had a motive, opportunity, and the means to have killed both Alva and Carl," Nana Jo said.

"I'm not sure where Alva's paintings fit into this, but I think we need to tell the police." I glanced around the table.

Chapter 37

I wasn't sure if Stinky Pitt was still out of town, but I decided to start with him anyway.

"I've been back in town for a total of two hours and my first call is from North Harbor's resident Nancy Drew."

I hate being called Nancy Drew. I would have called him Stinky Pitt if I didn't need his help.

"Detective Pitt, welcome home. How was your trip?"

"Save it. Whaddya want?"

My English teacher inner nerd cringed, but I was determined not to let him get under my skin.

"We have some information about the murder of Alva and Carl Tarkington. We learned—"

"Look, I can't do this on an empty stomach. I need to eat."

I gritted my teeth. "Would you like me to call back in an hour?"

"Make it two."

"Fine, but—"

"And don't call me. I'll call you."

"Okay, but—" I stared at the phone.

He hung up on me.

"I can't believe I was just saying that I wished he was back." I put my phone away.

"Maybe you should call Special Agent Brown too," Nana Jo said. "He might be interested in the information about the paintings."

She looked at her watch. "Okay, we'll meet back in the lobby in an hour and a half. Then Sam can call the chubby blowhard in the car."

"Great. I'm going to the bar and get myself a hunk." Irma touched up her makeup.

"My granddaughter is going to swing by to chat on her break. I'll meet you all at the entrance." Ruby Mae rarely gambled, instead choosing to sit and talk while she knitted. There was a massive fireplace next to the entrance with seating.

Nana Jo played blackjack while Dorothy usually played slots in the high-limit room.

I went in search of a quiet place to write. Experience taught me that the hotel area connected to the casino was the best place, so that's where I headed. When I found a chair in a quiet corner, I took out my phone and called Special Agent Warren Brown. My call went to voicemail, but I immediately got a text saying that he would call me back in ten minutes.

I glanced at the time and prepared to wait. It only took Special Agent Brown eight minutes.

"Good evening, Special Agent Brown."

"Please call me Warren and I will call you Samantha."

I could hear the smile in his voice, unlike the contempt I heard from Detective Pitt. It was a welcome change.

We spent a couple of minutes on the pleasantries.

"I would like to believe that you called to see how I liked the books I bought, but I don't think you did." He chuckled.

I explained what I'd learned from William Merkel about the paintings that Alva left to Isabella.

"Are you sure about the painting? He said it's the missing

Giovanni Bellini *Madonna and Child*. You're sure?" I could hear the excitement in his voice.

"That's what he said."

"And Isabella Sadat is leaving the country in the next day or two?"

"She said they're getting married. She plans to sell the paintings, but her boyfriend is flying in tomorrow and then they're going to Cairo."

"I can't take a chance that she might change her mind and the paintings could leave the country. I may not be able to keep Isabella Sadat in the country, but I can keep the paintings from leaving."

Gladys and Flossie stood in the hall of the guest wing. Mrs. McDuffie flicked a feather duster at a picture.

In a voice that was raised louder than needed, Gladys stood in a position that allowed the largest number of people to overhear her conversation. "I heard Thompkins say they're coming to move all that art first thing tomorrow."

"I'll feel better once that expensive art is gone." Flossie placed her hand to her head in a pose she'd seen Vivien Leigh use in her last film.

Gladys leaned close and whispered, "What're you doing?"

"Acting. You never know if anyone might be peeping," Flossie whispered. "Besides, it helps me stay in character if I act it and don't just say the words."

Gladys placed one set of the freshly polished

shoes she carried in front of one of the doors, then she pulled a handkerchief from her pocket and twisted it in her hands. "Good. I won't be able to sleep until that art's gone."

Both girls listened for a few moments before turning to glance in the direction of the house-keeper.

"Mrs. McDuffie," Flossie said. "Is it true? Will the art be taken away tomorrow?"

"Yes, it is the truth." Mrs. McDuffie said more formally than she'd ever spoken even when she'd met King George. "Tomorrow all the art will be taken to Australia. And good riddance."

The women paused for several beats.

"Now, you girls get those shoes delivered and get back downstairs. We've got work to do." Mrs. McDuffie paused and then shooed the maids down the back stairs.

The women hurried around the corner and waited. One by one each of the doors opened.

First, Sir Bentley Gardener opened his door and stuck his head into the hall. Lord Cecil Scott was next, and then Stanley Tate and Major Horatio Templeton. All of the men stood in their doorways. After a pregnant pause, each man reached down and picked up their shoes. They nodded a greeting before returning to their rooms.

Mrs. McDuffie breathed a sigh of relief and then hurried along the back stairs to the ser-vants' dining room. Mission accomplished. She walked through the dining room to the office. Thompkins and Lady Elizabeth were waiting.

"How'd it go?" Lady Elizabeth asked.

"Perfect. Gladys and Flossie did an excellent job."

"Now, it's up to Winston and the prime minister." Lady Elizabeth nodded.

Thompkins gave a discrete cough. "Excuse me, but what exactly will they do?"

"Each member of the war cabinet is being fed a different story. Do you remember Virginia Hall?"

The butler nodded. "The American."

"She's the one with the wooden leg," Mrs. McDuffie said.

"Yes. She's been working undercover," Lady Elizabeth said.

"Have the Americans joined the war?" Mrs. McDuffie asked.

"No, but let's just say there are people who are sympathetic to the cause." Lady Elizabeth sighed. "She's actually working with the French underground. She and Lord Browning have been monitoring communications. Whichever story makes its way to the Nazis will help identify the traitor."

Despite Mrs. Anderson's delicious meal, dinner was a somber affair. The conversation was stilted, and you could cut the tension with a knife. Lady Elizabeth invited Detective Waterstone and Nelson Wilmington to dinner. Thompkins brought one of Victor Carlston's dinner suits, which fit Wilmington nicely, but Detective Waterstone declined the offer and wore his rumpled suit.

After dinner, the group retired to the drawing room. Winston was the only member of the group who seemed completely at ease.

Thompkins entered with a tray of drinks. "Would you like whiskey or sherry?"

"Yes." Winston took a glass of each from the tray. He drank the whiskey and returned the empty glass to the tray.

Just as he had the night before, Joseph Mueller entered the room. He declined a drink. He hovered by a table and fiddled with a glass paperweight.

Nelson Wilmington sauntered to Mueller. "It's been a long time, Joseph."

"Yes." Joseph stared at the young man.

"Mr. Wilmington, how did you get started with art?" Lady Elizabeth asked.

"I've always loved art. Joseph can tell you that during school, I was always drawing. My brother Noah was more athletically inclined, but I would sit quietly with my pencils." He took a sip of his whiskey.

"Do you paint?" Lady Daphne asked.

"Only for fun. I'm afraid like many great men, I have an appreciation for good art, but I lack the talent." Wilmington grinned. "I've heard our illustrious First Lord of the Admiralty shares my passion."

Winston grunted and continued to drink.

"So, is that why you chose to be a curator?" Lady Daphne asked.

"Yes. I studied art at the Royal College of Art. Then, I went to Paris and studied at the Beaux-Arts. I tried to make a living painting, but . . . I had to face the reality that I just wasn't good enough. I would never make my mark on the world with my paintbrush, so I had to find another path."

"I'm intrigued by modern art," Lady Penelope said.

"Can't make heads or tails of that hogwash," Lord William said.

"Modern art isn't for everyone." Nelson Wilmington chuckled. "I have to admit that I'm not a big fan, but . . ."

"No matter what way I looked at it, I couldn't figure out if Waterhouse's *The Lady of Shalott* was a person or an animal," Lady Elizabeth said.

"I hear that a lot at the museum. Modern art is an acquired taste." Nelson Wilmington sipped his whiskey.

"What's the point of art if there's no one around to enjoy it?" Stanley Tate asked. "The Luftwaffe has shown they're invincible."

"The power of an air force is terrific when there is nothing to oppose it." Winston Churchill stared into the fire as he smoked his cigar. "We can't surrender. We won't surrender."

"We could still survive this . . . this bloodbath. It's not too late. Appeasement could still work. With the right incentive, we could walk away with the empire still intact," Stanley Tate said.

"An appeaser is one who feeds a crocodile, hoping it will eat him last." Winston pulled himself out of his seat and refilled his glass. "The end result is the same. Britain will be eaten up by the Nazis, and I don't plan to hand Hitler the British Empire on a silver platter."

"We can't afford another war with Germany." Major Horatio Templeton pulled out a gold lighter and lit a cigarette. He took a long drag and slowly exhaled.

"That's my point. Instead of hiding valuable paintings away in a cellar or shipping them across the world to Australia, maybe we need to sell them," Stanley Tate said.

"Gentlemen, I'm not a member of Parliament, but I could certainly help to liquidate some of the art. In my capacity as curator, I have come into contact with private collectors who would be willing to pay handsomely for this art. Selling just a few pieces would more than cover the cost of several tanks." Nelson Wilmington appealed to the prime minister.

Neville Chamberlain stared into the fire.

"We shouldn't be hiding art in caves across the empire. Or our women and children in the countryside," Stanley Tate said. "The only way to save our nation and our people is to work with the Germans."

"No." Neville Chamberlain stood up and walked over to where Winston stood near the fireplace. "The time for seeking to appease Hitler and the Nazis has passed. I didn't want to be the one to lead this nation into another war, but that is where we are. I see that now. The time for concessions has passed. Now is a time for action."

Silence filled the room.

Detective Waterstone entered. He paused and looked around at the somber faces. "Anyone care for a friendly game of cards?"

Stanley Tate, Lord Cecil Scott, Major Horatio Templeton, and Winston all sat down at the table to play cards.

Winston turned to Joseph Mueller, who was standing near the fireplace. "Mueller, toss me that deck of cards, would you?"

Joseph Mueller picked up the deck of cards that was lying on the mantel and tossed them to Wilmington, who caught them.

Lady Daphne moved close to her aunt and whispered, "It looks like the trap is set and we've got one rat."

"One down. One to go." Lady Elizabeth nodded and pulled out her knitting.

Chapter 38

The alarm I set on my phone went off and I was catapulted out of 1939 England and back to the United States. I packed away my notepad and headed to meet Nana Jo and the girls at the entrance.

I gave the valet my ticket and waited.

It was a slow night, and my car was here in record time. I slipped a tip to the attendant, and we all piled in.

We were cruising down I-94 when my phone rang. I pushed the hands-free and answered.

"Good evening, Detective Pitt. I'm in the car with my grandmother, Dorothy, Irma, and Ruby Mae."

"Yeah. Yeah. I'm tired and cranky, so let's just get this over with. What do you want?"

I shared what we'd found out. I explained that we believed that the paintings were valuable and what they might be worth.

"You told this crazy story to the FBI?"

"Surprisingly, Special Agent Warren Brown was very supportive. Isabella is getting married. She says she's selling the paintings, but regardless of whether she does or not, Special Agent

Brown is going to get some type of order preventing the paintings from leaving the country," I said.

Detective Pitt huffed. "So, you're saying Bethany killed her husband and her husband's aunt."

"Well . . . no."

"Whaddya mean?"

I ground my teeth at the slurred speech. "I'm not saying Bethany is the murderer, but I think she's involved with embezzling. Look, I think I have an idea how we can set a trap to catch the killer."

Chapter 39

"All right, Nancy Drew."

I hate when he calls me that.

"Detective Pitt, I—"

"Hold your horses." His mouth was full and his words were slurred more than usual, which made me want to puke even without seeing him. "I logged into the system and pulled up the file."

Nana Jo and I exchanged a glance. The surprise that I felt was reflected on her face. Neither one of us expected him to be so responsive. We waited. After a few moments, he mumbled.

"Looks like Alva Tarkington had an unusually high amount of arsenic in the hair samples . . . Carl Tarkington was stabbed with a long, thin blade," he said.

"Does it say what kind of blade?" I asked.

"Nah, but most likely a stiletto."

Something flashed across my mind, but it was gone before I could catch it.

"Look, I'm tired and I need to sleep. Why don't you and the rest of the Scooby-Doo Crew give it a rest and let the police handle it. I'm going to bed and I suggest you do the same." Detective Pitt swallowed and then belched.

He disconnected the phone.

"Eww. That was disgusting," Irma said from the backseat.

"He's an imbecile—a pig and an imbecile," Nana Jo said. "I don't know what Camilia sees in that man."

"They say love is blind." I shrugged.

"Blind maybe, but she'd have to destroy a lot of brain cells to have a conversation with the man."

"I don't know. He irritates me, but he did save my life." I drove toward Shady Acres.

"Hmm. He did." Nana Jo got out of the car and walked toward the house. "There's also the fact that when you and Frank get married, there's a good chance that he could be your stepfather-in-law."

"Stepfather-in-law? Is that a thing?"

"That's a thing."

I turned to my grandmother. "You need to promise me that you won't karate-chop him at Thanksgiving dinner."

Nana Jo shook her head. "I can't make any promises, but if Stinky Pitt behaves himself, so will I."

"I'm more likely to stab him with one of my knitting needles," Ruby Mae said.

I glanced in the rearview mirror and saw her holding up one of her knitting needles as she went through the motions of stabbing someone. Looking at the long, thin, metal needle that she used, I had a flashback. My mind wandered back to LIMA. On the mantel by the wall was a display of daggers. Long, thin, deadly daggers. Carl Tarkington had been stabbed.

My phone pinged. I had a voicemail. I had my car play the message.

Isabella's voice filled the car. She was excited and, in my head, I could see her bouncing with enthusiasm as the message played.

"Hey, Samantha. I got a message from Ethan Linton, he wants the paintings right away. At first, I was going to give them to him later, but he really wants them now. Plus, with Ahsan coming, I guess it makes sense to just get it over with."

"She seems pretty happy for someone who didn't want to sell them," Nana Jo said as we continued to listen.

"Ahsan said the money will come in handy," Isabella said. "Plus, Mr. Linton was willing to give me two thousand more dollars if I brought the paintings tonight. For my inconvenience. That's seven thousand dollars!"

"What on earth?" Dorothy said. "There's no way those paintings are worth half of that amount."

"Ahsan said we could use it for the wedding or to go on a nice honeymoon." Isabella squealed. "Plus, Mr. Linton told me that he would do a display at his museum for local artists. That way, Mrs. Alva's paintings will be seen and enjoyed by more people and not just put away in a closet someplace. So, I told him I would go to the appraiser and pick up the paintings. Ahsan said I should take them over to Mr. Linton before he changes his mind. So, I'm going now." Isabella thanked me and hung up.

That's when the pieces started to click in my mind. The stain on the rug, which Linton had tried to clean. The display with the Victorian household objects included an ice pick. A long, skinny, sharp object similar to a stiletto.

I turned the car and headed to the Linton Museum of Art. I called Detective Pitt again, but his phone went to voicemail. "Detective Pitt, this is Samantha. Ethan Linton killed Alva and Carl Tarkington. He figured out Alva's paintings are hiding expensive art and he's luring Isabella there. We're on our way to LIMA—"

I must have met the time limit for my message because I was prompted to start over. I hung up as I pulled in front of the museum.

We rushed inside.

Isabella stood in the foyer holding a check while Ethan Linton held Alva's paintings.

"Samantha, did you get my message?" Isabella tilted her head to the side and giggled. "I guess you must have since you're here . . . but *why* are you here?"

"Isabella, I don't think you should sell your paintings. This isn't a good deal," I said.

"That's not your decision to make. The paintings were left to Miss Sadat and she has already sold them to me." Ethan Linton sneered. "The museum is closed, so you and your friends should leave."

Isabella frowned at the cruel tone. "Samantha, what's going on?"

"You're right. We'll leave." I held out a hand to Isabella. "Isabella, why don't you come with us. I can drive you back."

Isabella took several steps toward me.

Ethan Linton narrowed his gaze, and then reached into his pocket and pulled out a gun.

Chapter 40

"You're too smart for your own good." Linton reached out and grabbed Isabella. He put his arm around her neck and pulled her to his chest.

Isabella screamed in fear.

"Quiet!" Linton ordered. "Now, unless you want me to blow your young friend's brains out, I suggest you move slowly away from the door." He waved the gun to indicate he wanted us to move into the parlor.

Isabella gasped.

Nana Jo, Dorothy, Irma, Ruby Mae, and I slowly made our way into the parlor.

"You'll never make it out of here," Nana Jo said.

"I think I will." Linton snarled. "It's certainly going to take more than a few nosy old women to stop me. Now, we're going to move down to the cellar and I'm going to enjoy a long vacation on a sandy beach. With any luck, someone will find you all in a few months."

Isabella whimpered.

"There's no way you can shoot all of us." Nana Jo bent her knees and widened her stance.

From the corner of my eye, I saw Dorothy make a similar stance as she inched closer to Ethan Linton. I needed to keep him talking. I needed to distract him. If he was focused on me, then maybe he wouldn't pay attention to Nana Jo and Dorothy, who were both aikido experts.

"Why did you kill Alva?" I asked. "She promised to leave you money in her will. Why not just wait?"

Ethan Linton scowled. "I've already waited years for Oliver and Alva to kick the bucket. Finally, Oliver was gone and Alva was dying. But then I found out Carl was spending Alva's money faster than a speeding train."

"How did you learn about the embezzling?" I asked.

Nana Jo and Dorothy inched closer to Linton.

"Bethany Tarkington is a lovely woman with many . . . admirable qualities. A woman of passion." Linton smiled, but it looked more like a grimace.

"You're having an affair with Bethany. That makes sense. Were you the one who suggested that she decorate Alva's room with wallpaper made with arsenic?" I asked.

Linton raised his brow. "You figured that out? I'm impressed."

"What was the plan? Arsenic-infused wallpaper would take time to kill." I scanned the room for a weapon. There was so much clutter, I could barely think straight, but I zeroed in on a collection of glass paperweights on a nearby table.

"Margery Brooks is a lonely woman, but she was willing to wipe down the wallpaper with a brush that would cause flakes, and then light the fireplace in Alva's room." Linton grinned.

Isabella gasped and a tear ran down her face.

"Alva was dying, the wallpaper would just speed things up. If it hadn't been for Carl, I could have waited. But not only was he a thief, he was a clumsy thief. They were on to him. Once they learned of his embezzlement, they would have to investigate all of the accounts he managed, including Alva's. So I had to rush my plan and give her a bigger dose of arsenic."

Nana Jo inched closer and one of the floorboards creaked.

"What are you doing?" Ethan Linton asked. "Back over there with the rest of them."

Nana Jo and Dorothy took two steps backward.

"Why Carl?" I asked. "Why'd you kill him?"

"Carl found out that Bethany and I were having an affair and came here making threats. Can you believe the audacity?" He laughed.

"So, you killed him with the ice pick"—I pointed to the one on the display table—"and then moved his body to the beach."

"You're smarter than you look," Linton said. "Now start moving."

We slowly backed out of the parlor toward the foyer.

A blur appeared in the window behind Linton. *Is someone there?*

"How did you figure out about the paintings?" I asked.

Ethan Linton grinned. "That was a touch of good luck. I just happened to be in downtown South Harbor when I saw you take Isabella's paintings to the art appraiser. After you left, I went into the shop and had a nice long chat with Mr. Merkel. He's a very friendly man. When I learned he was going to have the paintings X-rayed I came home and took a closer look at the paintings Alva bequeathed to me. Sure enough, she painted over valuable paintings." He shrugged. "I guess she tried to honor her late husband's wishes after all."

"Alva was smart. She knew Carl was stealing her money, but since she was dying and the money would be his when she was gone, she didn't try to stop him." *Was that a car outside?*

"She wasn't as batty as she pretended." Linton shrugged.

"Miss Alva was smart. She was smarter than you," Isabella said.

"Yes, well, thanks to Alva, I can retire. Now move." Linton waved his gun.

The front door swung open, and Detective Pitt pushed inside his gun raised and pointed at Ethan Linton.

Linton turned to the door and that's when Dorothy and Nana Jo made their move.

Dorothy reached out and grabbed Linton's hand holding the gun while Nana Jo pulled Isabella and pushed her behind her into Ruby Mae's arms.

Working as a team, Nana Jo landed a karate chop to Linton's neck, while Dorothy did a sweeping kick that knocked him on the ground.

Irma picked up a vase and smashed it over Linton's head.

He was out cold.

Chapter 41

Detective Pitt wasted no time getting handcuffs on Ethan Linton while he laid prostate on the ground. When Pitt stood up, he turned and scowled. "What exactly do you think you're doing? You could have been killed."

"I wasn't sure you got my message."

Within minutes, the Linton Museum of Art was swarming with police and Special Agent Warren Brown of the FBI.

Isabella's knees were wobbly and she was sitting in an uncomfortable-looking chair in the red room across the hallway from the police activity in the green room.

The paramedics gave Isabella the all clear and declared Ethan Linton fit to be taken to jail.

Detective Pitt and Special Agent Brown had a private conversation before they joined us.

"Samantha, do you feel up to telling us what happened?" Special Agent Brown asked.

Between all of us, we shared the details of what we knew. Neither Special Agent Brown nor Detective Pitt interrupted. When we were done, Detective Pitt looked as if he was going to explode while Special Agent Brown looked as if he was struggling to keep from laughing.

"Wait, so Alva Tarkington died and her twin sister, Zelda, had been passing herself off as Alva?" Detective Pitt asked.

I nodded.

"If she wasn't dead, I'd arrest her for identity theft." Detective Pitt rubbed his hand down his face.

"Please tell me Miss Alva didn't steal those paintings," Isabella said.

"We don't know for sure what's underneath them. Plus, there's a chance that we may never know for sure which paintings were purchased legitimately." Isabella looked ready to object, but Special Agent Brown raised a hand. "I'm not saying she stole the paintings. She may have purchased them and everything is clear. A lot of valuable art disappeared during World War Two. The Nazis stole tons of art from private collectors, churches, and museums as they marched across Europe. There were also people like Hildebrand Gurlitt, an art gallery director who acquired art for the Nazis. Some he purchased from Jewish collectors, for a fraction of their value for the Nazis, but the bottom line is it's still theft."

"That's despicable," Nana Jo said.

"Gurlitt . . . that name sounds familiar," I said.

"That's because his son, Cornelius Gurlitt, was in the news in 2010 when authorities discovered he was hiding more than fourteen hundred works of art in an apartment in Munich that he *inherited* from his father." Dorothy used air quotes around "inherited."

"Plus, we know some art was sold by the Russian government to raise funds. As you can imagine, the Russians aren't very forthcoming with providing proof of ownership or access to records." Special Agent Brown chuckled. "So, it's possible that Alva or Zelda may have owned the art, which means you will get your paintings, Ms. Sadat. But first we need to remove the overpaint and see what's underneath. Are you okay with that?"

Isabella nodded. Then, she reached into her purse and pulled out a book. "This is Miss Zelda's journal. She wrote poems and notes. Maybe there's something in here that will help."

I scanned the book and found a handwritten letter tucked inside the back cover. I opened the note and read. "This is from Zelda. She said that Alva wanted her to use the money and enjoy life." I glanced at Isabella. "She also said that Oliver Tarkington was Isabella's father."

Isabella gasped.

"He had an affair with your mother when she was his secretary. He broke off the affair, but it was too late. She was already pregnant. Alva couldn't forgive him for having the one thing she could never have—a child. But before she died, she wanted Oliver's daughter to have her inheritance. Zelda bought the paintings when she was in Russia. Zelda painted over them to hide them." I handed the diary to Special Agent Brown.

"When we verify ownership, the paintings will be returned."

"Thank you," Isabella said.

"What will happen to Bethany Tarkington and Margery Brooks?" I asked.

"Bethany has already been picked up for embezzlement. We'll pick up Margery Brooks, but I don't know how big a role she played in the murder of Alva . . . or Zelda." Detective Pitt rolled his eyes. "Whoever she was."

"Can I ask a question?" I looked at Warren. "What brought you here?"

"I went to get the paintings from William Merkel and learned that Isabella told him she was selling them to Ethan

Linton. So, I came here in time to see the final takedown."
Special Agent Brown winked at Nana Jo.

"Don't encourage them." Detective Pitt rolled his eyes.

I turned to Detective Pitt. "What brought *you* here?"

A red flush rose up his neck. "I got your message that you
were coming here. I figured you wouldn't leave things to pro-
fessionals and would get yourself in hot water—again." He
paused. "Besides, I figured Camilia would be furious if I let
anything happen to her son's fiancée."

I struggled to contain my smile. I gave in, stood up, and
kissed Detective Pitt's cheek. "Thank you."

"Yeah . . . Just make sure you come in tomorrow and give
a formal statement." He rushed away.

"Who would have thought Stinky Pitt has a soft side,"
Nana Jo said.

I dropped the girls off at Shady Acres and then Nana Jo
and I made our way home. Despite the time, I was too amped
up to sleep. So, I sat down to spend time in the British countryside.

Thompkins entered quietly, walked to the
prime minister. "Telephone."

Neville Chamberlain rose and followed the
butler out. After a few moments, he returned.
He stood in front of the fireplace for several moments. He'd aged ten years in the short time
that he was out of the room.

Two constables stepped inside and waited
by the door.

"Arthur, are you okay?" Lady Elizabeth asked.

The prime minister nodded. "Detective Water-stone, would you please arrest the Not-So-Honorable Stanley Tate."

"What the Devil—" Stanley Tate stood quickly, knocking over his chair.

One of the constables secured the MP while the other one and Detective Waterstone hov-ered nearby.

"What's this all about?" Major Horatio Tem-pleton asked.

"This is about treason." Neville Chamberlain took a deep breath. "I've felt for some time that there was a leak within my war cabinet."

"What?"

"Are you mad?"

"I couldn't prove it, so my hands were tied . . . until now. With the help of the Marsh Family I have finally identified the traitor." The prime minister bowed to Lady Elizabeth and Lord Wil-liam. "I have to admit, when Lady Elizabeth told me she wanted to play a game of telephone with my war cabinet, I thought she was . . ."

"Spit it out. You didn't think she was playing with a full deck." Winston laughed.

The prime minister bowed to Lady Elizabeth again. "Please forgive me."

Lady Elizabeth nodded. "I'm sorry that I was right."

"You were." Prime Minister Chamberlain stood and turned to the men of his war cabinet. "Today, Winston and I met with each of you sep-arately. Each of you was given a 'secret' which you were instructed was of vital importance to the nation. Each message was different. And each message was, I'm glad to say, false. Only one of you betrayed the trust you were given and reported false information. I just received a call that confirms that the message given to Mr. Tate was relayed to the Nazis earlier today."

The color drained from Stanley Tate's face and his legs buckled. "I was desperate. I have gambling debts that could ruin me . . . they had me by the throat. There was nothing I could do."

"There's always something you could do. You could have come to me. You could have resisted. You could . . . you could have done many things. Instead, you chose to betray your country."

The prime minister turned to Lady Elizabeth. "And have you determined who Tate's accomplice really is?"

"Accomplice? Good Lawd." Lord Cecil Scott stared at the prime minister.

"That would be Noah Wilmington." Lady Elizabeth pointed to the young man.

"Noah is my brother. We're twins. I'm Nelson."

"You and your brother are identical, and it was challenging, but thanks to Joseph we were able to identify the one thing that differentiated you from Nelson," Lady Elizabeth said.

"And what was that?" Noah Wilmington sneered.

Lady Elizabeth turned to Joseph Mueller.

"The one way we could always tell you from Nelson is that you're left-handed while Nelson was right-handed. When I tossed you that deck of cards, you caught it with your left hand. When you were keeping score, you used your left hand," Joseph said.

"That's ridiculous. So I used my left hand. That doesn't prove anything," Noah Wilmington said.

"Of course, the clincher for me was when you called John William Waterhouse's classic painting *The Lady of Shalott* 'modern art.' The real Nelson Wilmington would never have made that mistake," Lady Elizabeth said. "You killed your brother and took his place, thinking you could get away before anyone found out."

Noah Wilmington shoved the table and ran toward the door.

Winston stuck out his leg and Wilmington tripped and fell to the ground.

Detective Waterstone and the other constable secured him and removed him and Stanley Tate.

Lord Cecil Scott and Major Horatio Templeton both looked shaken.

Lady Elizabeth turned to Thompkins. "I think we could all use drinks."

"Agreed," Winston said.

Thompkins bowed and poured whiskeys and passed them around.

Neville Chamberlain bowed to Lady Elizabeth. "Britain and yours truly, we owe you a great debt."

"Nonsense. I was just doing my duty as a British citizen," Lady Elizabeth said.

Winston reached out and took his cousin's

hand. "If Britain is fortunate, we will find many citizens like my dear cousin with the intelligence, the courage, and the heart to stand up for what's right. If we do our duty as citizens of this great nation, then there is no army on earth that will be able to defeat us."

Chapter 42

After all the excitement from the previous night, I was happy to spend a day shelving books and helping customers in the bookstore while Nana Jo went to karate class. It was peaceful.

"Samantha!" Isabella yelled.

I turned to see her pulling a tall, handsome young man behind her. "You must be Ahsan. Isabella has told me so much about you."

Ahsan grinned. "Thank you so much for all that you did to protect Isabella. She was telling me about her harrowing experience."

"You're getting a wonderful woman, and I hope that the two of you will be extremely happy."

Isabella beamed and hugged me. Then she floated out of the store with the man of her dreams on her arm.

She was young and in love. The future was bright and nothing was impossible. I said a silent prayer that she would have more sunshine than rain, and the years would be kind.

Acknowledgments

Special thanks to my agent, Jessica Faust at BookEnds, and my editor at Kensington, John Scognamiglio. Thanks also to Dr. Alexia Gordon for medical advice and Kellye Garrett for leading the sprints with Crime Writers of Color that kept me writing. I also want to thank friends and fellow writers, Debra Goldstein and Tammy Layman Hall, for the brainstorming and encouragement.

Visit our website at
KensingtonBooks.com
to sign up for our newsletters, read
more from your favorite authors, see
books by series, view reading group
guides, and more!

Become a Part of Our
Between the Chapters Book Club
Community and Join the Conversation

Submit your book review for a chance to win exclusive
Between the Chapters swag you can't get anywhere else!
https://www.kensingtonbooks.com/pages/review/